Just a Littl

The Daring Dc

By Emma V. Lec

Published by Emma V. Leech.

Copyright (c) Emma V. Leech 2022

Editing Services Magpie Literary Services

Cover Art: Victoria Cooper

ASIN No: B09HQ1SGZG

ISBN No: 978-2-492133-39-8

About Me!

    I started this incredible journey way back in 2010 with The Key to Erebus, but didn't summon the courage to hit publish until October 2012. For anyone who's done it, you'll know publishing your first title is a terribly scary thing! I still get butterflies in the morning when a new title released, but the terror has subsided, at least. Now I just live in dread of the day my daughters are old enough to read them.

    The horror! (On both sides, I suspect.)

    2017 marked the year that I made my first foray into Historical Romance and the world of the Regency Romance, and my word what a year! I was delighted by the response to this series and can't wait to add more titles. Paranormal Romance readers need not despair, however, as there is more to come there too. Writing has become an addiction and as soon as one book is over, I'm excited to start the next, so you can expect plenty more in the future.

    As many of my works reflect, I am greatly influenced by the beautiful French countryside in which I live. I've been here in the South West for the past twenty-four years, though I was born and raised in England. My three gorgeous girls are all bilingual and my husband Pat, myself, and our four cats consider ourselves very fortunate to have made such a lovely place our home.

KEEP READING TO DISCOVER MY OTHER BOOKS!

Other Works by Emma V. Leech

Daring Daughters

Daring Daughters Series

Girls Who Dare

Girls Who Dare Series

Rogues & Gentlemen

Rogues & Gentlemen Series

The Regency Romance Mysteries

The Regency Romance Mysteries Series

The French Vampire Legend

The French Vampire Legend Series

The French Fae Legend

The French Fae Legend Series

Stand Alone

The Book Lover (a paranormal novella)

The Girl is Not for Christmas (Regency Romance)

Audio Books

Don't have time to read but still need your romance fix? The wait is over…

By popular demand, get many of your favourite Emma V Leech Regency Romance books on audio as performed by the incomparable Philip Battley and Gerard Marzilli. Several titles are available and more added each month!

Find them at your favourite audiobook retailer!

Acknowledgements

With special thanks to my lovely sensitivity readers, Crystal Carr-Chennupalli and Rebecca Vijay. Ladies you are so generous with your time and advice, thank you for your help with this title.

Thanks, of course, to my wonderful editor Kezia Cole with Magpie Literary Services

To Victoria Cooper for all your hard work, amazing artwork and, above all, your unending patience!!! Thank you so much. You are amazing!

To my BFF, PA, personal cheerleader and bringer of chocolate, Varsi Appel, for moral support, confidence boosting and for reading my work more times than I have. I love you loads!

A huge thank you to all of Emma's Book Club members! You guys are the best!

I'm always so happy to hear from you so do email or message me :)

emmavleech@orange.fr

To my husband Pat and my family … For always being proud of me.

Table of Contents

Family Trees

House of Cavendish
To Break the Rules

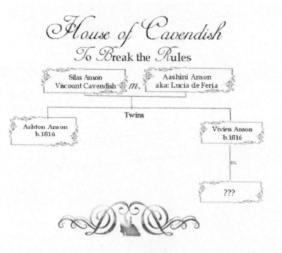

Silas Anson
Viscount Cavendish

m.

Aashini Anson
aka: Lucia de Feria

Twins

Ashton Anson
b.1816

Vivien Anson
b.1816

m.

???

House of Bedwin
To Dare a Duke

Robert Adolphus
Duke of Bedwin

m.

Prunella Adolphus
nee Chuffington-Smythe

Lady Elisabeth
b.1815

Jules
Marquess of Blackstone
b.1819

Lady Victoria
b.1825

Lord Harry
b.1833

Lady Charlotte
b.1817

Lady Rosamund
b.1823

Lord Frederick
b.1827

Lady Octavia
b.1838

m.

Cassius Cadogan
Viscount Oakley
b.1815

Nicolas Alexandre
Demarteau

House of Hunt
To Steal a Kiss

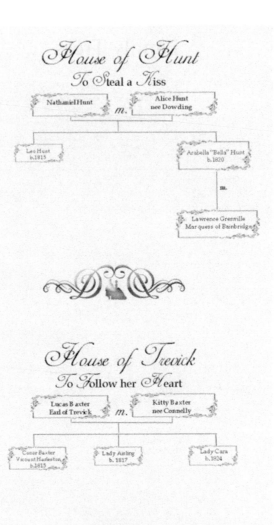

Nathaniel Hunt **m.** Alice Hunt nee Dowding

Leo Hunt b.1815

Arabella "Bella" Hunt b.1820

m.

Lawrence Grenville Marquess of Bainbridge

House of Trevick
To Follow her Heart

Lucas Baxter Earl of Trevick **m.** Kitty Baxter nee Connelly

Conor Baxter Viscount Harleston b.1815

Lady Aisling b. 1817

Lady Cara b.1824

House of St Clair
To Wager with Love

Jasper Cadogan
Earl of St Clair

m.

Harriet Cadogan
nee Stanhope

Cassius Cadogan
Viscount Oakley
b.1815

m.

Lady Charlotte Adolphus
b.1817

House of Cadogan
To Dance with a Devil

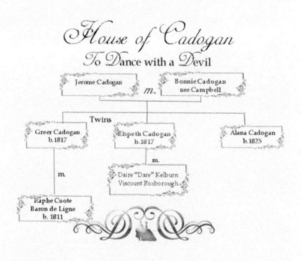

Jerome Cadogan

m.

Bonnie Cadogan
nee Campbell

Twins

Greer Cadogan
b.1817

Elspeth Cadogan
b.1817

Alana Cadogan
b.1825

m.

Daire "Dare" Kelburn
Viscount Roxborough

m.

Raphe Coote
Baron de Ligne
b. 1811

House of Morven
To Winter at Wildsyde

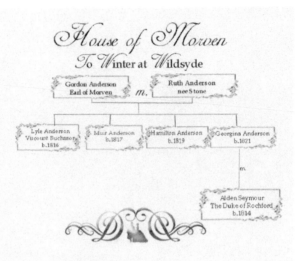

| Gordon Anderson Earl of Morven | m. | Ruth Anderson nee Stone |

- Lyle Anderson Viscount Buchanon b.1816
- Muir Anderson b.1817
- Hamilton Anderson b.1819
- Georgina Anderson b.1821

m.

Alden Seymour The Duke of Rochford b.1814

House of de Beauvoir
To Experiment with Desire

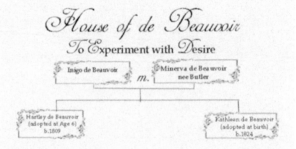

| Inigo de Beauvoir | m. | Minerva de Beauvoir nee Butler |

- Hartley de Beauvoir (adopted at Age 6) b.1809
- Kathleen de Beauvoir (adopted at birth) b.1824

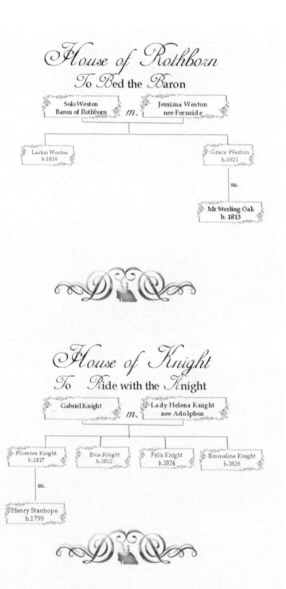

House of Rothborn
To Bed the Baron

Solo Weston
Baron of Rothborn
m.
Jemima Weston
nee Fernside

Larkin Weston
b.1816

Grace Weston
b.1821

m.

Mr Sterling Oak
b. 1813

House of Knight
To Ride with the Knight

Gabriel Knight
m.
Lady Helena Knight
nee Adolphus

Florence Knight
b.1817

Evie Knight
b.1822

Felix Knight
b.1824

Emmaline Knight
b.1826

m.

Henry Stanhope
b.1799

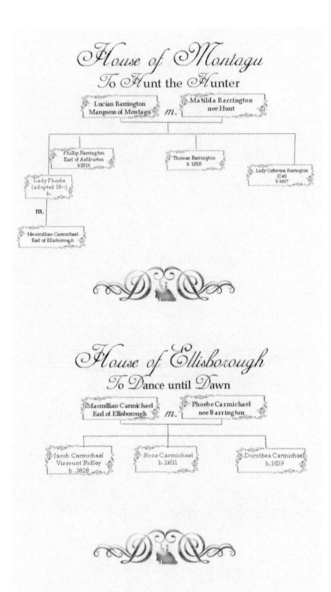

House of Montagu
To Hunt the Hunter

Lucian Barrington
Marquess of Montagu

m.

Matilda Barrington
nee Hunt

Phillip Barrington
Earl of Ashburton
b.1816

Thomas Barrington
b.1818

Lady Catherine Barrington
(Cat)
b.1827

Lady Phoebe
(adopted 18--)
b.

m.

Maximillian Carmichael
Earl of Ellisborough b.

House of Ellisborough
To Dance until Dawn

Maximillian Carmichael
Earl of Ellisborough

m.

Phoebe Carmichael
nee Barrington

Jacob Carmichael
Viscount Ridley
b. 1828

Rose Carmichael
b.1831

Dorothea Carmichael
b.1839

Chapter 1

August,

*~~I am~~ Anna <u>Brown</u> is in the most dreadful fix.
You must send her brother, <u>Bill</u>, at once to get
her out. She's being held at the gaol in Battle.*

Please hurry.

**—Excerpt of a letter from Miss Anna Lane-
Fox to her older brother Mr August Lane-
Fox.**

28ᵗʰ December 1840, Cavendish House, The Strand, London.

"I do like the orange satin," Ash said, a wistful expression on his handsome face.

"That is because you're an unfeeling monster with no regard for anyone around you," Viv said mildly, smothering a grin. She watched her twin brother with amusement as he pulled a face at her, sticking out his tongue. She gave a sad shake of her head. "Such a child."

Ash scowled and continued looking at the fabric samples Nani Maa had ordered sent to the house. The siblings were very much alike in looks, with dark indigo eyes like their father, and thick black hair and golden skin that spoke of their mother's heritage. Their mama, Aashini, was the illegitimate daughter of the Earl of Ulceby and one of his Indian servants. Aashini's marriage to their father, Viscount Cavendish, had caused an almighty stir back in the day, not that their father had given a tinker's cuss. He had turned his back on the *ton* years earlier and didn't give a damn. Viv suspected his utter disdain for them was the main reason they still welcomed him among their ranks. Well, that and the fact he was disgustingly wealthy and powerful. He was also a loving father and fiercely protective, while anyone wishing to cross swords with their mother—let alone their wicked grandmother, Nani Maa— could only be certifiable. The Anson family were close-knit and did not suffer fools.

Ash had inherited their maternal grandmother's love of fine fabric and vibrant colours, an appreciation which Vivien had little time for. Not that she didn't appreciate a well-cut gown or pretty things, but there always seemed more important and exciting ways to spend her time than choosing a gown for the next dratted ball.

"You know, if I'm that much of a monster, I ought to have left you to wear that yellow creation you were so taken with that made your skin appear sallow to Mama's New Year ball. Instead, you have that lovely pink gown that will have all the men sighing over you," Ash grumbled, returning Viv's thoughts to the task at hand.

"Just what I need," Vivien muttered, though she perked up at the idea it might make a certain someone sigh over her. If he accepted her mother's invitation, that was.

"Are you going to tell me who he is?" Ash asked, proving he was not half as daft as he liked to make out, though Vivien knew that well enough. Her brother acted the happy-go-lucky dandy, but there was far more to him than that.

"Who said—" Viv broke off at the impatient glance Ash sent her. Crossing her arms, she gave a huff of annoyance. "Fine. But if I tell you, it means you are complicit in my plans and are honour bound to help me ensnare him."

Ash slapped his hands over his ears. "No! I take it back. I don't want to know. La la la!" he said desperately as Viv tugged his hands free.

"Idiot," she said, rolling her eyes.

"Oh, Viv, leave me out of it," Ash said, a pleading glint in his eyes. "You know it always ends badly when you come up with some mad scheme, usually with my head in the basket."

"Don't be silly. I only need you to befriend him, and... and tell him how wonderful I am."

"So you want me to lie through my teeth, too!" he retorted.

Viv folded her arms and levelled a look at him that could etch glass. It was one she'd learned from Nani Maa, and it never failed.

Ash threw up his hands. "Ugh! Very well. Who is the poor dolt?"

Vivien hesitated, feeling uncharacteristically shy.

"Good God! Blushing, Viv?" Ash said in astonishment. "It's serious, then. Oooh... That fellow we met at Beverwyck? Lane-Fox? It is, isn't it?"

Viv nodded. "I got Mama to invite him to her New Year's ball," she admitted. "But I don't know if he's accepted. I can't ask her because then she'll know it wasn't just any old request and she'll take an interest."

Ash regarded her curiously. "Well, he seemed a decent chap, though rather tame by your standards, sis. Are you quite sure he's the fellow for you?"

Viv bit back a retort, because in fairness, she knew what he meant. She did not want a quiet life, at least not an *entirely* quiet life. Moments of calm were lovely, but needed to be interspersed with regular doses of excitement and adventure.

"I know he seems that way," Viv admitted, wondering why she had been so immediately taken with him herself. "He also

9

seems kind, a truly gentle gentleman, but there was something else, like he was hiding something. I... I can't put my finger on it."

"And you'd best not, unless you want Papa to chop him into tiny pieces," Ash said, smirking.

Viv rolled her eyes. "Don't be puerile."

Ash shrugged. "Why not? It's what I do best."

"Oh, Ash, don't tease. You will help me, won't you?"

With a long-suffering sigh, her brother slung his arm about her shoulder and hugged her. "When have I ever refused you?" he demanded, sounding a tad exasperated.

"Never," she admitted, hugging him back.

"And I have a lifetime of regrets to prove it," he added darkly.

Vivien laughed.

28th December 1840, Rother House, Burwash, Etchingham, East Sussex.

August tugged the rough woollen cap over his blond hair, straightened the cheap, well-worn waistcoat, and scowled at his reflection in the mirror. This was the last straw. Truly. He ought to leave the lot of them to their own devices. Lord knew they wouldn't miss his interference. Well, not unless he was being useful and hauling one of them out of gaol or breaking them out of some building they'd *accidentally* got locked in, or smuggling them out of a village on the verge of riot for spreading pamphlets of an incendiary nature. Good God. Could he not at least get through an entire week without one of his female relations exploding some blasted scandal in his face? Apparently not.

Muttering furiously under his breath, August stomped down the stairs, heading for the kitchen and the servants' entrance. His mother caught sight of him on his way through the hallway and perked up.

"Ah. Bill Brown, how good to see you again," she said, beaming at him.

August snorted. "It was only three days ago, Mother, and I swear I shall burn this infernal disguise and Bill Brown alongside it, and then where will you be?"

"You say that every time, August, dear," his mama said affectionately, reaching up to pat his cheek. "But every battle requires sacrifice."

"Yes, but why am I always the fatted calf?"

"Oh, pish. It's your poor sister languishing in that horrid cell, and for what, I ask you? Speaking her mind, as any free-thinking individual ought to do."

"Yes, Mother, but must she speak her mind so loudly that she causes mayhem and disorder, and in front of so many witnesses? It's only a matter of time before people realise Anna Brown is Anna Lane-Fox, and then I shall be a laughingstock, and she and Gwen will be completely unmarriageable."

Though what manner of poor fool would marry them as it was, August could not imagine. It boggled the mind to envisage either of his sisters as wives and mothers. Warrior-queens of ancient Britain, yes, but docile, well-behaved spouses? Not on your life.

"Oh, no. Bill, dear, is that you again?"

August sighed as an ethereal figure dressed all in pale grey floated into the hall like an elegant phantom, bringing with her the faint scent of peppermint. "Yes, Aunt Lettice. Anna has got herself into a bit of a scrape."

Again, he added silently.

Aunt Lettice made a sound of distress and pressed her ever-present lace hanky to her lips.

"Don't fret, love," Mama said cheerfully, giving her beleaguered sister a hearty squeeze. "Bill will get her out of gaol and no one the wiser."

"Gaol! Again? *Oh!* The scandal! We'll be ruined. *Ruined!*" Lettice wailed and fled down the hall sobbing. Oh, Lord. Could this day get any worse?

"Mother," August reproached her, for Letty's nerves were fragile things, and existing within Dante's lesser-known tenth circle of hell as she did—August lived with the conviction his mother had created a new one—was a constant strain upon them. He sympathised.

His mother just grinned and pressed her ink-stained fingers to her lips and then upon his cheek. "Run along now and free your sister from tyranny. There's a good boy. I must get back to my book. It's flowing marvellously well at the moment."

August groaned and hurried away. At least this debacle would get him out of the madhouse for the afternoon.

"There's no need to scowl so. It worked, didn't it? And it didn't cost half so much as last time. In fact, I thought the guard was rather sweet. He let me send you that letter after all, and he paid the boy over the odds to get it to you quickly."

August regarded his younger sister with impatience. "Yes, for which I have now repaid him with an exorbitant amount of interest. That get up doesn't fool anyone, you little twit. Anyone can see you are a lady, not... not a—"

"Flower seller," Anna said, quite unperturbed. "I had to get my paper into the hands of Lord Selby, and I discovered he buys his wife flowers every Monday on his way home. As an apology for all the vile things he did over the weekend when he was in town, I don't doubt."

"Oh, my God. Anna, you didn't?"

Anna beamed at him. "I did! I wrapped the flowers in my paper. Wasn't that clever of me, August? For even if he doesn't see it, his poor wife will—the servants are bound to show it to her—and do you not think she is tired of being made a laughingstock by the disgusting old satyr? Perhaps it will give her the motivation to join our fight."

"Or hit him over the head with the fireside poker." August sighed gloomily. "And then we'll be taken up for inciting a riot or murder, or something equally appalling."

"My, but you are a little ray of sunshine today." Anna tutted. "It wasn't my fault that big brute pinched me. Why must men see a single woman and think she is fair game? Must I be a prostitute because I do not have a man standing beside me? And it was hardly my fault he fell against that drunken lout and his friends. Did I make the lot of them start hitting each other or breaking windows? No, I did not."

"No, love, of course not, and the bastard needed a clout around the head for laying a finger on you. I should have gladly done it myself... but if you'd not been there alone, dressed as a flower seller, it would never have happened," August pointed out, not unreasonably in his view.

"No. If I had been a good, well-behaved, obedient young lady, I should be at home crocheting or doing needlepoint whilst my brain died by slow degrees and I screamed silently inside until I was dead," Anna remarked. "Is that what I should do, August, so I don't invite men to pinch my bottom simply by being in the same street as them?"

August felt the powerful desire to dash his brains out against the nearest brick wall, but took a breath. "No, Anna, of course not. The fellow was an ignorant brute, and it's wretchedly unfair. I know it's unfair, but it is how the world is. I cannot change it for you, and you cannot change it either. You can only make yourself and the rest of our family into pariahs. I don't wish to be a pariah, Anna."

His sister sent him a mutinous look he recognised only too well. "I might not change things in this lifetime, or even for the next generation, but perhaps I can build a steppingstone, as Mary Wollstonecraft did, a small but solid step up for women everywhere, something to lean upon. The echo of a voice that speaks for those who cannot."

August stared at his sister, and not for the first time he envied her. She had such purpose, such fire inside her, such a definite view of what was right. August had never felt so sure of his place in the world. Their father had been a brute, and he could not blame his mother or his sisters for jumping for joy when he'd died. Indeed, his closest male role models had been disgusting excuses for humanity, never mind anything higher minded. His friends' fathers had been little better, and the more his mother and sisters harped on about how the male of the species was ruining the world, the more August had questioned what the devil it meant to be a man, let alone a gentleman, a label he was finding increasingly difficult to hang on to.

The trouble was, he agreed with them. Christ, he'd have run howling into the wilderness a decade ago if he didn't. Women ought to be allowed to own property, ought to be educated, ought to be considered a man's equal, but those kinds of opinions got a fellow blackballed, humiliated, and shunned by his peers, and August had endured quite enough of that at school, thank you very much. No, far better he leave his female relations to cause whatever havoc pleased them and marry a nice, quiet young woman. The peaceable kind who wouldn't cry revolution if he expected her to be at home having dinner with him, instead of breaking into some influential fellow's home to leave papers demanding education for girls upon his desk. August grew hot and then cold at the memory of how close they'd come to getting caught for that little lark.

The touch of a hand on his arm brought his attention back to his sister.

"Ah, come on, Bill. Let's go 'ome and 'ave tea an' cakes," she said, in a ludicrous lower-class accent he could not believe would fool anyone. She grinned at him, eyes sparkling with mischief.

"Fine," he said, unable to remain cross with her for long. She was his little sister after all and he loved her, even if she was a pain in his arse and always had been. "But if there's any jam tarts left, they're mine. I've earned them."

"Not if I get to them first," Anna squealed, and broke into a run, holding onto her hat and tearing down the road like the hoyden she was.

"Brat!" August yelled after her and set off in pursuit.

Chapter 2

Mother, Anna, Gwen,

Just because I want you to be happy, to see both my sisters settled with someone they love, does not mean I have any intention of 'selling them to the highest bidder'! Most young women would wish to be brought out into society, and I would be remiss in my duty as your brother if I did not offer to do so. Anna, I understand you dislike the idea of being paraded about 'like a prize cow' but, as I would never allow a man whom you did not love and esteem to offer for you, it would be you doing the choosing and awarding the blasted rosettes! I am hurt and offended that you believe me capable of doing anything other than wishing to see my sisters safe and happy.

I cannot endure another Christmas like this last and I do not doubt you will go on far better without me. I shall take up Bainbridge's offer to stay with him in town for a few days before going to stay with Roxborough. I believe I will seek rooms of my own after this, so we may have a chance of coexisting peacefully in the future. I have no doubt I will hear from you if ever I become useful to your cause again.

Please give my regards to Aunt Lettice and my apologies for not bidding her goodbye in person. I quite understand her leaving the madhouse too and do not blame her in the least for relocating to Bath. I wish her a peaceful time with her cats.

I offer you my heartfelt wishes for a Happy New Year.

—Excerpt of a letter from Mr August Lane-Fox to his female relations.

31st December 1840, Axton House, Piccadilly, London.

"About bloody time," Bainbridge said, regarding August with satisfaction. "You look like a fox that's escaped the hounds by too narrow a margin."

"I couldn't have put it better myself," August said, accepting a glass of brandy with gratitude. In truth, guilt was weighing him down, for he did not like leaving his mother and sisters alone, for fear of what they might do in his absence. They were adult women, though, and as they never tired of telling him, they did not need a man to oversee their daily lives. Well, so be it. If he hadn't left, he might have said something he'd regret.

"You'll stay, I hope? You need a break from those infernal females."

August shook his head. He was already fretting about what trouble Anna might get into next if he wasn't there to curtail her more enthusiastic insanities. At least Gwen was a little less proactive, preferring to spend her time painting… though heaven help him if those paintings ever saw the light of day. He shuddered.

"No, just a few days. I thought I'd pop down and spend a weekend with Dare, but I'd better not leave them for too long. Too terrifying to consider what I might come back to. I'm thinking of taking a small place nearby, though, to give us all a bit of breathing space."

Bainbridge tsked his displeasure but said nothing. "Can't you find some fellow to marry one of them? At least then they'd become his responsibility."

August snorted. "Exactly. Do you ever see Anna putting her life in the hands of the male of the species? Not that I blame her when I look around at some of the sorry specimens on offer. I wouldn't let them watch after livestock, let alone give them the power to order my sisters' lives as they saw fit. Seriously, put yourself in their shoes and imagine having your every decision made by some twit like Humphrey Price."

"I take your point, a horrifying idea. All the same, it would be amusing to see him try," Bainbridge said dryly. "Anna would run rings about him."

August laughed as he imagined it and then sobered abruptly as he realised it wasn't the least bit funny.

"Well, enough of that," Bainbridge commanded in his usual overbearing manner. "You're not to think of them for the next two days, at the very least. We shall have some fun and drink too much and generally misbehave, as is the prerogative of any despicable male. Starting tonight. It's the Cavendish New Year ball, you may remember. New Year, new start, and we may as well begin with a God-awful hangover. So run along and get your finery on quick smart or we'll be late, and my lady will not be pleased, which will annoy me."

August sighed and set down his empty glass. He had not intended to go to the Cavendish affair, but it was clear Bainbridge would not allow him to spend New Year's Eve alone. Still....

"But you will undoubtedly be late if you wait for me. There's barely time—"

"Then you'd best hurry," Bainbridge said, grinning and showing his teeth. August sighed.

"No misbehaving, Bainbridge," he said firmly. "And don't try to manoeuvre me into doing something dreadful. I intend to find myself a wife this season, and so I'll be on my best behaviour."

Bainbridge frowned. "Yes, fair enough, but there's no need to be a dull dog. I'm a dashed paragon these days, but even so—"

"No misbehaving," August repeated, his tone brooking no argument. "I mean it. Those days are behind us, and I mean to keep them there."

"Stop fretting. I'm sure he'll come."

Viv sent her brother an indignant glance. "I'm not fretting," she objected, a statement he greeted with a pitying expression. "Much," she amended, for honesty's sake, because she had no secrets from Ash. How could she when they seemed to know what the other was thinking so often? They were very close, and though Viv had friends she trusted implicitly, her twin was always the first person she turned to when she needed a confidant.

"Well, Mama ought to be pleased. Parliament doesn't open until the end of the month, so she feared everyone would still be in Brighton or in the country, but it's a crush. It will be the talk of the *ton* for weeks."

Viv nodded her agreement, too distracted to say more whilst her brother kept up an amusing commentary upon the guests, their attire, who they were talking to—and about.

"Goodness, will you look at Evie?" he exclaimed. "Such a change has come over her recently. I swear she gets prettier every time I see her."

Viv turned in the direction Ash was staring and smiled with pleasure. "So she does. Another new gown. My, but she looks lovely."

"I can't believe she is still seeing Madame Blanchet. The old bat never designed that. The cut of the bodice is exquisite and quite out of the ordinary. I'd lay money on that being someone else's work."

"Ash!" Viv said with a choked laugh.

Ash shrugged. "Well, really. She's not half so talented as she thinks she is. It's all very well designing for the standard English rose, but give the woman anyone out of the ordinary and she doesn't know what to do with her. A one-trick pony is the expression, I believe."

Viv bit back a smile, remembering the irritated words Ash had exchanged with the woman when he'd seen the yellow gown. Viv had thought it beautiful, but had understood it did not suit her the moment Ash had held it up to her before a looking glass. It was perhaps not in the ordinary way of things to take one's brother to help choose her gowns, but Viv didn't much care. She found the entire process tedious, and Ash got so heated when she chose badly that it was far easier to let him be a part of the process. How a man could choose so well for her and wear such hideous waistcoats, however, was one of life's great mysteries. Tonight's was a deep purple with tiny golden suns embroidered all over, and quite restrained by her brother's standards.

"Miss Knight!" Ash called, grinning as Evie spotted them and hurried over.

"Good evening, Mr Anson. Viv," she said, dipping a curtsey to Ash and embracing Viv. "Oh, Vivien, how beautiful you look. Simply ravishing," she said, staring at Viv.

"We were just saying the same of you," Viv said with a laugh. "What a lovely gown. That shade of sea green matches your eyes perfectly. Wherever did you get it?"

To her surprise, Evie blushed. "Oh, Madame Blanchet made it for me," she said, though she avoided Viv's gaze. Ash glanced at Viv, eyebrows raised.

"Does she have a new designer?" he demanded.

"Oh, er… no, she doesn't. Do excuse me, I said I'd dance with Mr Godwin."

Evie hurried off again as her partner came to claim her. The mystery of Evie's new gown was swiftly forgotten, though, as Viv saw some late arrivals appear in the grand entrance to the ballroom. Their names resonated around the room as the butler announced them, and many heads swivelled to stare.

"The Most Honourable Lawrence and Arabella Grenville, Marquess and Marchioness of Bainbridge, and Mr August Lane-Fox."

"Just breathe, Viv. Shall I fetch the sal volatile?" Ash asked with mock concern.

"Oh, hush up," Viv said, not feeling half as unconcerned as she tried to sound.

To her discomfort, she felt her heart pick up speed. He was here, and looking devastatingly handsome. Truly, he was splendid, his hair shimmering like old gold beneath the blaze of the many chandeliers. Viv watched him covertly as he made his way around the ballroom with his friend Bainbridge and Arabella. He moved with easy grace, all long elegant limbs and broad shoulders. Viv's mouth felt unaccountably dry.

"How do I look?" she said, turning to Ash, who returned a startled glance, having never been asked such a question before.

"Viv!" he said, laughing. "You're not truly so nervous you've forgotten how beautiful you are? I mean, just glance at me if you need reminding. We're gorgeous."

Despite her nerves, Viv burst out laughing. "Oh, Ash. You are dreadful. What would I do without you?"

"Wear something appalling and die of boredom, I should think," he replied earnestly.

Too anxious to find a suitable retort, Viv let the comment go, instead concentrating on trying to appear as if she was not fidgeting with anticipation as they grew nearer. She felt certain Mr Lane-Fox knew very well where she was and was avoiding eye contact on purpose. Indeed, she felt certain he would not have approached her at all if it were not her mother's ball. As it was, they were duty bound. Bainbridge, having greeted her parents, made a beeline for her, grinning broadly as his friend followed with every outward appearance of pleasure. Though she could not have said why, Viv did not believe it.

"Mr Anson, Miss Anson, a pleasure, as always. Miss Anson, may I say, with the obvious exception of my beautiful wife, you are quite the most ravishing creature in the room."

"My Lord Bainbridge," Viv said, sinking into a curtsey. "You are too kind."

"No, that I'm not," Bainbridge said, a wicked glint twinkling in his eyes. "In fact, I think you ought to dance with this handsome chap at once. You'll make everyone stare with astonishment at such a fine sight. Don't you think so, my love?" he asked his wife.

Arabella turned an exasperated expression his way, and Bainbridge spoke over her before she could reply. "Yes, of course you do."

He then clapped Mr Lane-Fox jovially on the back with such force that Viv suspected the poor fellow's teeth must have rattled. His friend was too polite to show anything but pleasure at Bainbridge forcing them to dance, but Viv did not doubt he would have a strong word with his friend later.

"It would be a pleasure, Miss Anson," Mr Lane-Fox said, holding out his hand to her.

Viv ignored the faint choking sound coming from her brother and smiled graciously, taking the proffered hand and following him to the dance floor. As the first strains of a waltz filled the room, she felt certain Mr Lane-Fox's jaw tightened. No doubt he would have preferred a country dance, which would have been far less intimate. He took her in hold, her hand clasped lightly in his, his other hand barely touching her waist. A moment later, he swept her into the dance, and it took her a full minute to catch her breath. Yet he did not look at her, did not attempt conversation, and Viv's heart sank.

"I'm sorry," she said, watching his face.

He did not react at first, and she felt she had pierced his concentration in speaking to him. His brow furrowed in confusion. "For what?"

"You didn't want to dance with me," she said shortly, seeing no reason to beat around the bush.

"I assure you—"

"Oh, you made all the right noises, indeed, if I let you go on I'm certain you will continue to do so, but I assure you I know when a man wishes to dance with me, and when he does not."

"Do men ever not want to dance with you?" he asked, a dry tone to his voice that at least sounded genuine.

"No," she replied, seeing no point in dissembling. "Which is why your reluctance is so apparent. Have I offended you?"

"No! No, of course not," he said with a sigh, and she felt as though perhaps he had let his guard down. "Forgive me, Miss Anson. I assure you the fault is mine, and none of yours. The truth is, I'm in rather a bad skin at present and I did not wish to come tonight."

"You did not wish to see me again," she guessed, and watched his reaction, wondering if he would lie to her. Why she felt so certain this was at the heart of his reluctance she did not know, for surely it was hubris on her part, but she believed it all the same.

"No," he admitted. "I did not."

Viv had to admit she was surprised. Though it was as she'd expected, it still stung to hear it said out loud. "I see," she said, unable to hide her reaction.

"No. I don't think you do," Mr Lane-Fox replied. "Please don't take offence, for I assure you there is no need. Quite the reverse. I admire you, Miss Anson, very much. Good heavens, I'm not blind, and you are clearly witty and clever and vivacious."

"But you didn't want to see me again?" Viv repeated, confused now and not a little dizzy as her concentration faltered and he guided her into a series of quick turns.

"No."

Viv pondered this and then gasped. "*Oh*," she said, stiffening, for it had occurred to her too late that Mr Lane-Fox might be one of those gentlemen who did not approve of mixed blood marriages. Both Viv and Ash were privileged enough and protected by her father and by their powerful friends to escape much of the prejudice their mother had faced in the past, but that did not mean it didn't exist.

His gaze shot to her face, for her posture had become so unyielding he must know he had caused her deep offence.

"You need not dance with me again, if my existence offends you, sir," she said, her voice tight.

A look of startled horror crossed Mr Lane-Fox's face, so obviously genuine that Viv relaxed a degree. *"No!"* he said, shaking his head. "Oh, good Lord. No, nothing… Hell, I'm making a pig's ear of this. I shall murder Bainbridge for making me come. I knew I ought not."

"Why don't you just make a clean breast of it and tell me the truth?" Viv suggested, torn between mortification and amusement at his discomfort.

He made a pained sound and nodded. "The truth," he agreed, and took a breath. "The truth is, Miss Anson, that you are the type of woman that causes a stir wherever she goes. You are beautiful and outspoken and, if I am not mistaken, have a will of iron."

"You are not mistaken," Viv admitted, her lips twitching as she studied him. He was even more handsome at close quarters, she decided, and he smelled delicious, though she could detect no cologne. A blessing, that. Some men seemed to pour an entire bottle of scent over themselves until the stench was so overpowering it made your eyes water. Mr Lane-Fox just smelled of shaving soap and clean linen, and something warm and tantalisingly musky that made her want to move closer and nuzzle the place beneath his ear, and then press her lips to his neck and… She jerked her head back, realising she had been subconsciously leaning closer. Good heavens.

"Yes, well, that's the trouble, I'm afraid. I'm sorry to be blunt, but… you are not what I'm looking for."

Viv blinked, jolted from her inappropriate musings by his rather too candid admission.

"What are you looking for?" she asked, to mask the uncertainty crashing about in her chest. Viv provoked two standard reactions from unmarried men who were not friends or relations: desire for her because she was beautiful and rich, or disapproval of her mixed heritage. In her experience, those were the only options. Mr Lane-Fox had just opened a new category, and she did not know what to call it.

"Someone rather more biddable and… ordinary. Quiet," he admitted, looking somewhat sheepish about it, as well he might.

"Perhaps you should get a cat?" she suggested tartly.

A tinge of colour crested his cheekbones. "You asked me to be honest, Miss Anson. I am doing my best."

"Then you ought to practise deception. It might make you better company." Viv pressed her lips together and took a moment to calm her temper. "I beg your pardon, Mr Lane-Fox. That was uncalled for."

He sighed and shook his head. "No, I don't blame you in the least. I know how it sounds and, to a spirited woman like yourself, I can well imagine your desire to bludgeon me with the nearest heavy object."

"It is a temptation I am striving to resist," Viv replied with a tight smile.

"I know that, but I beg you put my dilemma in context before you condemn me outright."

"What context is that? A weak mind? Or is it a weak spine?"

His expression darkened a degree and Viv sensed he would not take much more if she continued to insult him. She closed her mouth and gestured for him to continue.

"I cannot explain the problem in detail, Miss Anson, but suffice to say my mother and two sisters are spirited females with prodigious intellects, a great many opinions on how the world ought to be, and a burning desire to take action, not just talk about it over tea. I adore them, I admire them, and I want to be as far away from them as I can get most of the time. I just want a bit of peace and quiet instead of being dragged into their daily dramas, and marrying a woman with as much spirit, verve, and intellect as they have does not bode well for my remaining shred of sanity."

Vivien gaped at him, admittedly a little taken aback. "They sound fascinating."

"They are fascinating," he said fiercely. "They're marvellous. They're also exhausting, and I waver constantly between pride and mortification at the things they get up to. They'll destroy my reputation entirely one of these days, though by then I won't care because my reason will be a distant memory, and yet I wouldn't have them any other way. I just don't want to live with them."

"How do they think the world ought to be?" Viv could not help asking. The dance was ending, much to her regret, and she hoped he would not run away before the end of this fascinating conversation.

Mr Lane-Fox offered his arm and led her from the dance floor, his expression one of resignation, though his voice was still warm and friendly. "They believe girls and boys should receive the same level of education, that the female brain is as capable as any man's. They believe men and women are equal and ought to be treated the same way, with women allowed to own property, and have autonomy over their own bodies, and their children."

Viv watched him, captivated, as he calmly expressed her every frustration and belief in a few short sentences. "And you, Mr Lane-Fox," she said, feeling suddenly breathless at the possibility. "Do you believe they are correct?"

"Damnation," he muttered crossly, rubbing a hand over his face. "I just knew you were going to ask me that."

Viv clutched at his sleeve, staring up at him, wanting to believe it was possible. "And so…?"

Mr Lane-Fox made a terse sound of frustration and disengaged her hand from his sleeve. "Yes, Miss Anson, I believe they are quite correct, God help me, but that does not mean I am prepared to turn the entire world upside down to change it for them, or for you. I pray you will forgive me for it. I'm certain I must be a dreadful disappointment to you. Now, if you'll excuse me. I must go and see… *someone*."

He bowed and left her, clearly eager to escape her company. Viv watched him go, and knew it was not disappointment she felt, but hope.

Chapter 3

Ashburton, you dog,

Don't think for a moment I swallowed that guff about a previous engagement any more than your Pa did. You've ensnared that gorgeous opera dancer. haven't you? And you knew dashed well I had my eye on her. All's well in love and war, I dare say, but I shall pay you back, Pip, old fellow. You see if I don't.

Well, you may have a Happy New Year's eve with your pretty mistress, but I comfort myself with the thought of you facing your father when he figures out where you spent the coming evening instead of the Cavendish ball. Ah, I should like to be a fly on the wall for that confrontation. Shirking responsibilities is one of those things fathers do get dreadfully het up about. I know mine does, and I can only imagine Montagu's reaction. Quite makes my blood run cold. Do remember to leave me that fine gelding you bought last week when you make out your last will and testament. It's been nice knowing you.

——Excerpt of a letter from The Most Hon'ble Jules Adolphus, Marquess of Blackstone (Eldest son of Prunella and Robert Adolphus, Duke and Duchess of Bedwin) to his friend, The Right Hon'ble Philip Barrington, Earl of Ashburton (Eldest son of Lucian and Matilda Barrington, The Marquess and Marchioness of Montagu).

31st December 1840, Cavendish House, The Strand, London.

"Oh, I say, I beg your pardon!"

Louis César bit back an oath as a man careened into him, nearly knocking the glass from his hand. By some miracle, he avoided being drowned in champagne and only spilled a little over his fingers.

"Dreadfully sorry," the man said, his face flaming scarlet. "Someone pushed me, and it was you or the lady dripping diamonds, and I figured you were the safer bet all things considered."

Louis let out a huff of laughter, unable to fault his reasoning. The stern-looking matron standing to Louis' left—and indeed dripping diamonds—would undoubtedly have given the poor fool a fine set down.

"No harm done," Louis replied.

The man beamed at him. He was a stout fellow, of average height and with a plain but friendly face framed by wavy chestnut hair: the kind of nondescript, average English gentleman that would pass unnoticed at a grand affair like this. Well dressed, if not exactly elegant, he had an affable air about him, and he was staring at Louis with undisguised interest.

"You're that comte fellow, aren't you? Villen. That's it, I think? Barnaby Godwin," he said, grinning and holding out his hand. "Pleased to crash into you."

"A pleasure," Louis replied, rather wishing the fellow would go away and find whatever party it was he'd come with. He'd just caught sight of Evie for the first time that night, dancing with bloody Hadley-Smythe, and he was not in the mood for polite chitchat.

"Knew it had to be you. Couldn't be two fellows with a face like that in one place. The handsomest man on three continents, is what the ladies say. Did you know?"

"No," Louis replied, endeavouring not to sound impatient.

"Oh, yes. They're all talking about you. Taking bets on who'll be your next mistress, or who'll you'll wed. Do you know they keep a book? Must say I was a bit shocked. Just like at White's! You don't think of ladies doing such things, do you? Well, I don't, leastways, but then I'm not very clever with females. Always get my tongue in a knot. Invariably say something stupid. Still, I don't suppose you need say much, with a face like that, I mean. Wish I could borrow it," he mused.

Louis tried counting to ten.

"Ah, there's Miss Knight. Dancing with Cyril, ain't she? Mr Hadley-Smythe, I mean. Now, she's a jolly female. I like her a good deal. She's kind, too. Never makes a fellow feel a fool, but always smiles and seems pleased to see you, and she laughs at my jokes, even when they're not funny. My jokes are never very funny," he said wistfully. "Always forget the punchline."

"She is kind," Louis said, the words out before he could think better of them.

Mr Godwin nodded, perking up now Louis was taking part in the conversation. "I know! The kind of gal that makes one feel better, even if you didn't realise you were blue devilled. Do you know what I mean?"

"Yes," Louis said with a sigh. "I know just what you mean." He shot Mr Godwin a sideways glance, wondering if he too had designs on Evie.

"Reckon Cyril is after courting her. Don't you?"

"Certainly. Aren't you?" Louis asked, though he wondered why he would punish himself with the discovery of another man after his Evie.

"Me?" the fellow said, wide-eyed. "Oh, no. I mean, she's splendid, don't get me wrong, but she don't look at me that way. I know I'm no oil painting, but a fellow likes to be wanted all the same, don't he? No, I shall find a lady one day who looks at me like I've hung the moon, or I'll stay a bachelor, I reckon. No point in settling for less, to my mind."

Louis brightened and felt a rush of fellow feeling towards the loquacious young man. "None at all," he agreed. "I think you are very wise."

"Crikey," said Mr Godwin, his mouth quirking with amusement. "I'd be careful saying things like that out loud. People will think you're queer in your attic."

Louis laughed and then turned his gaze back to the crowd, seeking out Evie once more. "Do you think Mr Hadley-Smythe in with a chance?" he asked, telling himself he was a fool but unable to stop all the same.

"Perhaps. Though she could do better if you ask me," Godwin said frankly.

Louis decided he liked Barnaby Godwin.

"Monsieur Godwin, would you care to seek some refreshment? I appear to be out of champagne."

To Louis' amusement, Mr Godwin looked at him rather like he'd just been invited to drink ambrosia on Mount Olympus. "Oh, I say. That's dashed decent of you. I should like that, only do call me Barnaby. I mean, if you'd like to, that is?"

"Certainly, Barnaby, and I am Louis César," Louis added, feeling magnanimous. Barnaby looked like he might burst with pride and just stood there gaping, with his mouth opening and closing. Louis patted the fellow on the back and guided him toward the refreshments room, praying he'd find a waiter en route to save him the bother. He needed a drink.

"Where is he?" Evie whispered to Viv as the two of them strolled arm-in-arm around the enormous ballroom.

"Over there, to the right of the Russian minister and Baroness Brunow."

Evie craned her neck to no avail until an elderly lady in a revolting puce gown moved and revealed Mr August Lane-Fox speaking to the Earl of Vane. "Oh, yes, I see him now. Yes, he is handsome, I agree. They both are, actually," she added, observing the two men together.

"Vane is too much an enigma. One never knows what he's thinking. I find Mr Lane-Fox more appealing. He is refreshingly honest, for one. Perhaps a touch too honest for my vanity. I find him very handsome indeed, though perhaps not when compared to Monsieur le Comte," Viv said, tilting her head to regard the two men critically.

"No one is as handsome as Louis," Evie said with a laugh. "He's an anomaly. We cannot hold mere mortals up for comparison. It's unfair."

"Ashburton could perhaps match him, though I admit they are very different. He is light and ice to the comte's dark fire. My, can you imagine the two of them side by side? Half the women in the room would faint," Viv said with a snort of amusement.

Evie chuckled. "I'd arrange it for you, but Ashburton cried off at the last moment. I suspect Montagu is *not pleased.*"

"Poor Pip," Viv said, smirking. "He'll have hell to pay if he's displeased his father."

"I know. Even though I doubt Montagu will so much as raise his voice. He never shouts, you know. Thomas says his quiet admonition is far worse and that he'd rather be pilloried than disappoint his father, but that's only because they admire him so."

Viv nodded, though it was clear she was no longer listening, her rapt gaze focused on the man across the ballroom.

"So, he said he admires you, but you are too much for him," Evie said, summing up the conversation Viv had relayed to her.

"Yes," Viv said with a sigh.

"Well, if he likes and admires you, that's half the battle won. You must only convince him you can be quiet and docile—"

Viv pulled such a face that Evie burst out laughing. She had a point, though. No one would believe that in a million years.

"Or—" she said, her voice trembling with amusement. "Convince him he doesn't want a wife like that at all."

"That is my only option, I know," Viv said thoughtfully. "How, though? Oh, drat it, here comes Lord Barclay to claim his dance. I'll see you after."

Evie nodded and watched her go, and was about to return to the refreshments room for a drink when she was startled to discover Mr Lane-Fox and Lord Vane in front of her.

"Miss Knight," Lord Vane said, giving an elegant bow and commanding her attention before Mr Lane-Fox could open his mouth. "Please excuse my unseemly haste, but I must get my request in for a dance with you this evening before my companion here can speak, as he too requests your indulgence. I suspect you must have few, if any, dances remaining."

Evie blushed, a little taken aback at being sought out by the pair of them, especially as Vivien had told her of her desire for Mr

Lane-Fox, but then, perhaps she could do Viv some good if she danced with him and told him how wonderful she was. Fumbling nervously with her dance card, she glanced up. "I-I have two dances left. The waltz that is about to begin, and a mazurka, if that suits you, Mr Lane-Fox?"

"I would be delighted, Miss Knight," he said, smiling at her warmly. A little too warmly. *Oh.* He was looking for a quiet, docile wife, one that wouldn't cause him any difficulties. Evie's blush deepened. Lud. Now she was in trouble.

"Miss Knight, you are looking a little over-warm. Shall I take you for some refreshment?"

Evie turned to see Louis had appeared at her elbow and wished very much she could accept his offer. "You are most kind, monsieur," she said, smiling at him. "But—"

"But my dance is about to commence," Lord Vane said firmly, giving her his arm and shrugging apologetically to Louis. "Beg pardon, monsieur."

Louis' gaze darkened and Evie returned a small smile, but took Lord Vane's arm, and walked with him to the dance floor with no little relief.

"I am astonished you had any spaces remaining on your card, Miss Knight," he said, taking her in his arms as the first notes of the orchestra heralded the next dance.

"Many of my friends are here this evening," Evie said, a little distracted by the sensation of being observed. She glanced back to find Louis, Mr Godwin, and Mr Lane-Fox watching her. Frowning, she turned her attention back to Lord Vane.

"You are too modest, I think," he said, smiling at her. "No one speaks of you without smiling. Did you know that?"

Evie looked up at him. "Have you been speaking to my father, then?" she said, a little uncomfortable.

He laughed and shook his head. "No, and stop being coy. I think you have caught Mr Lane-Fox's eye for one, and I know for a fact Mr Hadley-Smythe has spoken of little but you for days now."

Fighting not to blush again, for she'd look like a tomato if he kept this up, Evie regarded the man with interest. She understood what Viv meant by him being an enigma. His reputation was not a good one. Women and drink, gambling, all the usual vices had been attached to him, though he had been in polite society far more often of late and appeared the model of gentlemanly behaviour. There was a world-weary air about him, which was at odds with his good looks and vitality. He was certainly handsome, but she did not know what to make of him.

"Forgive me. I did not mean to make you uncomfortable. I was only interested in dancing with the young lady of whom everyone speaks so warmly. Though we were introduced some time ago, I have not had the pleasure of speaking with you since."

"Well, here we are," Evie said nervously, fighting not to laugh when Vivien caught her eye as she spun past.

Viv waggled her eyebrows in a mock lascivious expression that made a giggle bubble up inside Evie.

"Here we are, and with your suitors watching us with avid interest."

Evie glanced back at the three men and chuckled. "Oh, they're not my suitors."

"But I have just told you I suspect Mr Lane-Fox has an interest, and the others seem mighty fascinated by our progress."

Evie laughed and shook her head, but was not about to explain that Louis was only being protective of her because he was her friend.

"You are close with Lady Elizabeth Demarteau, I think?" Lord Vane said, returning her attention to the conversation.

"I am," Evie agreed.

"I should like an introduction, if I could be so presumptuous as to ask such a thing of you," he said, his expression hesitant. "I will not be offended if you wish to seek advice before doing so. I am aware of the inherent risks, but my intentions are quite honourable," he added with a rueful smile.

Evie considered this, deciding his manner was polite, and he appeared genuine. Besides, Eliza's husband would be certain to frighten the man off if Evie made an error of judgement.

"Very well. I shall ask her if she objects. Lady Eliza can make her own mind up, I assure you. She's very astute."

"I know."

Evie studied him with interest but could gauge nothing from his expression. When the dance had ended, he guided her not to where Louis, Mr Godwin and Mr Lane-Fox were still speaking, but to Vivien and Ashton as she requested. Then he thanked her politely for the dance and left her with her friends.

"Well?" Viv demanded.

"Just as you said," Evie replied, still a little breathless from the dance. "An enigma. He wants an introduction to Eliza."

"Interesting," Ash said thoughtfully. "I wonder if it's about her school."

"The school? What on earth would a man like Vane want to know about her charitable school for?" Viv asked, which was a fair question. Vane's reputation was not one for philanthropy. Indeed, he was something of a devil if half of the stories were to be believed, though after dancing with him, Evie wasn't certain she *did* believe them. She'd rather liked him.

"I have a dance with Mr Lane-Fox later," Evie told Viv. "I shall spend my time telling him how marvellous you are."

Viv laughed and took her arm. "Thank you, darling. That's sweet, though I think I shall need more help than that." She gave her brother a pointed stare. He groaned.

"Very well. I shall go and ingratiate myself," Ash muttered, and set off to befriend Mr Lane-Fox.

Viv nudged Evie. "I believe your next dance partner approaches."

Evie turned to see Louis had found her in the crush.

"Are you avoiding me?" he asked, crooking one elegant eyebrow. "Or have you forgotten you gave me the next dance?"

"Of course not!" Evie protested, before spying Mr Godwin at his elbow. He was a nice man, good natured, if rather too talkative. She wondered if he had driven Louis mad yet. "Oh, good evening, Mr Godwin. How lovely to see you."

"Miss Knight, a pleasure as always. You look in prime twig this evening, if you don't mind me saying so." His gaze drifted to Vivien and his colour rose dramatically. "Miss Anson," he added reverently as he gave a deep bow.

Viv smiled in return, and Godwin looked as if he might pass out. Louis exchanged an amused glance with Evie, who hurried to put the fellow at his ease.

"Are you enjoying the ball, Mr Godwin? Mr Hadley-Smythe mentioned you returned from Brighton especially."

"Oh, yes, marvellous," he agreed, returning his attention to Evie with relief. "Good time to make merry and be with friends. Never liked New Year. Makes me gloomy. Don't know why. Don't like things ending, I suppose. Seems sad, don't it? Like saying goodbye to an old friend."

"Or perhaps greeting a new one," Evie suggested.

"Oh, I say. Yes, that's a better way of thinking of it," he said, brightening.

Louis looked around as the orchestra struck up once more. "My dance," he said, offering Evie his arm.

Evie smiled and nodded, though she felt rather guilty at leaving poor Mr Godwin with Viv, who obviously intimidated him. With one anxious glance over her shoulder at them, she followed Louis onto the dance floor.

Chapter 4

Dearest Aisling,

I am sorry to hear Mr Cootes has made your stay at the Hall so uncomfortable. What a beast he sounds. At least you must be free of him now. Will you remain at Trevick for a while, or shall we expect to see you in town this season? I know you are not overly fond of society, but there is some pleasure to be found after all – my company being the most compelling naturally! Ash will be delighted too. Are you still besotted with him, you poor addle-pated creature?

I feel quite certain your mama will insist on you coming eventually, for such a perfect bloom cannot hide away in some vast castle to wither and gather dust. Oh, dear, and now I've made you sound like an unwatered aspidistra. My apologies. You must come to town at once and scold me for my impertinence.

Oh, do come Aisling. I have so much to tell you.

—Excerpt of a letter from Miss Vivien Anson (Daughter of the Right Hon'ble Silas

*and Aashini Anson, The Viscount and
Viscountess Cavendish) to Lady Aisling
Baxter (Daughter of the Right Hon'ble Luke
and Kitty Baxter, the Earl and Countess of
Trevick).*

31st December 1840, Cavendish House, The Strand, London.

Viv turned to Mr Godwin, who had a panicked, glassy look in his eyes. She offered him a warm smile in the hopes of putting him at ease.

"I believe you are acquainted with Mr Lane-Fox?" she said, having observed the two men speaking while she danced with Lord Barclay.

"August? Oh, yes. A good fellow. Known him since school. Not pals, mere acquaintances. Never brave enough to get up to the larks those four loved so much, but they're good sorts, all of them. Bainbridge is a bit daunting, mind, but never cruel, not like some. They hauled me out of trouble too, come to think on it," he added with a sigh.

"August? I mean, Mr Lane-Fox helped you?" she asked with interest, pleased to find proof of her conviction he was a kind man.

Mr Godwin nodded. "They all did, at one time or another. I was often in trouble, I'm afraid to say. Boys being boys, they like to pick on the smaller ones, which I was then. Didn't catch up until later. Bit of a dunce at school, too. Good at sports, though. My saving grace," he added with a grin and then blushed furiously as he realised he'd given her his life story.

"Shall we go and speak with him? You could reminisce," she suggested, laying her hand on his sleeve. Mr Godwin stared at it in some alarm and swallowed.

"Certainly," he said weakly. "But don't you have a dance partner searching for you?"

Viv shook her head. "No. I've kept the next two dances free this evening. Too fatiguing otherwise."

And she had been determined not to give Mr Lane-Fox the opportunity to avoid claiming one of them. She still had the polka remaining, which she had mentally labelled as belonging to him... if only he would ask her.

"Right you are, then," Mr Godwin said, darting an anxious glance at her before walking through the crowd in search of their quarry. "Do you know him well?"

Viv shook her head. "No," she said with a sigh, glancing at Mr Godwin and deciding to take a chance. "I should like to, but... I intimidate him."

Godwin gave a startled laugh and nodded. "By gad, I don't doubt that. It's hard on a fellow, you know, to look at someone as beautiful as you and not get his words all in a muddle. It's awful distracting, not to mention a frightful strain on the nerves, always wondering if some other fellow is going to steal a march on you. My ma always says not to marry a beautiful gal if you want peace of mind. I've pondered that often, and wondered if there's not a bit of sense in it, but just 'cause a girl is pretty, don't mean she's disloyal, or shallow any more than a homely one is likely to be kind and sweet-natured. Leastways, I don't think it does," he said, looking deeply confused. "Not that I'm looking for a pretty one or a homely one especially, only one that likes me, which is dashed hard enough, I might tell you."

Viv bit her lip to stop herself from laughing, for he was quite in earnest and so affable she decided he was an absolute darling.

"I don't think you'll have any trouble finding one that likes you, Mr Godwin. You just be yourself and she'll make herself known to you."

"Oh, I say. Thank you, Miss Anson," he said, puffing up visibly and grinning as he escorted her through the crowd. "Ah, there's the fellow. August, old man, look what a prize I've on my arm. Prettiest gal in the room, eh?"

Viv could see no visible sign of dismay on his face, but she felt certain Mr Lane-Fox was groaning silently.

"Miss Anson, we meet again," he said, humour lighting his eyes, though he must be cursing her, must know she'd manoeuvred Mr Godwin into seeking him out again.

"She's got some dances free, August. Ought to claim one whilst you still can," Mr Godwin said in an all too audible whisper, unwittingly forcing the poor man into asking her again.

Viv gazed about the room, pretending she hadn't heard, and tried her best to appear as though she were an innocent bystander. She failed. There was a smile tugging at her lips that refused to be vanquished.

"Is that so?" Mr Lane-Fox said, regarding Viv with a mixture of exasperation and... and something she very much hoped was anticipation.

August knew he ought to be annoyed, or at the very least irritated. He had tried his best to avoid Miss Anson ever since their dance, not even allowing himself to look for her in the crowd. He'd wanted to, though. That was the devil of it. No, not wanted to, *longed* to. He ought never to have danced with her and was very much looking forward to pummelling Bainbridge for putting him up to it. Holding her in his arms had been the biggest mistake he could possibly have made. The feel of her lithe body so close to his, the scent of her, the way her silken skirts had whispered against his legs, every detail of every moment of the dance was etched upon his brain for the rest of his days. She had taken his attention the first time he'd met her at Beverwyck. Well, and why not? He had a pulse, didn't he? Any fool could appreciate beauty when he saw it and she... well, she made it hard to breathe. It almost hurt to look at her, like a painting so lovely it made your

42

chest tight. She wasn't a work of art, though. That he could have managed. No, she was a flesh and blood woman with a mind of her own, and a quick-witted, intelligent one at that. She made his pulse leap and his heart crash about, and that was the last bloody thing he needed. Yet here she was again, and fool that he was, he could not wait to take her in his arms.

Of course, he asked her to dance—not that he had a choice — and Barnaby stood there beaming as if he'd wrapped them both in a great red ribbon and now his work was done.

"Are you furious?" she asked as he led her back out onto the dance floor when couples took their places for the polka.

He smiled and shook his head, not trusting himself to speak. He could only feel some relief that the polka was an energetic dance, and whilst partly in hold, it did not have the intimacy of the waltz. Small mercies.

"I'm afraid I'm dreadfully stubborn," she said as they waited for the dance to begin.

She gazed up at him, her great indigo eyes as inviting as a warm blue sea, and just as dangerous if he swam out too far.

"I'm spoiled, too. I always get my own way."

"Or else?" he suggested.

She nodded, grinning at him. "Or else I shall stamp my foot and have a temper fit."

"I should like to see that," he said, before he could think better of it. What the devil was he saying? That was the last thing he wanted!

"I could arrange it," she said, laughter in her voice, but then the music began, and they needed all their breath for the polka.

A few minutes in and she started laughing, a joyous, infectious sound that made his lips curve upwards. Soon, he joined her, unable to stop himself, absurd as it was, but there was something vital and life affirming about this ridiculous, frivolous dance with her and the way she made his blood sing in his veins. Around and around they went, dizzy with pleasure, with August drunk on her in a way too many glasses of champagne had not managed. She was glorious, filling his senses and making him want to shout with happiness… except such overblown sensations were only ever fleeting, and eventually one came down to earth. Finally, the music faded, the dance ended, and the crowd cheered and shouted as everyone realised it was almost midnight. Miss Anson stared up at him, her beautiful face flushed with happiness and exertion, her eyes sparkling with delight. August's heart gave a lurch in his chest as he saw he had indeed swum out too far, out of his depth, away from safety and peace and a quiet life.

He let go of her and took a step back.

"Thank you for the dance," he said over the roar of the crowd, and then hurried away as the chimes of midnight rang out through the ballroom.

Evie laughed as the ballroom erupted and the clock struck midnight.

"Bonne Année, ma petite," whispered a voice in her ear. She grinned, not needing to turn around to know who spoke to her, his breath fluttering against the back of her neck.

"Happy New Year, Louis," she replied softly, though she did turn then, to see him smiling at her, his expression warm and pleased.

"I have hardly seen you this evening," he said, a touch of reproach in his voice. "You have been like quicksilver, always slipping away."

Evie reached out to take his hand and give it a brief squeeze. Everyone was too busy celebrating to notice them now. "I am sorry, truly. I don't know where the time has gone. It's flown past far too quickly, and now it's next year already!"

His lips curved into a rueful smile and Evie decided she must persuade him to sit for a portrait. Such a man ought to be recorded, supposing anyone could capture his presence, and not simply his beautiful face.

"So it is, and you are well on your way to achieving your New Year's resolution… and eighteen forty-one hardly begun. Though you promised I could help you on your quest to have fun, I might remind you. It is hardly kind of you to leave me out."

"And you *have* helped me," she protested as he moved to shield her from the overexcited jostling of some inebriated young men. Louis sent them a murderous glare and the men lurched away in the opposite direction.

"You only danced with me once," he said with a heavy sigh, taking her hand and placing it on his arm.

"I did not intend it that way, only everyone was so insistent it was impossible to refuse them," she said, regretting now that she had not saved him a second dance.

"You found a dance for Vane and Mr Lane-Fox," he said lightly, though she could feel tension in the flexing muscle beneath her fingers.

Evie nodded. Her dance with Mr Lane-Fox had been a tad awkward, what with her gently rebuffing his attempts to flirt with her—not that he'd seemed dreadfully bothered—and then with her trying to tell him how wonderful Viv was without being obvious about her intentions. She would much rather have been dancing with Louis. However, there was that other matter….

"Well, I only had the two left, it's not my fault. If you'd wanted another you should have asked me earlier. Though I must tell you Papa said I ought not dance with you so often," she admitted. Not that she had the slightest intention of listening to that piece of advice, but she'd thought it might be prudent not to disregard his request so soon.

Louis' gaze sharpened, his expression growing serious at once. "He said that?"

She nodded. "He says I ought not favour you so. I've told him repeatedly we are only friends, that you have no designs upon me, but he doesn't pay the least bit of attention!"

He was quiet now, his tension unmistakable, and Evie wondered if she ought to have told him. She hoped she had not hurt his feelings. Louis was far more sensitive than most people realised. They saw the beautiful face and elegant figure, the wit and the charm, and assumed he was utterly confident. It wasn't true, and he was easily hurt—not that he'd ever admit it—but especially so if the remarks came from those he esteemed, and he held her father in high regard.

"Papa is dreadfully overprotective, Louis. You know that. It's not because he doesn't like you."

"Monsieur Le Comte," he corrected, appearing distracted as he guided her through the over-excited crush of people… not that anyone could overhear them with the din being made by the revellers.

"I haven't offended you, have I?"

"*Non, non. Ne t'inquiète pas,*" he soothed, though he did not turn to look at her.

"Where are we going, *Monsieur Le Comte*?" she asked, realising they were heading away from the ballroom.

"To get some air. It is too hot in here." He looked at her then, his expression clearing. "If you wish to?"

"Oh, yes, please. It's far too stuffy. I should like some air, though do you think we ought? We don't have a chaperone."

Evie glanced around, a little unnerved, wondering if they were being observed.

"Don't you trust me, *ma chérie?*" he asked, quirking one dark eyebrow at her.

She pulled a face. "Silly. Only people will talk."

"Half the world is on the terrace, I regret to inform you," he said dryly. "We shall be far from unchaperoned."

"Oh, look. It's snowing!" Evie exclaimed as they moved through the open doors.

Though 'half the world' was rather an exaggeration, there were certainly enough couples here for propriety. Evie laughed and tipped her head back, turning in a circle as tiny flakes of snow left their chill touches upon her overheated skin. She straightened to see Louis gazing at her, a look in his eyes she could not read.

"You have snowflakes in your hair," he whispered, and then reached up to brush them away. "There," he added, before stroking her cheek with the back of his fingers. His touch was warm and gentle against her rapidly cooling skin, far too intimate, and brought the colour rushing back to her face.

"Thank you," she said uncertainly as he took a step back.

Evie looked away from him, her gaze falling to the large sapphire pin she'd given him for Christmas, nestled in the folds of his immaculate cravat.

"Are you too cold?" he asked, his gaze moving over her bare arms and shoulders.

Evie shook her head. "No. Not in the least. It's a relief to be out of the heat. Actually, I'm also glad to have the chance to speak to you privately."

"You are?" he said, his voice soft, his gaze never leaving hers. He had remarkably thick eyelashes. How had she never noticed that before?

"Yes. I wanted to thank you."

"Oh." Those thick lashes swept down now, shielding that vibrant blue from her gaze and whatever it was he was thinking.

Evie thought he sounded a little impatient, and sensed he did not wish her to thank him.

"For my Christmas presents, I mean. Madame Blanchet is beside herself with curiosity to know who designed them for me. So am I to tell the truth? Was… Was it you, Louis? It seems impossible that you could have done such a thing, but I cannot think who—"

"Do they please you?" he asked, evading the question.

"You know they do. They're exquisite. I've worn nothing so lovely in my life and so many people have asked me about them, who designed them. It makes me furious to give that wretched woman the credit, but it was the only way I could persuade her to make them up for me and hold her tongue. Otherwise Mama and everyone would start asking awkward questions."

"You did right," he said, nodding. "Better she have the credit and no one the wiser. I am glad they please you. The world is finally taking notice of you as it ought to do, for you are lovely."

Evie smiled, touched by the comment. "That's kind of you to say so."

He gave a huff of laughter that did not sound the least bit amused and shook his head.

"Louis," she tried again, wanting him to answer her.

"Monsieur Le Comte," he said wearily. "Come along, *ma petite.* I had best take you back inside before you catch a chill."

Frustrated but aware he would not give her an answer tonight, Evie followed him back inside.

Chapter 5

Dearest Viv,

Yes, I shall come to town. Mama insists, and even Papa has begrudgingly admitted my chances of making a match will diminish if I don't hurry up and get on with finding a husband. You know how he hates the idea of me leaving home, so I <u>must</u> be in danger of becoming an old maid! I think on balance; I prefer being a wilting aspidistra, so I shan't scold you for the comparison. In any case, I shall keep you informed of when we will arrive. Nothing has been settled yet.

I will scold you for teasing me about Ash, though, you horrid girl. How unkind you are to me. I know he is your brother, but even you must be aware of how handsome and funny he is. Sadly, I adore him still. Sorry, love. No matter how I tell myself it is merely a childish infatuation that has endured too long, I cannot make my heart heed me. I am not a fool, though. I know he does not return my affections, and as much as I would love to be your sister, I promise I do not harbour any illusions of it coming to pass. Do you think there is another man out there, someone kind and sweet, who will take my mind off him and engage my foolish heart?

—Excerpt of a letter from Lady Aisling Baxter (Daughter of the Right Hon'ble Luke and Kitty Baxter, the Earl and Countess of Trevick) to Miss Vivien Anson (Daughter of the Right Hon'ble Silas and Aashini Anson, The Viscount and Viscountess Cavendish).

1st January 1841, Cavendish House, The Strand, London.

"There, there, love. You have a good cry," Ash soothed as Viv snivelled and blew her nose. "It's only the hangover making you blue devilled, and January is such a vile month to have stretched out before one. All those grey skies and drizzle, it's enough to give anyone the pip."

"It's snowing," Viv said crossly, too out of sorts to be reasonable.

"Even worse, though it's pretty to look at, I'll grant you."

Viv sighed and told herself to buck up. She was not a watering pot by nature and Ash was right, her head was throbbing, and she was tired after all the excitement which was making her wretched. It wasn't the only reason, though, not when remembering the way Mr Lane-Fox had walked away from her without a backwards glance, after the wonderful time they'd had dancing together it made her feel weepy all over again.

Ash took one look at her glum expression and sighed. "Well, the fellow has told you the problem, hasn't he? You cannot pretend he's led you up the garden path, so either you leave him be and find someone else, or you must expect things will not go entirely your way. If you want him to change his mind about you, the only thing to do is show him what he'd be missing out on, which is a great deal."

Viv swallowed hard and reached for her brother's hand, giving it a squeeze. Though they bickered and teased each other mercilessly, underneath it all was the knowledge they would do anything for each other. If one was down, the other one would always do whatever it took to lift them back up again. Taking a deep breath and determined to heed her brother's sound advice, Viv nodded.

"Yes. You're right, of course. I'm being foolish because I'm tired and my head hurts. I shall have another cup of tea and some toast and feel much more the thing, I promise. I'm sorry for being such a bore."

"You are never a bore," Ash said with a laugh. "Many, many things, but never that."

Viv snorted with amusement, and her brother grinned.

"That's better," he said with approval, reaching for the teapot and pouring her another cup. He added two generous lumps of sugar, a dash of milk and stirred before handing her the cup. "The sugar will help your head."

"And did you meet any lovely young ladies?" Viv asked him, sipping the oversweet brew with a grimace.

"Dozens," Ash said, smirking.

"Arrogant devil. I suppose they batted their eyelashes at you and sighed and flattered you."

"Certainly," he agreed, a devil dancing in his eyes.

"But no one special."

"I am not yet looking for anyone special," Ash reminded her. "Unlike you, my poor darling, I have longer before I am considered past my best."

Viv huffed with irritation and lounged back against the pillows. "It's so unfair."

"Life is, *meri shona*," said a familiar and amused voice. "Though I am far from past my best yet, you young pup. In my prime, rather."

"Good morning, Nani Maa," Ash said, leaping up to arrange the pillows on his grandmother's favourite chair as her maid, Mary, helped the old lady to sit down. Mary, who admired and was extremely fond of her cantankerous mistress, fussed about making sure her cushions were plumped and her spectacles were in reach, as well as whatever scandalous novel she was currently engrossed in.

Their grandmother sighed with relief as she settled her feet on a padded footstool. "Ah, that's better, and good morning to you, *mera tota.*"

"Nani Maa, must you?" Ash grumbled whilst Vivien smothered a grin, knowing how the childish nickname *tota*, meaning parrot, annoyed him.

He bent over the old woman, arranging a cashmere shawl over her knees with care. No one knew exactly how old their grandmother was, as she refused to tell them. Anywhere between seventy and a hundred seemed possible, but her skin was the warm dark of well-loved mahogany and her hair a startling white in contrast. Now her head tilted to one side as she considered Vivien, bright, intelligent eyes putting her in mind of a blackbird listening for worms. The wicked old woman missed nothing, and they never had pulled the wool over her eyes, no matter how clever they thought they'd been. They both adored her.

"Well?" she demanded of Vivian, shooing her maid away with a little wave of her hand to get the woman to stop fussing over her.

"Well, what?" Viv asked, perplexed.

"Tell me about him."

Heat rose under Viv's cheeks, and she darted a glare at Ash, who shook his head. "Never uttered a word, I swear."

Viv sighed. Nani Maa knew everything. She ought to be used it by now.

"He's lovely. Tall and handsome, hair the colour of ripe wheat, blue eyes, kind and funny and, I suspect, just a bit wicked. Utterly perfect," she added with a dejected huff.

"No man is that," Nani Maa said with a snort. "Not even you, *tota*," she added, ruffling Ash's thick black hair until it was all mussed.

"Argh!" Ash exclaimed, leaping to his feet. "Now I must do it again," he complained, heading for the nearest mirror.

"Perhaps I should call you my dear peacock," the old woman mused, her eyes alight with amusement.

Viv sniggered.

"Who is he then, this paragon of male virility?" Nani Maa asked, picking up a small bell and ringing for Mary, whom she'd only just dismissed.

"Mr August Lane-Fox," Viv said wistfully, as Mary hurried back in and looked expectantly at her mistress.

"A fresh pot of tea, Mary, and some of that gingerbread, and don't tell me there isn't any. I smelled it baking," Nani Maa said.

"The doctor—" Mary began, but might as well have saved her breath.

"That silly quack is more of an old woman than I shall ever be," Nani Maa retorted. "Now run along."

"Yes, ma'am." Mary hurried away again.

"Lane-Fox," Nani Maa mused, thoughtful now. "Isn't he one of those naughty boys that were always causing trouble? Friend of the Marquess of Bainbridge."

Vivien's eyebrows went up, though she didn't know why she was surprised that her grandmother knew of their exploits. It was amusing too, to hear the men referred to as boys. "Yes, that's right."

"Mmm. That Bainbridge is a fine man," the old woman said with a happy sigh. "So big and virile. I do like a man with such a large—"

"Nani Maa!" Ash exclaimed in horror, finally turning away from the mirror.

"I was going to say personality," she said, looking the picture of innocence.

Viv didn't believe her for a moment.

"Anyway," the dreadful creature said with a dignified sniff. "You want this fellow. Is he courting you?"

"No," Viv replied, unable to keep the despondency from her voice. "He doesn't want me, thinks I'm too much bother."

To her dismay, far from being sympathetic, Nani Maa gave a bark of laughter. "Oh ho! The fellow has sense, *meri Shona!* I like him already. It's about time you found a man who doesn't faint at the sight of your beautiful face. Working for his attention will be good for you."

"What a rotten thing to say!" Viv folded her arms indignantly.

Nani Maa shrugged, unrepentant. "If you don't have to work for something, you don't appreciate what you have. It won't do you the least bit of harm, and likely a deal of good. Him too, perhaps, if he thinks he can't handle you, or doesn't want to. Perhaps he needs the challenge."

Ash took his place again, finally satisfied his hair was just as it ought to be. "There, see, Viv? I told you. You just need to show him what he's missing."

"Ah, *mera tota,* you are not so foolish as you look," Nani Maa said with affection, her eyes glittering with mischief as she reached out to ruffle Ash's hair once again.

21st February 1841, Rother House, Burwash, Etchingham, East Sussex.

Although he had known it was a bad idea, August stayed away from his mother and sisters for over six weeks. Dare and his lovely new wife, Elspeth, had made him most welcome. Indeed, August found himself enchanted with his friend's bride. She was everything a wife ought to be, to his mind, and he congratulated Dare heartily on his good fortune. With that thought in the forefront of his mind, he wasted no more time pining for Miss Anson. Not at all. The vision of her beautiful face never, *ever* entered his head. Not once. Really, he had completely forgotten about her. It wasn't as if his heart skipped if ever anyone mentioned her in conversation, or he looked for her wherever he went, always hoping to catch sight of her, no matter how unlikely. No, no. There was absolutely *no* silly behaviour like that. None. Not a bit.

Six weeks might easily have become eight, if not for the rumours.

It began, as it often did, with a few sly remarks dropped within his hearing. He ignored it at first, too used to his female relations causing indignant muttering of some kind or other to fret unduly.

It soon became clear ignoring it would not make it go away. So, steeling himself for the worst, he went home. Rother House was a grand manor house built by August's ancestors in the early seventeenth century. It was a handsome building, built of local sandstone, with hipped roofs and six towering chimney stacks on the main roof alone, all made of Weald clay. Coming back here always provoked a confusing tangle of emotions for August. The first sight of the building he loved so dearly relieved his heart and made him feel he truly had come home, back to the place he had known as a boy, and yet it was generally accompanied by the knowledge there was a drama of some variety that needed his attention.

Much to his frustration, this time was no different. The gossip was entirely true.

"Couldn't you stop her?" he demanded of Anna, once they were ensconced in the cosy if well-worn parlour with their sister, Gwen, and a large tray of tea and cakes.

They had obviously decided he'd be easier to manage if he wasn't hungry after his journey. They weren't wrong.

"Don't be daft, August," Anna said mildly. "You know it's impossible to stop her once she's made her mind up. Besides, she's happy."

August pinched the bridge of his nose and wished his family would occasionally consider the wider consequences of their actions. "Yes, she's happy. That's very nice for her, I'm sure. However, I can't go anywhere without people whispering and laughing behind my back. And, rather more to the point, you two are unmarriageable."

He folded his arms, awaiting their reaction.

"I don't want to get married anyway," Gwen said, shrugging. She scratched her head with the pointy end of a paintbrush. There was a blue smear on her nose, a dab of vermillion red on her chin, and the powerful scent of linseed oil and turpentine clung to her.

"Well, good, because no one will have either of you now. Hell, I don't know if they'll have me!" he added with frustration. He didn't bother to point out that he would be forced to keep the pair of them for the rest of their days. It wasn't as if he begrudged them the money. It ought to be partly theirs, anyway. He begrudged the impact such outrageous behaviour had on his own life, however. "Why did she not just tell everyone her friend had come to stay?" Anna smothered a grin.

"Well, everyone knows Charlie too well. She's rather notorious. Besides, if you see them together, it's obvious, and Mama can't abide lying and deceit, not after Papa."

August huffed and bit into a tea cake, chewing irritably. Charlie Brooks, or more accurately *Charlotte* Brooks, was indeed notorious. She lived and dressed as a man, smoked cheroots, and generally caused uproar wherever she went. Clever and witty and outspoken, she was the darling of the artistic set, and naturally set the rest of the world on their ears. Now, it appeared she had moved into their home as their mother's... *companion.*

"Charlie is a dear," Gwen said, picking thoughtfully at the dried paint on her nails. "I don't see why everyone must get in such an uproar about it. It's none of their business who Mama goes to bed with."

August winced, not wanting that particular image in his mind. Frankly, he didn't care either, but he'd rather not have to think about his mother in such a light. Too disturbing.

"Neither do I, but they do, and that uproar reflects on the rest of us," he explained patiently. "So, it might be best if I took rooms in town and you two came and stayed with me, put some distance between you and Mama until this latest affair is over."

"Certainly not," Anna said at once, bristling. "I have my own life to lead. I certainly don't want to go to London under your chaperonage."

"But there's so much to see and do," August said hopefully, turning to Gwen as being the more reasonable of the two, if the least practical. "Think of all the wonderful art galleries and museums you could visit."

For a moment, a wistful light brightened Gwen's lovely face, but then she shook her head and sighed. "No. Mama would be unhappy if we left, and you know how forgetful she is when she's writing. She'll forget to eat."

"Surely Charlie can help with that. If she cares for Mama as much as you tell me she does?"

"Oh, no," Anna said, helping herself to another cup of tea. "I mean, yes, she adores Mama, but she's writing a play and utterly absorbed. The two of them would starve, I swear, if I didn't have regular meals sent into them."

August bit back an oath and tried to ignore the fact he had another invitation from Bainbridge burning a hole in his coat pocket.

"Have you told him—" Gwen began, only to hush up at a furious glare from Anna.

August looked between them and narrowed his eyes. Alarm bells were ringing in his ears at a terrific pitch. "What? Told me what? What's going on?"

Anna glared at Gwen, who only shrugged. "It's not like you can hide the fact the place is going to be full to the rafters any day now."

"Gwen!" Anna exclaimed.

The bells were clamouring wildly now. "What place? *This* place? Full to the rafters? Why? Who's coming?"

"Now, don't get upset," Anna said, which in August's view was the most upsetting thing she could have said. Nothing good ever followed those words in his experience, and he'd had enough of it to form an opinion.

"Anna," he growled as she hesitated.

"Mama and Charlie have started a retreat for artists and free thinkers and… and people like themselves," she blurted, the words tumbling over each other.

August stared at her. "Here. In *my* house?"

Anna's chin went up. "Well, it's only your house because of unfair laws and—"

August held up a hand. "Yes. Yes, forgive me. Forget I said that, but… I *do* still live here. I, in fact, pay the bills… yes, yes, because of unfair laws, etc. I know that too, but did no one think to ask me if I *minded?*"

Anna chewed at her lip. "No, er, and actually, we were rather hoping you'd stay away longer as... we need your room."

A muscle in his jaw twitched.

"I see." August stared at the fireplace. Really, he ought to have expected something like this. It served him right for going away.

"He's furious," Gwen hissed at Anna in an all too audible whisper.

"No," Anna said thoughtfully, as though he wasn't there. "He's in shock. For now. Then he'll be furious. Then he'll wash his hands of us."

"Oh good. Does that mean we can use his room?" Gwen asked, perking up.

"Yes." August got to his feet. He had the firm conviction he'd best leave now. Things would not get any better if he stayed. "Yes. You can have my room. You can have the whole damned house. It's for the best. I see that now. I can't help you. I love you all, but I'm not your keeper, and have no wish to be. You never listen to my advice, and I'm not a tyrant to bully you all and demand you marry or live life as society thinks you ought. I wish you could do as you please and not make my life so damned difficult, but as you live as you please, no matter what the consequences, it's a moot point. So, have at it. It's yours. Paint the place purple if it pleases you."

"Is he all right?" Gwen asked Anna dubiously as August moved towards her.

Anna shrugged, looking anxiously between them.

"Perfectly," he said, embracing her and kissing her cheek, before doing the same to Anna. "I feel much relieved, actually. You're free, and so am I. I shall pack and be on my way. Forward any correspondence to Bainbridge, will you?" he added, and hurried from the room.

Chapter 6

Miss Knight,

I was most distressed by your absence from last night's rout party. Miss Anson assures me you are only a little under the weather — a head cold I believe? Is that so? Have you seen a physician? Is there anything I can do for you? Please reassure me of your wellbeing before I fret myself to death.

You missed nothing of note last night, I assure you, for it was a deadly dull affair, but perhaps that was because you were not there to enliven it.

I hope the accompanying parcel is of some benefit to your spirits. I assure you I will be quite inconsolable until I see you back to your usual self and in my company. For my sake, hurry and get well.

Take care of yourself, ma petite.

LC x

—Excerpt of a letter from Louis César de Montluc, Comte de Villen to Miss Evie Knight (daughter of Lady Helena and Mr Gabriel Knight).

22nd February 1841, Cavendish House, The Strand, London.

"Are you sure she's all right?" Viv asked her mother anxiously as servants hurried in and out of the house, loading her parents' carriage with luggage.

"I'm not dead yet!" Nani Maa protested before the countess could reply, glowering and folding her arms. She was not at her best, however, despite her protests. The damp weather and cold had half the *ton* down with various ailments and Mama would take no chances with Nani Maa's health, or the cough that had persisted for a little too long.

Mama rolled her eyes. "No one is suggesting you are. We are *trying* to ensure you remain fighting fit. Which is why we are taking you to see Pippin, you dreadful creature! And much thanks we have for escorting you to see your best friend," she added, shaking her head.

Nani Maa pouted, quite unrepentant. "Well, better her than that fool quack again. Idiot didn't know what he was talking about. Pippin will see me right."

"Yes, I am certain she will," Mama said, patting her hand with a reassuring smile before returning her attention to Vivien. "Now, don't you worry about us. You and Ash will have a lovely time with Arabella whilst we're gone, though I rely on you to behave as you ought, Vivien. I know Bainbridge's aunt is quite respectable, but... Well, Nani Maa liked her a good deal. Shall we leave it at that?"

Vivien laughed, knowing full well Lady Beauchamp and her friend and companion, Mrs Cora Dankworth, were perfectly outrageous. "I'll be good, Mama, don't fret."

Her mother nodded and embraced her. "We ought only to be away ten days, but I shall write and let you know how she's getting on."

Once they had waved their parents and Nani Maa off to the countryside, Viv and Ash went back indoors to wait as the servants next loaded their belongings on a carriage for the short journey to Axton House.

"A stroke of luck, Arabella asking us to stay when she did," Ash mused thoughtfully. "I'm afraid I would have abandoned you as well and stayed with a friend here rather than mouldering in the countryside."

Viv laughed. "Oh, I know, brother dear, believe me. As it is, you're stuck with me."

"And glad of it," Ash said soothingly. "Though I do wonder what life at Axton House will be like. The old duke is said to be something of a tyrant, you know. I wonder what's brought him to town? I thought he was a recluse these days?"

"He's not been seen in town for almost a decade," Viv agreed as Ash handed her up into the carriage. "But he adores Arabella. Apparently, he moped about and drove all the servants to distraction the last time she went away, and they had to cut their visit short and go home. So she persuaded Bainbridge it would be less bother to get him to come with them."

Ash laughed and shook his head. "Well, it makes sense. Bella always was good with troublesome children."

🎩 🎩 🎩

22nd February 1841, Axton House, Piccadilly, London.

"About bloody time!" Bainbridge said, slapping August on the back. "I can't believe it's taken you this long to wash your hands of them. They'll sort themselves out, you'll see."

"This from the man who brought his father to town rather than leave him at home to cause chaos in his absence?" August queried, deadpan. He had been tucking into a lavish breakfast, all by himself until now, as the rest of the household had not yet shown themselves.

Bainbridge huffed and waved a hand as he took his place at the head of the table. "Not guilty. That's Arabella on both counts. She's spoiled the old reprobate so thoroughly he can't bear her to go away, and it was her that brought him. Not me."

"So you say," August chuckled, amused by his friend's indignation.

Bainbridge scowled. "It's true. She made me feel sorry for the wicked old goat being left all by himself. As if he doesn't have an army of servants to torment, not to mention my brother lives five minutes away. Anyway, enough of that. Sorry I wasn't here when you arrived yesterday, by the way. Some business to take care of that couldn't wait. I trust you've been comfortably settled?"

August snorted. "Comfortably? In this palace? I may never leave. I've been treated like some indolent pasha, my every whim anticipated. Is this what life is like as the Marquess of Bainbridge?"

"It's my wife," Bainbridge said simply. "I never met a female more able to motivate and organise staff. If Wellington had married a woman like Arabella, the war would have been over in half the time, I swear. They fall over themselves to please her."

"Just the staff?" August asked, quirking an eyebrow.

Bainbridge grinned at him. "Shan't even bother denying it, old man. I'd do anything for her. Do you think it's mesmerism? Animal magnetism and all that?"

"Do you care?"

Bainbridge considered this as a footman set a plate piled high with eggs, bacon, sausages, mushrooms, and fried tomatoes in front of him. "Not a bit," he admitted, reaching for a slice of fried bread and taking a large bite. "I'm happy. She's happy. No point worrying why, is there? Enjoy it, I say."

August sighed and nodded. "I never thought I'd see the day. You, Dare, *and* bloody Raphe all happily leg-shackled and me still a bachelor. I felt certain I'd be the first to go. I *wanted* to be the first, dammit," he grumbled, cutting off a sizeable chunk of sausage and stuffing it in his mouth.

"Well, you looked mighty pleased with yourself when you were dancing with Miss Anson on New Year's Eve."

August felt a jolt lance through him at the mention of her name, but schooled his face to remain immobile. "It was just a dance, Laurie."

"Was it?" Bainbridge asked nonchalantly, reaching for his coffee. "Looked like the stuff dreams are made of from where I was stood. Never seen a fellow with more stars in his eyes."

"Oh, stow it," August said irritably. "She's gorgeous, I admit that. She's also funny and witty and clever, but she will not want the life I wish for. She is not the kind of female to sit at home and embroider. She'll want to be involved in… in *things*. She'll arrange parties and say outrageous things and ruffle the feathers of people who are best left unruffled. Do you not understand why I'm even here, Bainbridge? I want a rest from scandal. I don't want to be the fellow in the room that everyone is pointing at and whispering about. I'm tired of it."

"No, you don't," Bainbridge said, not looking up from his considerable breakfast.

"What do you mean, I don't?"

Bainbridge shrugged. "Just what I said. You don't want to sit at home embroidering either. You *think* it's what you want. You've always thought it, but it's not true."

"I didn't mean *me* doing the embroidering, halfwit, as you well know, and what do you mean by that, anyway? Are you calling me a liar?" August demanded, offended by the implication.

"Oh, no," Bainbridge said, his voice soothing. "Merely deluded."

"Oh, well, that's all right, then," August retorted.

"Well, I see you've upset our guest already, darling. Well done. How long have you been home?" Arabella asked her husband, smiling kindly upon August as he stood to greet her.

"'Bout five minutes," Bainbridge admitted through a mouthful of bacon and eggs.

Arabella sighed, bent and kissed her husband's cheek, and sat down at the table. "Dear heart, you'll give the poor man indigestion."

"Only fair. He's giving me indigestion by being a clodpole," Bainbridge retorted. "He won't marry Miss Anson. I ask you, is that rational?"

"Not in the least, but it really is his decision, my lamb," Arabella said, sending August a mischievous grin to take the sting out of her remark. Her expression sobered, and she turned back to her husband. "Laurie, darling. You explained the situation to Mr Lane-Fox, as we discussed?"

"Oh, please, call me August. Laurie is like the annoying brother I never had. I consider you family, God help you," August said, giving her a wry smile.

She beamed at him. "Thank you. You're a dear. August it is, but Laurie," she persisted, turning back to Bainbridge. "You did explain?"

"Explain what?" her husband asked.

August narrowed his eyes, too well attuned to his friend's knack for pretending he was oblivious to things exploding around him. He had the awful foreboding that things were about to do just that. "Yes, Laurie, explain what?"

"How do I know? I just asked her that," Bainbridge protested.

Arabella sighed. "Oh, dear. Well, August, I do hope you will not let me down, for I feel certain I can rely upon you to act like a grownup, even if you find the situation a tad awkward."

"Awkward?" August repeated, the sensation of impending doom growing stronger by the second.

"Only a *little* awkward, I'm sure. For I'm certain you've made your intentions clear, being a gentleman, and so there's no possible way Miss Anson could misunderstand your presence here."

"Misunderstand my…?" August shook his head. "Sorry, you've lost me. Why should my presence here matter to her, anyway?"

"Because Miss Anson and her brother are staying with us too," Arabella said brightly, and took a neat bite out of a slice of plum cake.

🎩 🎩 🎩

"You sneaky bastard!" August exclaimed once he'd got his scheming friend on his own. He finally ran him to ground in his office, making out he was answering correspondence when he was only hiding from the inevitable.

"Oh, don't pretend you're not secretly pleased," Bainbridge said, waving his indignation aside like it was of little importance. "You're dying to see her again."

"That is entirely beside the point," he protested, trying to ignore the way his heart was still pounding, or the fact he leapt out of his skin every time he heard the door knocker… which was often. The blasted house was bedlam, with visitors coming and going constantly.

"No, it ain't. It's entirely the point. You like her, she likes you. Do I need to have a little talk about the birds and the bees?" Bainbridge asked gently.

August glowered at him. "I'm leaving."

Bainbridge's expression became mutinous. "No! No, you are not. My lady wants you to stay. So, stay you will."

66

"Oh, bloody hell, Laurie. Stop trying to manipulate me. It won't work and it isn't fair."

Bainbridge sighed. "August, have you ever stopped to consider why we are friends?"

"Because you won't take no for an answer?" August suggested, folding his arms and scowling at him.

"Partly," Bainbridge acknowledged. "But it's more than that. You've always been a part of our madness, but you never embraced it like we did. It was like your dirty secret. Something to keep hidden."

"It was hardly anything to be proud of," August objected, springing to his feet and stalking to the window. He glared out at a day shrouded in mist, grey and unwelcoming, unlike the cosy room he stood in.

Bainbridge laughed, shaking his head. "At twelve years old, it was. We were gods, August. Every boy at school admired us or feared us. They *all* wanted to be us. But you always kept your part in it secret, when you were the one who planned it all, nine times out of ten. Have you never wondered why?"

"Oh, my God." August put his head in his hands and groaned. "You've got a theory, haven't you? I swear, Laurie, if you start any sentimental nonsense, I shall run screaming from the house and never return."

"Sentimental? *Me*?" Bainbridge repeated, obviously stunned by the accusation.

"Yes, you. You are sentimental, you big oaf, or at least you're always the one that gets weepy when he's in his cups."

"I deny that!"

"Deny it all you like, it's true," August insisted.

Bainbridge narrowed his eyes at him. "I see what you're doing, but it won't work. You, my lad, have had to be the sensible one ever since your lying toad of a father kicked the bucket when you were a lad. Your mother went to pieces and your sisters were inconsolable, and you took all their problems on and sorted them out. You're still sorting them out now, even though you know they don't need or want you to do it—well, half the time. The other half, I admit they need you to bail them out, literally, but that is beside the point. Miss Anson isn't needy, August. She's...." Bainbridge hesitated, frowning, searching for the right word, which apparently eluded him. "She's wanty."

"She's *what?*" August demanded.

"Wanty," Bainbridge repeated, with all the assurance of a man raised to be a duke.

"That is not a word, Laurie."

"It is now."

August threw up his hands in exasperation. "What the devil does it mean?"

"It means she doesn't need you. She wants you, you great blockhead."

"And so?"

"And so why not give it a chance? Throw caution to the wind and, for once in your life, don't pretend someone else is responsible for doing it. Kick up your heels. A week in her company, August. Why not? It's not much to ask, is it?"

August sighed. He was uncertain if he was just giving in because he wanted to anyway, or because there was just no point in denying Bainbridge, who treated every problem in his path the same way. He mowed it down until it was gone. He suspected it wasn't standing up to Bainbridge that was the problem. He'd played immovable object to Bainbridge's unstoppable force before now and was not so easily mown. He *wanted* to see Miss Anson. That was the devil of it. Satan's balls! He was *wanty* too.

"Fine," he said ungraciously. "A week. And if it all goes to hell, you'd damn well better come and bail me out."

"Consider it done, old man," Bainbridge said, beaming at him. "Consider it done."

Chapter 7

Monsieur le Comte,

I did indeed succumb to a nasty cold, but I am much better now, helped in no small part by the lavish parcel. My word, whatever possessed you? I've had the devil of a job hiding it all from Papa. I even had to bribe two of the footmen into holding their tongues.

I have never received such a thoughtful combination of gifts, however. The books are marvellous, the chocolates divine, but the mechanical singing bird in a golden cage —Louis, words fail me. It is so lovely, yet I have been forced to hide it in the back of a cupboard which breaks my heart. I cannot begin to imagine how much it cost, but it is far too generous a gift. You know very well that I ought not to accept it, but I shall because you were so thoughtful as to choose it for me and I cannot bear to be parted from it.

—Excerpt of a letter from Miss Evie Knight (daughter of Lady Helena and Mr Gabriel Knight) to Louis César de Montluc, Comte de Villen.

23rd February 1841, Axton House, The Strand, London.

Ash looked at his sister as her maid put the finishing touches to her coiffure. "Stop looking so smug. If your smile grows any wider, you'll strain something."

Vivien shrugged, unrepentant. "I don't care. I'm too happy. He's here, Ash, and even if he didn't know I was coming—which Arabella says is true—well, he didn't run away screaming, did he?"

"Give it time," Ash murmured.

Vivien stuck her tongue out at him and marched past with her nose in the air. "Come along, or we shall be late."

Ash groaned, not being a huge fan of the coming ordeal. Arabella had been most apologetic but had asked that they show their support at her Fancy Fair. Her arch nemesis, Mrs Wibberley, the vicar's wife, with her tales of self-sacrificing charitable fundraising efforts, had goaded Arabella into raising some funds of her own. Despite Bainbridge's munificence and support for those who fell within his purview, and Arabella's generosity in the time she gave to local events and visiting the sick and the elderly, Mrs Wibberley continued to nitpick and undermine her wherever she could. Determined to shut the blasted woman up once and for all, Arabella had gone all out to raise a small fortune. Through her efforts, various items had been donated by—or sometimes blackmailed out of—the wealthiest members of the *ton*, and would now be sold off, with the funds going to charity. An impressive auction was to be held in the afternoon. The event revolved around the indoor Fancy Fair, where the smaller donated items and handcrafted gifts created by the ladies of the *ton* were to be sold at individual little stalls run by the ladies themselves, and tickets sold for admission to the fair. The sticklers among the *ton* were aghast at ladies behaving like common tradespeople, but as it was for charity, and merely a bit of fun, most people enjoyed it for the harmless event it was. There would also be some real tradespeople selling food and drink, and some entertainment, such as musicians and jugglers. Vivien was looking forward to it immensely. Not least because Mr Lane-Fox would be there, too.

Vivien hurried down the stairs, only to pause halfway down as she saw him waiting in the entrance hall. He looked up and smiled, and Viv's heart gave an odd little kick in her chest.

"Miss Anson. May I say how lovely you look today?"

Viv smiled, a little startled to feel a blush colour her cheeks. "Thank you, sir. You are most kind."

"Hardly," he said ruefully. "It's no more than the truth, though if I were being strictly accurate, I ought to say, how lovely you look *every* day."

"You wouldn't say that if you'd been stuck with her when she had a head-cold a few weeks ago," Ash said cheerfully, ignoring the incinerating glare Viv shot his way. "She looked wretched then, I promise."

Mr Lane-Fox laughed at Viv's obvious consternation. "There, there, Miss Anson, take heart. I have sisters, you know, and they love to make me seem a fool at every opportunity. I pay your brother no mind, I promise."

"You relieve my mind, and I commend your good sense. No one else pays Ash any mind either," she said, giving her twin a *serves you right* smirk as a footman helped her on with her pelerine.

They made it out to the carriage with no further bickering and arrived at the Fancy Fair in good time. Arabella had hired a large hall and had it decorated in the manner of a spring fair. Colourful bunting crisscrossed back and forth above the capacious area, and each individual stallholder had decorated their own stand, some with more finesse than others. That the competition between stall holders was fierce became increasingly obvious within moments, as Mr Lane-Fox was almost bodily dragged to a stall run by the Misses Rivenhall, the beautiful granddaughters of the Duke of Sefton. Before Vivien could make a comment to her brother about their audacity, he too had been nabbed, rounded up like a lone sheep and herded towards a stall selling crocheted… *things*. Vivien wasn't entirely certain what they were.

"Heavens, it's brutal," exclaimed a voice from beside her, and Viv looked around to find Evie at her side.

"You're not wrong. I've lost Mr Lane-Fox and Ash and we've barely set foot in the room," Viv observed.

Evie shook her head in wonder. "I tried to get to Rosamund's stall a moment ago and got so jostled by her admirers in their desperation to get to her, I'm sure I'll be black and blue in the morning. She'll have nothing left to sell by now, and she'll tell you herself her embroidery is hardly a thing of beauty."

"No, but she is, so the young bucks want to impress her by buying all her wares."

Evie laughed. "Oh, look. Mr Lane-Fox has made a bid for freedom, and… what *is* that he's holding?"

"What happened?" he asked, rather dazed as he returned to Vivien's side. "I was quietly minding my own business and the next minute… I don't even know what this is."

He held up a scarlet knitted object with a deal of frilly blonde lace and gold fringing.

Vivien peered at it with curiosity. "Ugly?" she suggested.

"Oh, is… is it a baby's bonnet?" Evie said, with sudden inspiration. She took it from Mr Lane-Fox and poked her fingers through two holes. "Perhaps not, unless the baby had horns. Good heavens," she spluttered, pulling a face.

Vivien smothered a giggle. "I don't suppose a duke's granddaughters have much use for knitting. They probably didn't know whatever it is ought to look like."

Mr Lane-Fox's eyes glittered with mirth. "Perhaps you could wear it as a muff?" he suggested, offering the dreadful thing to her.

"Not my colours, sorry. Though I think you could carry it off. It matches your eyes."

"It's red, Miss Anson," he said reproachfully.

Vivien shrugged. "So it is."

"I see. Like that, is it?" he murmured, offering her his arm.

Vivien pursed her lips, glancing up at him. "You abandoned me on New Year's Eve and have avoided me ever since. I believe I owe you a little retribution."

His expression sobered, and he nodded, lowering his voice. "What would you have of me? How can I make amends?".

"You might explain why you've decided not to run away from me today," she suggested.

"Who says I haven't?" He quirked one blond eyebrow at her, and Vivien could only laugh.

She tightened her hold on his arm. "Then I shall keep a firm grip upon you, sir."

"You do that," he replied, smiling, a soft tone to his voice that made her insides go all fluttery.

"Well, we had better face the hordes and spend some money, or Arabella will be disappointed in us," Viv said, looking around the bustling room for their best option. "Oh, look, there's Aggie."

"Where?" Evie stood on tiptoes and then gave an exclamation of delight as Aggie saw her and ran forward.

"Miss Knight!" Aggie squealed, hugging Evie with such enthusiasm she nearly knocked her flying. Le Comte de Villen, Agatha's guardian, caught Evie by the elbow, steadying her.

"*Alors,* Agatha, have a care, child. Poor Miss Knight is only just recovered from her illness. She does not need you throwing her to the floor."

"Monsieur!" Evie said, still hugging his ward, who was staring up at her with delight. "I did not realise you would be here."

"Neither did I," Louis César replied ruefully.

"I made him come," Aggie said, looking smug. "It took me all morning to persuade him, but I managed it."

"Persistence always pays," Vivien agreed, sending Mr Lane-Fox a coquettish glance, which made him laugh.

"And what have you bought, dear?" Evie asked Aggie, who opened a bulging fabric bag to show her treasures. "My, you have been busy."

"They're presents for the girls at school," Aggie said, grinning. "They'll be ever so pleased, but may we see the monkey now, *monsieur*?"

"Will I get any peace if I do not agree?" Louis asked mildly.

"No. Not a scrap, sorry," Aggie said with a heavy sigh.

"I thought not." His lips twitched a little, but he submitted gracefully, offering his arm to Evie. "Would you accompany us to see the monkey, Miss Knight?"

"I should be delighted to," Evie said. "Though I didn't know there was a monkey."

"Oh, yes," Aggie said, excited now. "Fred told me he saw it at another fair. Arabella did too. It was so adorable, doing little tricks and getting up to mischief. So she got the owner to bring it here."

"Monkeys are not to be trusted," Louis said darkly.

Viv laughed with surprise. "Do you have much experience with monkeys then, *monsieur*?"

"More than I wish for," he replied, but offered no more on the subject.

"Would you like to see the monkey, Miss Anson?" Viv turned to see Mr Lane-Fox watching her with interest.

"I would, rather," Viv admitted.

"Then we had better follow them." Mr Lane-Fox escorted her with the others to where a small crowd of onlookers had gathered around a man with an ornate wooden barrel organ. As he turned the handle, music filled the room, though this spectacle was far less interesting than the monkey.

"Oh, the dear little thing. He looks like a tiny old man!" Evie laughed as the monkey reached out a hand to a hesitant young woman who offered him a peanut.

Agile fingers worked rapidly to peel away the tough outer shell before the monkey popped each nut into his mouth, chewing furiously. His bright, dark eyes scanned the crowd for any more likely donations.

The comte studied the creature suspiciously and made a noncommittal sound.

"Oh, don't be so grumpy. He's adorable," Evie persisted.

Vivien laughed at the comte's silent if expressive rejection of this comment, which turned to a gasp when a sharp elbow struck her hard in the ribs as someone pushed forward to the front for a better view.

"Madam!" she said, clutching at her side, but the woman spared her barely a glance. As she passed, Vivien sucked in a breath as she recognised who had assaulted her.

"You ought to have let me through," Lady Steyning snapped coldly, as her daughter Hyacinth smirked and deliberately jostled Viv again as she passed.

Viv gritted her teeth, furious but determined not to create a scene in front of Mr Lane-Fox, who had not seen the little contretemps play out. Her rigid posture must have given her away, however.

Mr Lane-Fox turned away from the conversation he'd been having with her brother to look at her. "Miss Anson, are you well? Has something happened?"

Viv shook her head. Lady Steyning was the daughter of the Duke of Sefton, and aunt to the appalling Rivenhall girls. Lady Steyning hated both Vivien and Ash, and their mother. This was partly because she resented Mama's beauty and popularity despite the scandal she had created in marrying their father, and partly because of Mama's friendship with Matilda, the Marchioness of Montagu. Lady Steyning had once hoped of snaring the marquess herself, and had been rather too vocal in her confident pronouncements of becoming the next marchioness. Montagu's very public declaration of love and subsequent proposal to Matilda had humiliated Lady Steyning and, over the following years, she had tried to take the shine from Matilda's happiness, even attempting to seduce Montagu in the hope of becoming his mistress. Unsurprisingly, she had failed utterly. Mama had been vocal in her support of Matilda, and her unmasking of several of Lady Steyning's attempts to spread rumours and gossip had created an enmity which was decidedly vitriolic. The woman had not married well either, despite her rank, ending up with a mere baronet, an unpleasant fellow to boot. Viv knew her to be cruel and vindictive, and decided it was best to err on the side of caution for once.

"No, I'm quite well, thank you," she said, striving for calm.

August's obvious concern and his smile went a long way to easing her temper, and she took a deep breath, hoping to enjoy the rest of the fair.

The capuchin monkey was indeed very droll. The organ grinder had dressed him in little checked trousers and a blue tunic with a matching cap. When the man turned the handle, he danced to the music and then gave a bow, snatching off his cap to beg for peanuts which were being sold at an exorbitant price for five nuts. The crowd laughed and exclaimed, thoroughly entertained. Despite his obvious suspicion of the little beast, Louis César bought Evie a bag of monkey nuts, and Evie handed one to Vivien.

"Assuming the poor creature can get past the gorgon," Evie whispered, gesturing to Lady Steyning.

Vivien grinned. Her smile faded, however, as she turned back to discover Miss Hyacinth Steyning had captured Mr Lane-Fox's attention. She was a beautiful girl, as her mother had once been, before selfishness and disappointment had wrought hard lines on her pretty features. A coquettish nature tempered the beauty, however, and Vivien did her best to squash an unappealing surge of jealousy as the young woman batted her eyelashes at Mr Lane-Fox and toyed with her hair. She focused instead on Agatha, who had bent down to get a better look at the monkey, who reached out to hold her hand. This delighted the child, who gazed up at the Comte with happiness shining in her eyes. Louis César smiled back at her, his expression warm and indulgent, and Vivien wondered if he knew Agatha regarded him as her father. She hoped so. Anything less would break the poor girl's heart.

Though she tried not to, Vivien could not help catching a little of the conversation between Hyacinth and Mr Lane-Fox, especially when her name was mentioned.

"If you will excuse me, Miss Steyning. I accompanied Miss Anson today, and I should not wish to be thought a poor companion."

"Oh, her," Hyacinth said with a dismissive little sniff. "You really ought not. They do not receive her kind at the best affairs, you know. Scandalous family. It won't reflect well on you."

Vivien smothered a gasp, torn between outrage, humiliation, and not wanting to be caught eavesdropping. The desire to scratch the horrid creature's eyes out was also tantalising, but would do her more harm than the temporary satisfaction it would give.

Though she no longer held his arm, Vivien was aware of the way Mr Lane-Fox stiffened beside her, aware too of the sudden, prickling atmosphere.

"Really? Well, Miss Steyning, I would not wish to attend any affair that did not count itself fortunate for Miss Anson's presence, and as my own family is far more capable of creating scandal than hers, I shall enjoy her company as I have been doing. Good day to you."

Out of the corner of her eye, Vivien saw the anger in Miss Steyning's expression, the sudden flare of colour to her porcelain cheeks.

"As you wish. It's your reputation's funeral, after all. You cannot say I did not warn you," Miss Steyning whispered, turning away with a contemptuous swish of skirts.

Vivien dared a glance at Mr Lane-Fox. He was rigid with anger, his jaw tight. Tentatively, Viv reached out and laid a hand on his arm. His complexion paled as he turned and realised she had heard the exchange.

"Miss Anson," he said, looking utterly wretched.

"Thank you," she said, smiling up at him before he could say any more.

"She's a small-minded, spiteful little fool," he said, and the fury behind those few words soothed away any jagged edge of unhappiness that might have lingered.

Viv stared at him, at the obvious concern in his eyes, and at the stance of a man who would undoubtedly have done battle for her if his opponent had not been female. Something in her heart shifted, and the feelings that had begun as a warm glow flared into something hotter and more intense.

"I know that," she said to reassure him, for he looked so frustrated at being unable to do more to defend her honour. "It's all right."

"It isn't the least bit all right."

"I know that too," she said soothingly. "But the Miss Steynings of the world will not have their minds changed. You cannot argue with someone who has no wish to consider any opinion but their own, any more than you could make a blind man see again. It is not worth your time, and certainly not your peace of mind."

"What about *your* peace of mind?" he asked gently, laying his hand atop hers where it rested on his sleeve.

He wore fine kid gloves, and his heat seeped through the thin leather, reaching her skin, somehow warming her heart too.

"I am not so easily overset," Vivien said, which was true, especially in the light of this man and the words he had given her without so much as a moment's hesitation. "Please, let us forget it and enjoy our outing."

He nodded, and they turned their attention back to the antics of the monkey. In front of them, Miss Steyning had crouched down as Agatha had, and was trying to entice the monkey to her now, but the creature was hesitating, clearly uncertain whether the reward of a nut was worth it.

"Miss Anson," Mr Lane-Fox said, his voice mild. "Do you still have the nut Miss Knight gave you?"

Viv nodded and raised her palm to show him the monkey nut.

Without a second thought, he took the nut from her hand and dropped it onto Miss Steyning's bonnet. Her hat was a fancy affair with a large swathe of dark green feathers and the nut nestled comfortably like a little egg in a nest. Viv smacked a hand over her mouth to stop herself from giving a bark of laughter, but she was not the only one who'd seen him do it. The monkey's dark eyes widened, and he leapt.

Things happened quickly thereafter.

With astonishing speed and dexterity, the monkey landed and snatched up the nut. Miss Steyning screamed and leapt to her feet.

"Get it off me! Get it off me!" Miss Steyning shouted, tugging at her bonnet ribbons.

The screaming apparently upset the monkey, who shrieked indignantly and began pulling the feathers out of the bonnet and scattering them about. By this time, Miss Steyning had undone her ribbons and cast the bonnet aside, monkey and all. The little fellow did not wish to be so cast, however, and grabbed hold of her hair instead. Pandemonium. Women on all sides screamed and fled whilst little boys and grown men both doubled over with laughter. Some of Miss Steyning's admirers flapped ineffectually at the monkey, who ignored them.

Agatha, who had been watching all this open-mouthed with delight, tugged at August's sleeve.

"May I have that horrid woolly thing you bought?" she asked, pointing at the red knitted thing Mr Lane-Fox had tried to stuff in his pocket, though it didn't fit.

"Certainly," he said, handing it to her.

Agatha collected the remaining monkey nuts in the knitted object and held out the offering to the creature, rattling the nuts before dropping the bundle to the floor. The monkey looked at it with interest and leapt down for a better look. Miss Steyning fainted conveniently into the arms of one of her admirers.

"Oh, you horrid girl! That took me hours to make," exclaimed a shrill voice, and a moment later a girl of perhaps fifteen lunged at Agatha and pulled her hair, before knocking her to the ground.

"Let go of me!" Agatha shouted, trying to get up as the girl attempted to drag her about by her hair.

The girl failed to let go.

Agatha hit her.

The girl gasped and staggered back, clutching her nose. Louis César leapt between them before things could get any worse.

"Arrêter!" he said, his voice harsh. Turning to Aggie, who had found her feet, he jerked his head. "Go!"

Agatha nodded, bright enough to see the incoming tide of trouble, and hurried away, and just in time, as a florid faced man loomed in front of Louis, who steeled himself for a confrontation. The Marquess of Attingham was not a pleasant fellow under good circumstances, which these certainly were not.

"Where is that wicked girl? She hit my daughter!"

"It was self-defence. Your daughter attacked her for no reason," Louis replied calmly. "I suggest you teach your children better manners."

"How dare you! I'm not taking instructions on manners from a bloody frog!"

Before Louis could utter another word, someone leapt to his defence.

"You rude man! Is it any wonder your daughter is so ill-mannered?"

Louis turned an exasperated glare upon Evie. "I will handle this."

Vivien's gaze drifted from the ensuing argument and back to the monkey. Now the object of her ire had departed, the maker of the knitted article snatched it away from the monkey, who chattered at her angrily. The girl hurried away, taking the red knit creation with her. Looking around for something else to focus on, the monkey's eyes lit on a something that piqued its interest. Standing next to the angry man confronting Louis was a large lady—perhaps his marchioness—resplendent in a lavish burgundy velvet gown, which was rather *de trop* for such an affair as this. With skill that suggested training, the monkey climbed up the back of a woman's gown, undid the clasp of a glittering ruby necklace, and leapt up to the rafters of the hall.

"My rubies!" wailed the woman, her hands going to her throat. "Oh! Thief! Thief! That monkey took my rubies."

"What?" bellowed the florid faced man. At once, he forgot Louis and raised his fist at the scampering capuchin. "I'll have the little beast's head! Those damned rubies are worth a fortune. Ten pounds to the fellow who shoots the little rat down."

A murmur of interest rippled around the crowd.

"Oh, Louis!" Evie exclaimed, clutching at the comte's sleeve. "Don't let him hurt it."

The comte gave a sigh of resignation that suggested he'd known anything to do with monkeys had been bound to end this way. "As you wish, *ma petite.*"

Vivien stared at Mr Lane-Fox, who was looking deeply unhappy. Perhaps aware of her gaze, he turned to her.

"I ought not to have done it. I don't know what gets into me," he said, shaking his head. "You see? This is what happens. I cause chaos and other people take the blame for it. It must stop. I'm not a boy any longer."

Vivien bit her lip, trying to smother a laugh. "You ought not have, but I cannot pretend I regret it, though we must save the dratted monkey. Oh, August, it was marvellous. *You* are marvellous."

He looked startled by her declaration, as well he might, for it was dreadfully improper, not to mention addressing him by his given name. She didn't care.

"No," he said with a soft laugh. "I'm not the least bit marvellous. I'm just a troublemaker with a knack for avoiding trouble."

Vivien took his arm and leaned into him, her gaze upon his face unwavering. "I disagree, and I like you. Very much."

He studied her face for a long moment and then turned as a collective gasp fluttered through the room. "Devil take it. I'd best try to intervene. It seems this is not yet over," he muttered, and looked up.

Chapter 8

Louis,

What in the name of everything holy have you been up to?

—Excerpt of a letter from Monsieur Nicolas Alexandre Demarteau to his brother, Louis César de Montluc, Comte de Villen. Translated from French.

23rd February 1841, The Marchioness of Bainbridge's Fancy Fair, Mayfair, London.

Louis ignored the ranting marquess and turned his back on him as Mr Lane-Fox stepped into the breach and tried to talk the loathsome fellow down. Instead, he regarded the monkey and muttered a curse. There was a stir now among many of the menfolk and he didn't doubt some halfwit would produce a pistol in short order. If they killed the wretched monkey, both Evie and Agatha would be beside themselves. That was unacceptable.

The building that housed the Fancy Fair was an enormous barn with a ceiling that looked rather like the upturned belly of a great ship. Naturally, the monkey had climbed to the farthest point, about twenty feet high.

Louis' fingers twitched. He ought not. He *really* ought not. Yet the idea was so tantalising....

"Oh, Louis, they'll kill it!" Evie said, clutching harder at his sleeve. "The poor thing, and Aggie will be distraught."

Louis turned to her and ached with longing at the concern in her big green eyes. Such a tender heart this woman had, so full of love and affection, always trying to keep everyone safe and happy. Would she ever look at him as anything more than a friend?

"*Ne t'inquiète pas*," he said softly. "I'll get the little devil."

Evie stared at him. "But you can't, not now. Not from up there!"

"You think not?" he said, giving her a reproachful frown. "How you underestimate me, *ma petite.*"

Before she could say another word, Louis stripped off his coat, handed it to her, and then climbed up the heavily beamed wall, agile as a cat. It had been some years since he had done anything of this nature, but he kept himself fit with a daily regime of exercises he had begun when Nic had trained him for the circus so very long ago. This was child's play, though shocking to the crowd below, who gasped at seeing a nobleman do something so outrageous. His brother would have his head for this, he didn't doubt. He didn't care.

Louis looked down to see Evie watching him, a hand pressed to her mouth, the other to her heart. Was that heart beating faster merely out of fear? Did she truly never consider him as a lover? Perhaps she needed to see a glimpse of who he truly was, rather than the polite face he showed the rest of the world. Besides, he wasn't above showing off for the benefit of his beloved. A lowering realisation, to discover she had reduced him to performing tricks for her attention, but there you had it.

In a move designed entirely to shock and impress, instead of climbing the beams as a sensible soul might, he leapt from the end wall to catch hold of the long joist that spanned the width of the building, much as the monkey had done. Screams from below indicated it had looked as impressive as he'd hoped, though it had not been so very far. In the circus, he had performed from greater heights and done far more dangerous things, though that was a lifetime ago now.

Louis swung up onto the joist with ease and dusted off his hands. The mischievous capuchin, who was sitting in the middle of the beam, retreated to the far end, dragging his loot behind him. Louis grinned. This was like old times, climbing into impossible places to steal someone's jewels. *Mon Dieu,* Nic would have an apoplexy when he found out. At this moment, Louis didn't give a damn. He was having far too much fun.

"Monsieur! Please, be careful!" Evie's voice drifted up to him and he flashed her a grin before running across the beam in pursuit of the monkey.

More gasps from below, but the beam was wide and solid compared to a tightrope, and held no challenge. He could have turned a cartwheel and walked on his hands without a second thought, but he wasn't quite that far gone to good sense and propriety. Yet. At the far end, the monkey chattered and climbed the wall again, so Louis slowed, holding out a hand.

"Non, non, you do not wish to run away from me. I am here to save you from that big, angry fellow. He wants to shoot you down. Come, come, you little devil. You will be safe, and I will be a hero for my young lady. It is not such a terrible deal, *alors?"*

The monkey chattered, clutching the jewels tighter.

"I know. I sympathise, truly. They *are* pretty, but we cannot always have what we want. Believe me, I know. See? I have something sparkly too." Louis reached for the sapphire pin Evie had given him, turning it in his cravat so it caught the light.

The monkey's eyes lit up.

"Oui, it is beautiful. *Viens.* Come and have a closer look, come along," Louis crooned softly. Monkeys had often caused havoc in the circus, and having been bitten a time or two as a boy,

he was loath to get too close, but at least this one did not seem bad-tempered, only avaricious.

Finally, curiosity got the better of the animal, and the monkey leapt onto his shoulder. Louis inspected the rubies with a contemptuous snort, before tucking the necklace in his pocket, whilst the monkey tugged at the big sapphire in his cravat, which was hopefully securely pinned. A great cheer rose from beneath him, and unable to resist the temptation, Louis executed a theatrical bow before making things worse by dropping off the beam, catching it again with one hand, and then leaping gracefully to the floor. The monkey clung on throughout before running off into the arms of its relieved owner.

Screams, gasps, cheers, and general uproar filled the barn and Louis was immediately besieged by women. The most insistent of these was the owner of the rubies. The Marchioness of Attingham took Louis' hand and pressed it firmly against her considerable bosom.

"Oh, *Monsieur Le Comte,* how heroic of you! You might have been killed, and all to save my rubies. I declare I've seen nothing so selfless in my life. I owe you a great debt."

Louis smiled and decided it might be prudent not to tell her he was saving the monkey and didn't give a damn for her rubies, which were not rubies at all. He gave a hesitant tug at his hand, but the lady's grip was akin to being held in a vice.

"You ought to be rewarded for such heroism," she enthused, giving him a coquettish look.

As a large lady perilously close to her sixtieth year, the expression sat ill upon her heavily powdered face.

Louis cleared his throat and made another attempt to tug his hand free of its fleshy prison.

"Returning your property is reward enough, my lady," he said, holding out the necklace to her.

"Amelia, let the damned frog go," barked the marquess, snatching the necklace from Louis and stuffing it in his pocket. "It's time we left this madhouse and its occupants."

The marchioness flushed and released Louis' hand, which was a relief. But, bearing in mind the service he'd just rendered to the marquess, the added insult did not impress Louis.

"Madam," he said gently, lowering his voice and using his most seductive tone, playing up his accent to the hilt. "I regret to inform you that someone has done you a grave disservice, for those jewels are not rubies, but merely paste."

The marchioness' eyes widened with horror. "No! No, that is not possible."

"Don't be damned ridiculous," the marquess blustered, and Louis knew at once from his reaction that he knew very well they were paste. So the rumours of his gambling debts and monetary problems were true, then. From the furious glint in the marchioness' eyes, it was obvious she knew it, too.

"Gilbert," she said, a warning note to her voice that made the marquess pale somewhat.

Louis took advantage of the moment and left, making his way as best he could through the fluttering ladies as they alternately flattered, charmed and, in one case, groped him.

"Thank you, ladies. The spectacle is over. Give the comte room to breathe, would you?"

Louis let out a breath of relief as Mr Lane-Fox ushered the women away.

"Thank you," Louis said. "Where are Agatha and Miss Knight?"

"This way. Miss Knight and Miss Smith did not wish to leave, but once the women surged forward with such enthusiasm, they were in danger of being stampeded to the floor. I thought it prudent for them to seek shelter."

He led Louis through the throng to a small storeroom and opened the door. Miss Anson, Aggie and Evie were all within.

"Louis!" Evie flew at him, hugging him tightly.

For a moment, Louis' breath caught in his throat, but it was too quickly done, her embrace over before he had the chance to appreciate it. Evie blushed scarlet, remembering she had an audience and, much to his regret, let him go.

"Oh, I could throttle you. I thought I would die of terror," she said, half laughing, though her eyes were rather too bright.

"You worried for me, *ma petite*?"

"Of course, you dreadful man! If you had fallen…."

She shook her head, her voice trembling, but Louis had no time to discover what she might have felt if he had fallen before Aggie grasped his hand.

"Oh, Monsieur, it was marvellous," she said, staring up at him in wonder. "Everyone was dumbfounded. Every woman in the place has fallen head over ears in love with you, I promise."

Rather than being pleased by this revelation, Louis grimaced. There was only one woman he'd put on that ridiculous show for, and he wanted to know if she had felt anything beyond concern for a friend. He was pathetically desperate to get her alone. A frail hope.

"Wherever did you learn to do such a thing?" Evie demanded of him, having recovered her composure. "You never hesitated, just like a cat. In fact, I believe you climbed as quickly as the monkey did."

Ah. He ought to have prepared a response for such questions.

"Oh, monsieur loved to climb trees as a boy, didn't you, monsieur? He has told me many times," Aggie said brightly, chattering away and saving him by changing the subject. "I hope the marchioness was appreciative for your efforts at retrieving her jewels?"

Louis sent her a grateful smile, for Aggie knew of his rather peculiar past, or a little of it at least, and would never give him away.

Mr Lane-Fox laughed. "She was so appreciative I feared the comte would not escape with his life intact. Or his virtue," he added in an undertone.

Aggie appeared a little perplexed, but Evie flushed and looked rather indignant. Louis experienced a tiny flicker of hope that perhaps that was a touch of jealousy and felt somewhat better.

"She did seem rather—er—pleased, *oui*. Except then I rather spoiled things for her husband by letting the cat out of the bag," he replied, unable to hide a grin. "The marquess must have pawned her rubies to pay his gambling debts and replaced them with paste."

"No!" Evie said in wonder. "Oh, monsieur. You could tell such a thing?"

Louis nodded, realising he ought to have had an explanation for that too. Not everyone could tell genuine jewels from excellent copies. Would she tell her father of what had happened today? Would he explain what Louis could not? Too distracted to answer at all, Louis wondered what her father would say if the man knew of his intentions towards his daughter. Gabriel knew too much of Louis' past to be sanguine about the match, even if Louis ever persuaded Evie he was the husband she wanted. Her father knew about his years as a jewel thief, knew a little about the abuses he'd endured as a child, and about the circus. Perhaps he didn't know everything, but enough to damn him if he revealed his past to Evie before Louis did it himself. Gabriel might have supported the marriage of Bedwin's daughter to Louis' brother, Nic, but his own daughter would surely be another matter. Mr Knight had instructed her not to dance with him so often. Evie would ignore that, he felt sure, but then what? Would he try to keep them apart? Ought he to tell Evie everything, as he had once urged Nic to tell Eliza? But Eliza had been in love with Nic, and Evie....

"But how could you tell? *Monsieur?*"

Louis snapped out of the increasingly anxious thoughts circling his mind at the sound of Evie's voice.

"Oh, I could tell by the colour. Even inferior rubies have a warmth and depth of colour that fakes do not. They were too light, and a necklace of that quality of design would have used nothing but the best stones."

"How clever of you," Evie said admiringly. "But wherever did you learn such things?"

Louis shrugged, uncomfortable now. "Oh, one picks up such information here and there...."

Like from the fences who took the jewels he'd stolen and sold them on.

"He must have been furious," Miss Anson said, looking thoroughly delighted by the prospect.

"We can only hope," Mr Lane-Fox said, winking at her.

"I suspect so, though presently running scared from his wife and desperately trying to think of a good explanation for the loss of her jewels," Louis added.

"Well, the excitement appears to be over, so I had better escort you home, Miss Anson," Mr Lane-Fox said, holding out his arm for Vivien.

"Oh, and I must collect my bag of presents," Aggie said, dashing off.

Louis waited until they had walked off, smiling at Evie as she held out his coat for him.

"Thank you, *ma petite,*" he said as she helped him on with the snugly fitting garment.

Louis stared down at her as her small hands smoothed his lapels.

"There," she said, once she was satisfied.

"As efficient as my valet," he teased gently, wondering if he dare flirt with her. "Should you like the job?"

"And have poor Elton cut my throat whilst I sleep before casting himself into the Thames? I think not. That man guards you as jealously as the crown jewels," she retorted, laughing as she took his arm.

Evie looked up expectantly when he did not immediately escort her out.

"Would you have cared if I'd fallen, Evie?"

Her expression was one of horror. "Oh, Louis! How can you ask such a ridiculous question? We have been friends for too long. You are my confidant and the keeper of my secrets, no matter how foolish they are. You are irreplaceable and you know it, therefore I conclude you are fishing for compliments."

Not compliments, only a glimmer of hope, he begged silently. *Only the merest hint that I might one day be more than I am to you, mon coeur.*

"Ah, you see through me with such ease," he said sadly, though such an emotion was too easy to summon.

"No," Evie said thoughtfully. She stared up at him, her green eyes so piercing he wondered what it was she did see when she looked at him. "I do not believe that is true, Louis. Perhaps it was once, but no longer. I confide in you, but you no longer return the favour. Do you no longer trust me?"

Louis hesitated, uncertain of what to say in reply, for if he trusted her with his heart, would he not give it to her now, without question? But she was not ready for such a declaration, she was too young, too innocent for a man with so many secrets and so very dark a past, and he was too afraid she could hurt him like no one else had ever done before. The kind of hurt that he would not survive.

"I give you more than anyone else on this planet, Evie," he said, his voice grave, choosing his words with care. "And I trust you above anyone else, save my own brother. One day I hope you may be the keeper of all my secrets, but I would not burden you with them now, for they are not pretty things to be shared lightly. I am not so shabby a fellow that I would ease my own mind in return for causing you distress."

"Are your secrets so very grave, Louis?" she asked, and he cursed himself for the concern already clouding her beautiful eyes.

Louis lifted her fingers to his lips and kissed them. "My past is complicated, but it *is* in the past. The future is so much more agreeable, *n'est-ce pas?* Let us consider that for now."

"For now," Evie agreed, perhaps sensing she would get no more from him on the subject, but her expression remained wary as he escorted her out.

Louis prayed he had not done more harm than good.

Chapter 9

Nic,

I know, I know. I am a thousand times a fool and I beg you will forgive me. My judgement is not what it once was and the reason for my desperate bid for attention was to be found in the audience. What could I do but act like an infatuated boy showing off for his sweetheart?

Perhaps you should do me a kindness and shoot me, for I fear what I might be reduced to next. Perhaps I will call out Mr Hadley-Smythe, or pick a fight with any one of her growing legion of admirers. Mon Dieu, I am making myself crazy.

—Excerpt of a letter from Louis César de Montluc, Comte de Villen to his brother, Monsieur Nicolas Alexandre Demarteau. Translated from French.

6th March 1841, Axton House, Piccadilly, London.

The time passed in a flurry of activity, with Vivien delighted to discover August at her side more often than not. He was funny and attentive, and looked at her as if she were the embodiment of his every dream. She knew she was tumbling head over heels at a demented pace and did not care. In the last few days, Lady Compton Domville had held an assembly at her home at Number Five Grosvenor Square. The dancing—to Weippert's band—had begun at eleven thirty, with a lavish supper being served around one thirty in the morning. Next was a supper party held by the Bainbridges' neighbours, Lord and Lady Granger, which went on into the early hours. Lady Anne Wilbraham had also held a *soirée dansante* at the family mansion in Lower Brook Street, with over two hundred of the leading fashionables in attendance.

Little wonder that, by Sunday morning, everyone at the breakfast table was looking somewhat jaded. Vivien, in contrast, felt marvellous. A tad weary, perhaps, but Mr Lane-Fox had been so solicitous these past days, seeking her company constantly instead of running from it, and dancing with her twice at the Compton Domville affair, and once last night at the *soirée dansante.* The 'once' and not twice niggled at her a little, and she had been aware of a change in his demeanour as the evening grew late. He had disappeared for a while and, when he returned, there had been a spot of blood on his gloves. Something had been said, something had happened, she felt certain, and she determined to discover what had eaten at his peace of mind. Aware that he would likely not give her the answer she wanted, she turned elsewhere for information.

During the Sunday church service, Vivien sat next to Arabella and whispered the question to her whilst the vicar closed his eyes to pray for their eternal souls.

Bella darted August a look and waited until the vicar was intent on a rousing sermon before she replied. "His mother is living openly with another woman, as a husband and wife live. Between his mama and his rather scandalous sisters, poor August must put up with a deal of ridicule. Bainbridge told me someone said something to him last night that he took exception to, so he took the fellow outside. Knocked him out cold."

Vivien's eyes widened in surprise. August seemed such a gentle fellow. "Someone must have sorely provoked him to do such a thing."

Bella nodded and patted her hand. "It was done quietly, thank goodness. No one any the wiser on this occasion."

After church, at the Bainbridges' own private chapel, the party walked back to the house as a few desultory snowflakes fell to the frozen ground.

"There, you see, darling. The ground did not shudder and open to reveal the fiery pits of hell, nor did the sky fall in," Arabella said, soothing her husband who had attended the church service under duress and grumbled all the way to there.

"Hmph," Bainbridge muttered. "Just because I got away with it once, there's no need to make a habit of it. Tempting fate, I should say."

"But the vicar here is so much more interesting that Reverend Wibberley, and he was so pleased to see you," Bella insisted.

"No, he wasn't," Bainbridge retorted. "He looked horrified. Spent half the service staring at my boots, reckon he was checking for cloven hooves."

Arabella snorted and shook her head. "Dreadful man."

"Don't make out you don't prefer me that way," Bainbridge said loftily. "You'd be wretched with some dull dog who never put a foot wrong."

"I wouldn't dream of it," his wife said, giving his arm a soothing pat. "I adore you, just as you are."

Bainbridge looked smug. "There, see, August? Just because you're a devil with a scandalous family, don't mean you can't find some deluded angel to marry you."

"I am not deluded!" Bella retorted indignantly. "I am well aware of what you are and are not."

"Yes, and you love me anyway, you silly article," Bainbridge concluded cheerfully. "So August ought to find someone too. Especially as he's so much more adept at hiding his worst characteristics. Aren't you, old man?" he said, mischief dancing in his eyes.

August gave his friend a warning glare but said nothing.

"Does he have worst characteristics?" Vivien asked innocently, aware she was stirring the pot, exactly as Bainbridge had wanted her to do.

"Oh, loads of 'em. Most of our lot's dreadful behaviour stems from some idea of August's. We lured twenty cats into Almack's once at his behest. Do you remember, August? They had those revolting fish paste sandwiches that night, all curling up at the edges, and you said you had a better use for them. He left a trail up to the back of the building and a window open with a stash of the dreadful things tempting them in."

August tsked impatiently. "Bainbridge, I really don't think Miss Anson needs to hear—"

"Oh, yes, I do," Viv interrupted with undisguised glee.

"Have you ever tried herding cats, Miss Anson?" Bainbridge grinned. "Well, to watch some of the high sticklers of the *ton* doing just that was the highlight of an extremely dull evening."

"Yes, and then we were banned for life," August retorted crossly.

"No, no. Dare, Raphe and I were banned for life, thank the Lord. Lady Jersey reinstated you after you told that fool to hold his tongue when he was rattling on about her daughter's acting out an infatuation with Prince Nicholas, and her and her blessed mama's devious scheming for her to marry into royalty. Of course, August didn't know Silence Jersey was listening but defended her daughter anyway, and so regained her ladyship's favour."

August shrugged. "It was quite obvious the two of them were madly in love. There was no acting involved, and I despise gossip about anybody."

"You see, Miss Anson, August is so thoroughly noble and good-hearted he can be as dreadful as the rest of my wicked friends, but *he* is always forgiven. And what about that to-do at the balloon ascension at Green Park? They read the riot act that time."

Viv watched, fascinated, as August's eyes flashed with irritation.

"I did not mean it to go so far. If those bloody drunken sots hadn't started pushing people about, it would never have happened. They were violently out of control, and mean with it. They deserved to be taken in hand, the damned brutes."

August flushed, crests of colour at his cheeks as he realised he ought not to speak in such a forthright manner before the ladies. "I beg your pardon, Arabella, Miss Anson."

Bella only laughed—she *was* married to Bainbridge, after all—and Viv grinned at him.

"Ah, they did indeed deserve it, and I admit it was not your fault in the least. The best laid plans, et cetera," Bainbridge said mournfully, though he looked thoroughly entertained. "And yours were always that. What about the time you swapped the house master's sherry for vinegar, or the fireworks that went off exactly when that vile bully Travis was about to pound poor Barnaby Godwin for the third time that week? Exploded right up his arse, scared him witless, and gave Barnaby the chance to escape. I don't think I've ever laughed so much in my life."

"They thrashed us for that," August reminded him with a resigned sigh. "You worst of all, because you told the headmaster Travis had it coming, and it was about time someone took him in hand if the beaks kept turning a blind eye."

"True enough, but it was worth it. Travis broke your nose in retaliation, if I recall, though you knocked him down in the end. I'd do it again. Wouldn't you?"

"Yes," August said, though he didn't sound entirely happy about it. "I would."

Viv watched him, something warm and happy glowing in her heart. A good man. A kind one. One that would stand up for a friend, one that felt embarrassed for the pranks of his youth, and more recent trouble, but would risk it again for the sake of giving Vivien the retribution she had so desperately wanted but could not take for herself.

They walked on farther in silence, and Viv wondered why August still looked so troubled. Last night's fight, perhaps.

"What's wrong?" she asked him, daring to take his arm.

"Nothing," he said, mustering a smile.

Viv gave him a look that suggested he was a poor liar.

August sighed. "Family trouble. Nothing to concern you, Miss Anson."

"Vivien," she corrected him gently. "At least when there is no one to overhear and scold me for allowing you such familiarity."

"Vivien," he repeated, his gaze upon hers, though she could not read his expression.

"I heard about that night at Almack's," she said, smiling now. "Prue—the Duchess of Bedwin—was there, and came to tell us about it. She cried with laughter, telling of how the cats climbed the curtains and snatched the dreadful refreshments from the tables while everyone ran about like headless chickens. Mama was delighted. I don't think I have ever seen her laugh so much. We are not welcome at Almack's, naturally, so it was the most delicious bit of entertainment for us," she added in an undertone.

August frowned, clearly unhappy with this.

"Papa was banned from Almack's years before he even married Mama," she added soothingly, for he looked as if he wanted to do battle with society at large on her behalf. The thought added fuel to the warmth already simmering inside her. "He's not good *ton* either, thank heavens."

He nodded, but his distraction was such that Viv felt stirrings of unease. "How does your father bear it?" he demanded, after they had walked on a little way. "How does he not call out people left, right and centre for their rudeness? Is he not constantly rolling his sleeves up to pound someone?"

Viv shrugged. "Papa is a powerful man, wealthy and influential. Most are too sensible to speak so in front of him, for his retribution could be more damaging to them financially or socially than a black eye or broken nose. Though it has happened, and he has thrashed the rudeness from those men on a few memorable occasions. So memorable that sensible people do not wish to be at the receiving end of such a lesson. Women are harder to deal with, as you have discovered. Neither Papa nor Mama could break a spiteful woman's nose, no matter the provocation, though I think Mama has been tempted a time or two," she added with a grin.

August did not look the least bit amused, rather he looked furious, and rather pale and not entirely well. "You ought to have such a man as your husband. A powerful, titled man people would not dare to speak ill in front of."

Viv laughed nervously, uncertain of his tone. "For example?"

"The Marquess of Blackstone, the Earl of Ashburton. Men like that could protect you from such unpleasantness. You are close to them both, I think?"

Viv stopped in her tracks, staring at him. "Yes, we are good *friends,*" she said, emphasising the word. "Nothing more, and I have no desire to marry either of them. I would kill Blackstone within a week, or he me, and as for Ashburton, good heavens, no."

"It's what you need," August said, his voice firm, if bleak. "A powerful man with influence. You could marry a duke, Vivien. Any man in his right mind would be proud to have you for his wife and could protect you from the insults of those fools not worthy of your notice."

"I don't want a duke, or a marquess, or a blasted earl. What has got into you?"

"A bit of sanity, clarity, call it what you will," August said, though he did not look pleased by the revelation. He took a deep breath, turning back to face her. "I'm not what you need, Vivien. I see that now, though the revelation is a painful one. I am not powerful, or vastly wealthy. I do not have the kind of influence to keep you and any children safe from the slings and arrows life will inevitably throw."

"And if I don't care about such things?"

"You ought to care," he said, his voice sharp. "For the sake of any children you may bring into the world, if not for your own sake."

Vivien thought about that, knowing that she could not pretend there was no truth to his words, though she dearly wanted to deny them. There was more to it than that alone, though.

"And I would plunge you into an unsettled, scandalous, endlessly combative life, the kind you want so badly to avoid," Vivien said, her throat tight.

August stared at her, his expression one of misery. "I could not simply ignore it when some fool slighted you, male or female. It's not in my nature, though God knows I'm trying to behave. I would retaliate, I would cause a scene or call them out, riot and chaos would ensue as it always does. You can't want that any more than I do?"

No, she did not want that. She wanted excitement and adventure, yes, but not to fight for her position in society. He was right. Her parents had gently suggested Jules as a match, and though they would urge her to marry for love, to the right man no matter who he might be, they too had suggested she might look in the same direction that August had directed her. But she did not want Blackstone or Ashburton. The only man who had ever caught her eye, who had ever engaged her heart, was him.

"You are telling me we don't suit," she said, her voice somewhat unsteady.

August swallowed, and when he spoke, he too sounded shaken. "I wish I was in line for an earldom, or that some elderly relative was about to die and leave me a vast fortune, but it isn't the case. I am moderately wealthy, but no man fears me save those that occasionally find themselves at the wrong end of my fists. That is no way to earn respect among the *ton*. You should have a life full of happiness, as free of care as any life can be, and I cannot give you that any more than you can give me a life free of scandal and upset. We would be like fire and brandy, a potent mix. We would burn bright but not endure."

Vivien stared at him. "Yes. I see what you mean."

Somehow her voice was steady, but the warmth that had bloomed inside her had died a quick death, and the snowflakes falling with slow deliberation around them seemed to settle in its place.

"It's for the best," he said quietly.

"As you say," Vivien managed, praying she would not cry until she was alone.

"You should get inside before you catch a chill, Miss Anson."

His voice was gentle, kind as always, and she was Miss Anson once again.

"What about you?"

"Don't worry about me. I'll be on my way. Easier for everyone. Bainbridge will see my things sent on."

Vivien nodded. "Good day to you then, Mr Lane-Fox."

Oh, how polite they were, how very English. She wanted to howl and stamp her feet on the ground, but she would not. Instead, she turned away and walked back to the house alone.

Chapter 10

Bainbridge,

Forgive me for my unseemly departure. I could not stay. I ought never to have listened to you in the first place, though I blame myself for doing as I wished, rather than doing as I knew was right.

This little exercise has only made me wretched. Miss Anson is everything any man could want, and if I marry her, I consign us both to a lifetime of fighting society and causing a scandal. Neither of us wants that.

I must forget her and turn my attentions elsewhere. If only it were that simple.

Please forward my belongings to Mivart's. I shall take rooms there for now.

—Excerpt of a letter from Mr August Lane-Fox to The Most Hon'ble Lawrence Grenville, Marquess of Bainbridge.

31st March 1841, Cavendish House, The Strand, London.

Vivien sighed and stared at the rows of books in front of her. Usually such a sight was enough to gladden her heart and a visit to Hatchard's the very thing to brighten her day. Except in the dreary weeks since she had last seen August, nothing made her smile any longer. Worst of all, she had heard reports he had escorted Miss Cecilia Thrussell to a *musicale* last week. Miss Thrussell was a sweet girl, quiet and demure. She would make him the perfect, well-behaved wife.

Not that Viv was moping. Well, she was trying her best not to mope, for she hated being such a wet blanket, but the world seemed grey and dreary of late. Even the weather was awful, with no sunshine for weeks, instead a constant, grim drizzle that made everyone cross and fretful.

Ash had made her come out today, determined to get her out of the house and into a more positive frame of mind. Bless him, he had done all in his power to make her smile, even eschewing some of his invitations to stay at home with her when she was especially blue devilled. This simply could not go on. It was not fair to him, or to her. She deserved better.

Viv took a deep breath and picked a book at random from the shelf—she didn't much care what—and was almost knocked off her feet. The book fell with a thud to the floor and a young woman reached out to steady her.

"Oh!" the woman exclaimed. "Oh, I do beg your pardon, only… *lud*, he's coming! Please… *please* don't give me away."

Before Vivien could ask what the devil was going on, the girl flung herself to the floor in the corner of the bookshelf behind Viv. The young woman hugged her knees, making herself as small as possible and sent a beseeching look up at her.

Viv turned as she heard the heavy tread of footsteps grow closer. Turning, she was somewhat alarmed to see one of Mr Peel's burly policemen.

"Good morning, miss," he said. "Did you see a young woman come this way, dressed in grey, about so high?"

He gestured with his hand to indicate the approximate size of the woman huddled just around the corner of the bookshelf Viv stood beside. She hesitated.

"Good heavens, what has she done to have a Metropolitan Policeman chasing her? Is she dangerous?"

"To public order, aye. Ranting about the rights of women and causing a public menace she was," he said in disgust. "Women like that go about stirring others up, making them dissatisfied with their lot when they was perfectly happy before."

"Oh, yes, I see," Viv replied blandly. "Because we should all be at home stitching samplers before the fire where it is safe, and we can cause no bother to anyone. I should be getting back myself."

She gave the man a dazzling smile, the one that usually made men lose their wits. It worked this time too, and the fellow did not seem to heed the fact that she had laced her words with blatant sarcasm.

"Quite, miss," he said, sounding somewhat breathless. "So you've not seen her, then?"

"Alas, good sir, I cannot help you," Viv replied with another brilliant smile, disinclined to lie outright to an officer of the law.

He blinked, swallowing hard. "Right. Right you are then, I... I'll be on my way."

"Good day to you," Viv replied sweetly and watched until he was out of sight. "Insufferable half-wit," she muttered.

"I know," said the woman behind her, who got up and smoothed down her skirts.

Viv saw now that she was a pretty woman in her early twenties. Her hair was a soft gold, disordered and escaping its pins after her run in with the law, and her blue eyes danced with lively intelligence.

"They're afraid of us. That's the trouble. Socrates said it out loud, you know."

"He did?" Vivien said, looking at her with interest.

She nodded with enthusiasm and straightened her hat as best she could. "Yes. He said, 'Once made equal to man, woman becomes his superior.' That's what they're frightened of. They know that if they educate us and give us the tools to be independent, they won't be able to control us any longer, and that is terrifying to most males."

Viv nodded. "Yes, I can see the truth in that, though I think there are exceptions. My father is one, and my brother too. They value mine and my mother's opinions, and I was educated alongside my brother."

"You were? Well, I applaud your papa," the woman said, grinning at her. "Thank you, by the way, for hiding me."

"I was happy to help you, Miss…?"

She screwed up her nose and gave an apologetic smile. "Oh, best not share my name, just in case. I shall be in the suds if it gets about I was in trouble with the law again. I'm not even supposed to be in town. But it was a pleasure to meet you. If you'll excuse me, I'd better make myself scarce before that big lummox comes back and has another look. Good day to you."

"Good day," Viv replied, watching her hurry away with a sigh. What a pity. The most interesting person she'd met in ages, and she didn't even get to know her name. Ah well. She bent and picked up the book she'd dropped, turning it to see it was *Frankenstein, or, The Modern Prometheus*. Well, she hadn't read it and as she was certainly not in the mood for a romance, it would do nicely. With her selection finally made, Viv went in search of her brother.

🎩 🎩 🎩

8th April 1841, The Sea Front, Brighton.

"Well, this is grand. Sunshine, sea air, and the promise of some fine entertainments."

Viv turned to regard her twin, who was beaming at her.

"Yes, I'm glad Papa brought us down. It is a beautiful day," she agreed, enjoying the unseasonably warm sun on her face.

Though it was only April, it felt more like summer had arrived and after such a long and gloomy winter, this had the effect of a dose of effervescent salts on the humour of those enjoying all that the seaside offered. A substantial exodus from London had accompanied the adjournment of Parliament for the Easter recess and the removal of the Court to Windsor. Brighton subsequently had filled up with the great and the good of society, most of whom seemed to be promenading this morning in their finery.

"Well, would you look at that," Ash said, beaming and tipping his hat to someone along the street.

Vivien turned in the direction he gestured to see two elegant young women hurrying towards them, their faces full of delight.

"Evie! And Aisling! Oh, how wonderful to see you both," Vivien exclaimed, hugging each of them in turn. "But I didn't know you would be here?"

"Mama brought us down yesterday," Evie said, breathless with laughter. "Papa is tied up with some trouble over the railway, but Mama was desperate to escape London and get some sun and fresh air, so we came first, and Papa will join us in a few days. But we saw Aisling in town, and Mama said she might come with us if she wanted to."

"I wanted to," Aisling said with a soft chuckle, daring a glance at Ash. "Good morning, Mr Anson. How are you?"

"All the better for the company of two such lovely creatures," Ash said, offering each of the young women an arm. "Now we shall be a merry party, and Vivien needs some merriment."

"Is there aught amiss, Viv?" Aisling asked with concern as Viv took her free arm.

"No. Not in the least. Only it has been such a dreary winter, but the sunshine and your company were all that I needed. Are you staying long?"

Evie shrugged. "Everyone will disappear a few days before Parliament sits again on the twentieth, so I suppose that will be an end to the entertainments to be had. I imagine we'll return to town then, for Mama has several social engagements."

"Will you try the sea bathing?" Aisling asked, giving the bathing machines an anxious glance.

There were already people swimming out, enticed by the early warm weather and the lure of improving their health. Or perhaps it was a dare.

"Certainly not. It's far too early in the year, the sea must be icy," Vivien said with a shiver.

"Yes. Yes, it's certainly too early in the year," Aisling said firmly, looking vastly relieved.

Vivien frowned and glanced at Evie who mouthed the words, *'her dare.'*

Oh, of course. Aisling's dare was to swim naked by moonlight. No wonder she was relieved. Viv gave her shoulder a comforting pat.

"It is. Far too cold, though some brave souls are attempting it."

Ash shuddered and shook his head. "That's not bravery, but idiocy. I value my tender parts too dearly to put them through such an ordeal. I want to be a father one day, if not for a while yet."

"Ash!" Vivien hissed, widening her eyes at him, for Aisling had turned the colour of a cooked lobster.

"Beg pardon, ladies," he said, looking entirely unrepentant.

They enjoyed a pleasant walk along the front, sampled the fruit ices and retired back to The Old Ship Hotel for lunch, whereby some happy accident they were all staying. The newer Duke of York was the more fashionable venue, but The Ship had charm and a familiar elegance, and for some, happy associations.

"Mama has fond memories of this hotel," Evie said with a smile as they made their way to the dining room.

"Oh, of course, her curricle race from London with your father. How intrepid she was, and to win the race too! She's a remarkable woman," Aisling said with an admiring smile. "And it's such a romantic story."

Evie nodded. "Yes, though Mama says she nearly expired from the chill she caught. She told me she arrived frozen stiff and soaked to the bone, but she said it was worth it, for Papa carried her into the hotel, and he kissed her for the first time as he carried her up the stairs."

Both Aisling and Vivien gave a wistful sigh, and Ash laughed, shaking his head.

"Barmy, the lot of you."

"It's not barmy at all," Viv protested, feeling an unwelcome surge of melancholy. "Mr Knight was gallant in defeat, and it is romantic the way he carried her inside... and now coming back here, where they shared their first kiss all those years ago. It is splendidly romantic."

Something in her tone must have alerted Evie to her mood, for she took Viv's arm as Ash escorted Aisling to their table.

"Still nothing from Mr Lane-Fox?" she asked softly.

Viv shook her head, appalled to discover his name still sent a stab of longing through her heart, though it had been weeks since that scene at Axton House. "Of course not. We do not suit, Evie. I told you that."

"Telling me or telling yourself does not make your heart do as it is told, though, does it?" Evie said, squeezing her hand.

Viv swallowed hard and sent her a pleading look.

"So let us talk of other things," Evie said briskly, aware that Viv was on the brink of tears and anything kinder would have overset her. "What are your plans for the rest of the day?"

Vivien took a breath, grateful for Evie's rapid change of subject as they joined Ash, who was pulling out a chair for Aisling to sit down. "Well, Ash suggested…."

But whatever it was Ash had suggested flew from her mind as she saw two men enter the dining room. They were so intent on their conversation, they did not notice Vivien and her party until they were mere inches from their table.

The two men stopped in their tracks.

Chapter 11

Raphe,

Thank you for your letter. I am glad to hear you and the lovely Greer are muddling on in my absence. Even better to hear I am missed, even if that is not entirely true. Give Ollie my regards.

I arrived in Brighton on the 8ᵗʰ of April and have taken a room at The Old Ship Hotel, for which I thank you. I know you will tell me I have more than earned my wages, but you are a generous employer, brother mine, and I am grateful for it. It is good to be among society without fearing someone will notice my worn cuffs or too oft folded cravat.

It's an enjoyable treat to be back in society for a while and catch up with old friends, but it surprises me not to feel as at home here as I once did. Moreover, I miss the peace to be found at Marcross Manor and, strangely, the work, too. Never thought I'd say such a thing, but I think you understand. Still, I am glad you forced me into this brief holiday for that reason alone. It is good to realise what has become important to me. I must be getting old. I suppose your very tempting example of wedded bliss might make a fellow somewhat envious, though I doubt I'll ever be as fortunate as you have been in your wife, you lucky dog. Ah, well, a fellow can hope, and hunt, and speaking of which... I have a party to attend.

—Excerpt of a letter from The Hon'ble Mr Sylvester Cootes to his brother, The Right Hon'ble Raphe Cootes, Baron de Ligne.

8th April 1841, The Old Ship Hotel, Brighton.

"Miss Anson."

"Lady Aisling."

The two men spoke in unison, both sounding somewhat winded.

"Mr Lane-Fox," Vivien managed, though her heart was thudding so hard she could hardly breathe, let alone speak. She dared a glance at the others to find Aisling glowering at August's companion with undisguised hostility. This was such an extraordinary and unexpected expression to see on Aisling's sweet face that Vivien was momentarily diverted.

Thank heavens for Evie, who plunged into the awkward breach. "Mr Lane-Fox, how nice to see you again. I see the splendid weather has tempted you away from town, too. Good heavens, there must not be a soul left in London."

"Miss Knight, it is a pleasure to see you as always, and yes, the world appears to be here enjoying the sunshine, though my friend here invited me to accompany him. We've not seen each other this age, so had some catching up to do. If you would allow me to introduce him—"

"We've met," Lady Aisling said, giving the man a cool nod. "Mr Cootes."

The simmering tension was hard to miss, and Evie glanced first at Ash and then to Vivien, though they were both at a loss.

"We were about to sit down for some lunch," Evie said, and Vivien was certain the next words out of her mouth would have been, *if you will excuse us,* which would politely but neatly give them their marching orders, but then her blessed brother had to open his mouth.

"I do hope you'll join us," Ash said cheerfully.

Vivien didn't know whether to kiss him or hit him with the breadbasket. Judging from Aisling's expression, she was for the breadbasket.

"It would be a pleasure," Mr Cootes said, pulling out a chair for Evie, before August could reply. August sent Vivien an apologetic smile and did likewise for her as everyone took their places.

Vivien's composure was hardly helped when August took the only remaining seat beside her. There was a flurry of activity as waiters arrived and attended to napkins and brought wine and water whilst they passed the menus around. Silence fell as everyone surveyed their choices.

"How have you been?" he asked, and with such tenderness that Vivien wanted to weep.

Wretched. Miserable. Utterly blue devilled.

"Quite well, thank you, Mr Lane-Fox."

That had sounded rather cold and indifferent, which she had not intended at all, but it was all she could do to keep her composure. If she let it slip at all, she might do something outrageous and throw herself at him. Oh, but it was good to see him. Even though it hurt more than she had suspected it might, she drank in the sight of him. Had he lost weight? His handsome

115

features seemed a little sharper than usual, the cheekbones more prominent.

"And you?" she dared ask, hating herself for hoping he'd been as unhappy as she had.

He stared at the menu for a long moment, though she thought he did not see it.

"August?" she pressed, knowing she ought not to use his name. She no longer had the right.

He closed his eyes for a moment. "Wretched," he whispered, before turning back to her with a rueful smile. "Would you forgive me for wishing I had never met you?"

Though a lump rose in her throat, Vivien smiled, though she suspected it was a wistful expression. "Not in the least. I am afraid I am guilty of the same emotion."

"Well, we had best make the best of things," he said, a note of forced cheer to the words.

"Yes." Vivien nodded. They were adults. Just because they could not be together, did not mean they could not be friends, not treat each other kindly. "Perhaps you know why the sweetest girl on God's green earth is staring daggers at your Mr Cootes. Do I know him, incidentally? He looks familiar."

"You perhaps have seen his brother in town. Lord de Ligne?"

"Ah, yes," Vivien nodded, realising the resemblance was marked.

"As for the animosity between him and Lady Aisling, I believe they met at Christmas, at Roxborough's House party. Sylvester must have made an impression."

"Sylvester Cootes? Oh, *he's* the most vexing man who ever lived!" Vivien said, and then slapped a hand over her mouth.

August grinned at her and raised an eyebrow.

"I forbid you to tell him I said that," Vivien warned him.

"Oh-ho, but you cannot tell me something so intriguing and not explain why my friend has been so labelled. At least, not if you wish me to hold my tongue," he teased.

Vivien laughed, reflecting that it was far too easy to enjoy this man's company. "I am afraid I cannot, for I don't know, other than that they did not get along. Strange, as Aisling is shy and tender-hearted, and I have never known her take anyone in dislike before. She is the kind that has a good word for everyone and gives everyone the benefit of the doubt." Vivien hesitated, not wanting to insult the man but worried for her friend. "He... He isn't the kind of man who would—?"

"Good heavens, no!" August said at once. "He's got a devilish sense of humour, like his brother and he can be a little overbearing, but he's a decent fellow, good-hearted. He likes to tease, I'll grant you, but he would never importune a lady."

Viv sighed, shaking her head. "Well, something is causing her to react so strongly towards him."

"Well, perhaps he disturbs her peace of mind."

"I beg your pardon?" Viv said, frowning at him.

August returned a rueful smile. "You disturbed my peace of mind, Miss Anson. You did from the very start."

Viv's eyes widened, and she looked at Aisling again at the very moment she stole a covert glance at Sylvester Cootes. Vivian watched them both with interest, aware of August doing likewise. Mr Cootes had by now demolished his bread roll and, discovering the basket empty, attempted to steal Aisling's. He did it in such an obviously furtive way that he must have known full well she would discover his thievery. She did. Aisling smacked his hand.

"Mr Cootes, the waiter will bring more bread presently. There is no need to steal mine."

Sylvester returned a pleading expression. "But I'm famished, my lady, and your bread roll was just sitting there, forlorn and forgotten."

"It was not forgotten," Aisling said tartly. "I was simply not ready to eat it yet."

"Whereas I am fading away from a lack of sustenance," he said with a wistful sigh.

Aisling snorted. "You seem perfectly robust to me!"

A slow, pleased smile curved over the rogue's mouth. "Why, thank you, Lady Aisling. How kind of you to notice my virile masculine physique."

"I did no such thing," she spluttered, colouring.

"Yes, you did. You just said so. You said I was *robust.*"

The devil's eyes glinted with mischief.

Aisling's chin went up. "I only meant that you were in no danger of swooning from lack of nourishment."

Sylvester shrugged, giving her a pensive sigh. "Perhaps not from a lack of nourishment. At least, not of the kind you eat. My heart and soul, however, are withering away. Why do you treat me so ill when you know I admire you?"

Aisling sent him an incinerating glare. "Why are you such a pestilential nuisance?"

"I bother you, don't I?" he said, a satisfied glint in his eyes.

"Yes, you do, though why you should look so vastly pleased about it, I cannot fathom."

"Can't you?" His grin was growing wider by the moment, an event that seemed to undermine what remained of Aisling's composure.

"No. And I do wish you would cease speaking altogether rather than talk drivel," she snapped.

"I am pleased that I bother you, because it means I provoke a reaction," Sylvester explained with the utmost patience. "If you were indifferent to me, that would be truly devastating, but you are not indifferent."

"No. Not indifferent," Aisling agreed with a brittle smile. "I dislike you intensely."

"Intensely. How fascinating. But why? I do not believe I have done anything to cause great offence. I have teased you a little, perhaps, made you somewhat flustered, but to dislike me intensely without reason is a little odd. Don't you think?"

"Not in the least." Aisling put her chin up. "Perhaps you were cruel to me in a previous incarnation."

Sylvester choked on the wine he'd just taken a sip of. August pounded him on the back until he was breathing easy again. "Forgive me, Lady Aisling, but... but do you mean to tell me I am being punished for sins I committed in another lifetime?"

"No," Aisling said, looking as if she might leap across the table and strangle him with his own cravat at any moment. "I mean that sometimes one gets a feeling about another person, an instinctive reaction to their presence. In your case, my instincts tell me to run as far from you as possible."

Vivien shared an amused glance with August. Evie and Ash were deep in conversation and paid Aisling and Sylvester no mind. Viv knew they ought not eavesdrop either, but it was too interesting a conversation not to follow it. Sylvester lowered his voice, his tone intimate and only just audible.

"But perhaps your innocence means you are misinterpreting your reasons for running, my lady."

"What does that mean?" Aisling snapped, her eyes flashing with irritation.

Sylvester sat back in his chair, regarding her with a steady, contemplative expression. "I shall let you figure that out," he whispered, softly.

Aisling threw her bread roll at him. It hit him on the forehead, ricocheted across the room and landed with a loud splash in a bowl of soup on the table across from theirs. Sadly, it was tomato soup, which splattered the pristine white cravat and delicate pale primrose waistcoat of the diner. His companions, of whom there were three, burst out laughing. The soup splattered diner leapt to his feet with an exclamation of fury, and with such force that his chair toppled over with a crash.

Aisling froze in horror, her face draining of all colour. A public scene was the kind of thing to give her palpitations.

Sylvester got to his feet without a moment's hesitation. "I do beg your pardon, gentlemen. Entirely my fault. I cannot think how I came to do such a thing."

"You blithering idiot! How do you throw a bread roll that far by accident?" the diner demanded, and not entirely without justification.

"A stupid accident for which I hold myself entirely accountable. I beg you will send any cleaning bills to me. Just ask for Cootes at the desk."

"Cleaning? Those stains will never come out!" the fellow shrieked, becoming more incensed by the moment.

"You might try salt and baking soda," Vivien suggested, as it was her maid's favourite remedy for stubborn stains.

"Good lord, you're not only a buffoon but dining with the help," the man sneered. "A pretty piece I'll grant you, but you ought not to bring her into society."

Viv froze, adopting the expression she used as a shield whenever faced with such situations. The trick was to never let them know their words bothered you. If you reacted, they won.

The table fell very silent. At the same moment, August and Ash stood as Sylvester took a menacing step forward.

"That," Sylvester said, his voice very quiet, "is the daughter of Viscount Cavendish you've just insulted. Might I have the honour of your name, sir? For I should like to know where to send the wreath when his lordship hears of your insult."

The man turned a queasy shade of green. "Now, look here—"

"I'm not sure I want to wait for his lordship to deal with this," August said, and the restrained fury in his voice made all the fine hairs on the back of Viv's neck stand on end.

"Me either," Ash said, practically vibrating with anger. "I'd just as soon sort the fellow out myself. Pa need not get his hands dirty for once."

This could turn very nasty in no time at all.

"August," Viv said, reaching out and grasping his hand. He turned to stare down at her and she gave a small shake of her head. "Don't cause a scene. Not here."

"Come on, Frank, let's be on our way. I've lost my appetite," said one of the fool's more sensible friends, tugging at his arm as he stared at the three furious men ready to defend Vivien at the drop of a hat. He wore an objectionable puce waistcoat of a virulent shade even Ash would have hesitated to wear.

Frank's cheeks were flaming now, the splotches of red an odd sight set against his deathly pallor.

"Yes, do run along, Frankie, old boy," Sylvester said, grinning, though his smile showed entirely too many teeth to be friendly.

Frankie ran along, his friends following close behind.

"Blasted ignorant prick," Sylvester said in disgust, resuming his seat.

August sat too, still holding Viv's hand. His grip was reassuring, firm but gentle, his fingers warm. "All right?" he asked, his voice low.

Viv let out a breath and nodded. "Yes. Thank you for… for what you did, but he was not worth your anger, certainly not worth fighting. He would have insulted your companions for another reason had I not been here. I was just an easy target."

"He'd best hope I don't cross his path again when the circumstances are less public," August muttered.

Viv smiled and squeezed his hand. "Forget it. Let us enjoy our meal. Please," she added.

August nodded, smiling for her sake, though she knew he was still furious. She looked around, relieved to see Evie speaking earnestly to Ash, her hand on his sleeve. Evie would know what to say to diffuse her brother's temper. Turning her attention to Aisling, she found her friend looking utterly wretched.

"That was all my fault," she whispered, looking close to tears.

Viv opened her mouth to contradict her, but Sylvester beat her to it.

"It certainly was not. It was my fault for vexing you into throwing things at me perhaps, but that lamentable excuse for a man was a prick before the bread roll landed in his soup and he'll be a prick until the day he dies. That is not in the least your fault."

This rather inelegant speech had the strangest effect on Aisling, whose lips quirked up at the corners. "You have quite a way with words, Mr Cootes."

"I'm charming and intelligent. I told you that before. You have the most lamentable memory, my lady," he said with a world-weary sigh, though his expression was alight with amusement.

"You're insufferable," Aisling corrected, though the harsh tone was absent from her words now. "But you do, occasionally, have good instincts and act well. Thank you for what you did, for taking the blame for me and… and standing up to that horrid man."

Sylvester's eyes grew wide, and he pressed his palm to his chest, covering his heart. "Good heavens, Lady Aisling. Do you mean to say I have done something you approve of? *Again?* That's twice you've approved of me. I may swoon."

"Oh, I knew I was going to regret that," Aisling said with a sigh. "And no, Mr Cootes, this is not the beginning of a beautiful friendship. You are still the most vexing man that ever lived."

"Thank you," Sylvester said, beaming at her like she'd offered him the most profound compliment. "Not simply a vexing fellow, but the *most* vexing fellow that ever lived. I knew I bothered you, Lady Aisling. I just knew it."

"Lord, grant me patience," Aisling muttered, and rolled her eyes to the heavens.

Chapter 12

Monsieur,

I hope this letter finds you well.

I wanted to let you know Mama has swept us all up and taken us to Brighton. It was all done at the last moment, and I did not have the time to warn you of our departure.

The sun is glorious, like April and May have been pushed aside in favour of June. The sea glitters, almost as blue as your eyes, and the sunshine is a wonderful boost to one's spirits after such a tiresome winter of grey skies and drizzle.

Half the world is here, it seems, and I have already met the Anson twins, Mr August Lane-Fox and Mr Sylvester Cootes. Mr Hadley Smythe and Mr Price were strolling on the promenade this morning, and I also bumped into Mr Barnaby Godwin. He asked if I had seen you and seemed most disappointed that you were still in town.

Must you remain in London? There are many amusements to be found here at present.

—Excerpt of a letter from Miss Evie Knight (daughter of Lady Helena and Mr Gabriel Knight) to Louis César de Montluc, Comte de Villen.

11th April 1841, The Sea Front. Brighton.

He ought not to have done it, August reflected with a sigh. Asking Vivien and her friends to accompany him and Sylvester on a walk along the seafront was an exercise in futility and heartache, but he'd never been any good at resisting temptation. The result was the embodiment of allurement walking with her hand on his arm.

Vivien wore a delicious white gown that accentuated her lush curves. It was trimmed with lace and oddly charming little puffs of pink ribbon. Her hat was also white, a mad extravaganza of flowers and ribbons on one side. She looked edible, and there was a dull ache of resentment in his chest that he could not shake. He was still simmering from the scene in the dining room yesterday, an event that ought to have confirmed his instincts to stay away from her were sound. All it had done was make him want to take on the bloody world and change it one fight at a time, if that's what was required. Of course, the rational part of his brain—the part that wasn't ninety-five percent caveman—knew that was not the answer. Sadly, he did not know what was.

"Stop fulminating."

August looked around at Vivien in surprise. "I never said a word," he objected.

"I can hear you ranting in your head," she said gently, smiling at him.

He gave a huff of laughter. "That obvious, am I?"

"To me, yes," she said, her grip on his sleeve tightening a little.

Words burned on his tongue. Words he knew he ought not say.

I miss you. I want you. I am wretched without you.

"It's a glorious day."

Ah, yes, the weather. When in doubt, an Englishman could always rely on the weather as a safe topic of conversation.

Vivien giggled.

"Well, you try," he grumbled. "I am no good at this. I ought not have asked you to—"

He broke off, his gaze fixed on four figures splashing about in the sea like lunatics. August narrowed his eyes. They had walked some way from the fashionable end of town and there was no one else on the beach but them... —and the men in the sea. The tide was a fair distance out, leaving a good stretch of shoreline, but not so far that he didn't recognise the fellow Sylvester had aptly named an ignorant prick.

"Oh," Vivien said, her grip on his arm tightening a little. "Look."

She pointed to a neatly folded collection of clothing that included a revolting puce waistcoat.

August grinned at her.

"We ought not," she said, though excitement glimmered in her indigo eyes like starlight upon the sea.

"We really ought," August replied, the joyous sensation that always assailed him when he'd had a marvellously wicked idea rising like a tide.

Vivien looked thoughtful. "Well, yes. I mean, really, leaving that vile waistcoat out in the open like that, it's asking for trouble. And sporting about like little boys in the altogether! It's outrageous really. They must intend to cause a stir."

"They ought to have used the bathing machines rather than offend decent people. I mean, puce? It's enough to provoke anyone," August said earnestly.

Without another word, the two of them hurried to the pile of clothes, snatched them up, and ran from the beach, leaving the others to walk on without noticing their departure.

"Oh! Oh, that was dreadful of us, and... Oh, August. What a lark!" Vivien said, laughing so hard her eyes watered. "But ought we leave them something to cover themselves? Some poor maiden aunt will have a hysterical fit if she sees four naked men walking through the town."

"They're wearing their smallclothes. Those aren't in the pile," he said with a shrug.

"Even so. Perhaps a towel?"

August thought Vivien was far too kind-hearted. "I have a better idea," he said, eyeing a pawn shop down a corner street.

Not very much later, they found their way back to Sylvester, Evie, and Aisling, who were waiting in the fashionable part of town.

"Where did you two get to?" Aisling asked them.

"Tsk, Lady Aisling, surely you know better than to ask such a question?" Sy said, earning himself a stern glare from August.

"If you come this way, you'll see soon enough," August said, gesturing for them to follow him.

He treated everyone to dishes of fruit ice and they sat facing the seafront, enjoying the sunshine and a light breeze that made the ladies' frills and ribbons flutter enticingly.

"What, exactly, are we waiting for?" Sy asked, once they had all finished their ices.

"This," August said gleefully, his expression one of delight.

Sy turned in the direction he was staring and narrowed his eyes. "Is… is that the prick—"

"Yes," August said, grinning.

"He's wearing petticoats!"

"Oh, dear." Vivien put a hand to her mouth to smother a burst of laughter.

The four men, all wearing matching expressions of fury and humiliation, were hurrying up the street, each with a voluminous petticoat pulled up under their armpits. The lace hem frothed around their knees as they walked, white, hairy legs on display below.

"Goodness," Evie said, in tones of awed astonishment.

As the men drew closer, the one that had so insulted Vivien caught sight of August, who was far too delighted by the scene to rearrange his face.

"You!" the prick raged, purple with indignation. "You bloody bastard. You did this!"

Before anyone could react, he'd lunged at August, his friends looking as though they'd be delighted to take a hand in pummelling him too. August blocked a fist that would have broken his nose and dodged a surprisingly neat left. The fellow was handy with his fists, but then, so was August.

To his relief, and before the other three men could take him down, Ash and Sylvester waded into the fray.

"Go back to the hotel!" he yelled at Vivien and the other two ladies, who really ought not be subjected to such a scene.

"Not on your life!" she yelled back. "Oh, August, watch out!"

August ducked and struck out, delivering a punch to the solar plexus that had the fellow staggering back and sitting down hard on the ground.

"Oh! Nicely done!" Vivien exclaimed, apparently egging him on.

Unfortunately, the devil got up again.

August glanced around to see Sylvester grappling with a big fellow and, with some surprise, that Ash had knocked down his opponent and was holding off another with ease. Well, well. Those dreadful waistcoats he adored did not prepare one for the fact Ash could fight like a demon.

A shrill whistle and shouts alerted them to the fact they ought not be brawling in full view of the public as two constables ran full pelt towards them.

"Ash! Get the ladies out of here," August yelled, as Ash's opponent had already beat a retreat.

Ash nodded, herded up the women, ignoring their protests and shepherding them away with speed. The last thing they needed was to be caught up with such scandalous behaviour that would no doubt damage their pristine reputations. The prick had taken his chance to scarper too, but Sylvester and the big brute he was wrangling with were too caught up in the moment to heed the warnings to flee. August waded in, pushing his way between them, and caught a clip to the jaw that snapped his head back. Sylvester steadied him as he staggered.

"Oi, cut that out! You there, halt!"

The big fellow took to his heels with the second constable legging it after him. A little dazed from the blow, August had neither the time to run nor the inclination to abandon Sylvester, who was breathing hard and wiping his bloody nose on a torn sleeve.

"Right, my fine fellows. You're down to the station with me," the constable said with a grim smile.

Sylvester nodded and waved a hand at the fellow. "As you like, Constable, only... give a fellow a chance to catch his breath."

August sighed and leaned wearily against the wall. Well, this was just bloody marvellous.

11th April 1841, The Police Station Holding Cells, Brighton.

August shifted uncomfortably upon the hard bench, which comprised the only furniture in the holding cell the constable had happily thrown them into. He rubbed his jaw with tentative fingers, wincing a little. No loose teeth at least, thank the Lord. Sylvester sprawled beside him, head back against the wall, eyes closed. He looked like he had been wrestling a bear, with his nose all bloody and his coat ripped at the seams, but appeared otherwise unconcerned by his predicament. It seemed he was as used to the routine as August was. Over the years and usually in company with Bainbridge, Dare and Raphe, August had seen the inside of more cells than he cared to recall. That was without mentioning the ones he'd spent time in on behalf of his sister or to use her *nom de guerre*, Anna bloody Brown. August sighed and regarded the corner of the cell where what had, at first glance, appeared to be a malodorous pile of filthy clothing snored gently and without apparent worry.

The tromp of heavy footsteps and the jangle of keys had August sitting up somewhat straighter, and he elbowed Sylvester, who stirred and mutter. The snoring in the corner continued.

"Oh, Christ," August grumbled, starting to his feet with alacrity as he saw not only the constable who had escorted them here, but Viscount Cavendish. Vivien's father.

"That them, your lordship?"

"I believe so," Cavendish replied, eyeing August and Sylvester.

His expression was impossible to read, and August prayed he'd not blush like a schoolboy, for he felt horribly as if he was in short trousers again and about to get his backside tanned.

"Right, come on then, lads. His lordship has paid your bail, so you mind your manners else you'll find yourselves back 'ere afore too long."

"Thank you, Constable," August said, approaching Lord Cavendish. "My lord," he began miserably.

Cavendish silenced him with a curt wave of his hand. "Save it for now. I'd say you need a drink, and I want one. Come along with you."

Realising he was being saved from the humiliation of a set down in front of the constable, August did as he was told. Sylvester, the lucky dog, was allowed to go off on his merry way, whilst Cavendish *invited* August to accompany him to the private parlour of a tavern. August strongly doubted it was an invitation he could refuse.

It was a cosy room with thick, low beams and comfortable seating, and a fire had been lit to ward off the chill of the thick stone walls despite the unseasonal warmth outside. They were supplied with brandy, glasses and plates of bread and butter, cold meats and cheese, and left alone.

"Help yourself," Cavendish said, gesturing to the plates and pouring them both a drink.

"Thank you, I won't," August replied stiffly. His stomach rebelled at the idea of eating when Vivien's father was likely about to tell him to keep away from his daughter or else he'd chop him up into bite-sized pieces. Of course, he ought to keep away from her anyway. He'd already decided he would keep away from her, but that did not seem to be the point.

The viscount slid a glass across the table and August took it, staring down into the richly coloured liquid with a heavy sense of inevitability.

"So, you are the reason my daughter has been moping about the house like a sad little wraith."

August looked up and swallowed hard. His tone had been mild, but August knew this man's reputation too well to be lulled into a false sense of security.

"My lord, I never intended…"

"We never do, do we?" Cavendish said, smiling a little. "But all the same, the results are undeniable. Vivien is in love with you."

August jolted in his seat, the words striking him all the harder for the baldness with which they'd been spoken. He ought to be horrified or at the very least alarmed by her father throwing the accusation at him, except it had not been an accusation, more a statement of fact, and August's heart was soaring. It ought not, the stupid organ. It was a pointless reaction to an impossible situation.

"My daughter has not said so out loud, you understand. She would not do so, believing her case to be hopeless," Cavendish went on, as though he hadn't just flung August's entire world into turmoil. "But I know her. You are the only man she has ever spoken to me of with admiration shining in her eyes and such warmth in her voice. You have made quite an impression."

"As she has on me," August said, seeing no point in dissembling.

Cavendish nodded. "I should think so, and yet you are not courting her?"

August let out an unhappy huff of laughter. "A circumstance I should think you'd be grateful for," he said bitterly.

"Why would I be grateful to see my only daughter wretched?" he demanded, an edge to his voice August was not about to underestimate. "I confess to spoiling my children, Mr Lane-Fox. If they want something, they invariably get it. Vivien wants you."

Cavendish poked at some tender spot inside August with his sharp words, and it hurt. Pain and frustration bubbled up in an unpleasant surge.

"She agreed," August said furiously. "It's not like I don't want to court her, but we both agreed it would end badly. I am not you, Lord Cavendish. My family is a scandal, my mother is living openly with her female lover, one of my sisters is in trouble with the law more often than I am and the other paints indecent pictures of heroic women besting naked men. I spend far too much of my time defending the family honour, such as it is. Too often with my fists. I do not have vast wealth, a title, or a reputation that would make people think very hard indeed before offering Vivien the slightest insult, as was demonstrated all too vividly in the dining room of the Ship Inn."

August broke off, his chest heaving with emotion. He had not intended to speak quite so passionately.

"And so you are giving up?" Cavendish replied with perfect calm, quirking a dark eyebrow.

August very much wanted to throw the damned brandy in his imperturbable face.

"What choice do I have?" he demanded, too unhappy and frustrated to moderate his tone.

"Quite. Just as you say. Vivien ought to marry Blackstone, or Ashburton. I'll mention it to her." Cavendish said. He got to his feet, nodded to August, and headed for the door.

August stared as the viscount left without another word, totally off balance. Well, good. Cavendish agreed with him. As well he ought. He *had* agreed with him. Hadn't he?

Chapter 13

Miss Knight,

I have followed you, as you bid me to do.

I am also ensconced at the Ship Inn, though I might tell you I could have bought the Royal Pavilion for the price they charged me for my modest accommodation. Brighton is full and there is not a room to be had anywhere. However, my persistence appears to have paid off. I hope you are pleased. You snap your fingers and I come running like the most obedient lap dog.

I am only marginally mollified by your observation about the colour of my eyes. I admit, the sea looks positively Mediterranean today. It makes me long for warmer climes. Perhaps one day I shall take you to Provence. I believe you would like it.

—Excerpt of a letter from Louis César de Montluc, Comte de Villen to Miss Evie Knight (daughter of Lady Helena and Mr Gabriel Knight).

11th April 1841, The Old Ship Hotel, Brighton.

"Oh, Papa! Did you get him out?"

Vivien flew across the lavish rooms of their suite and into her father's arms.

"There, there," Papa soothed, hugging her tightly. The scent of bay rum clung to him as always, a scent she associated with happiness and security, and unconditional love. "Of course I got him out, though I got the feeling he'd rather I'd have left him there."

"Poor August," she said, her heart aching. "He's too decent, that's the trouble."

"He was taken up for brawling, love," her father said, amusement lacing his voice.

"And how many times have you seen the inside of a police cell, Papa?" Vivien demanded curtly.

Papa laughed. "There, there, my pretty tigress, put away your claws. I agree, he seems a decent young man with an overabundance of difficult relations and good intentions."

"I know," Viv said with a groan. "He thinks he must protect me from the world, and for a little while there, I agreed with him we would not be a suitable match."

"So he said." Papa went to stand by the window, admiring the late afternoon sun glittering on an expanse of cobalt perfection as the sea sparkled before them. "But I collect you have changed your mind."

Viv nodded. "Yes. At least, no, not exactly. It's more a case of accepting the inevitable."

Her father frowned at her. "Explain."

"He's the one, Papa. I know he is, and it doesn't matter if life would be easier with Ashburton or Blackstone or one of their ilk. It doesn't matter if his family is mad or outrageous or indecent or whatever it is he is so worried about. It doesn't matter if we create scandal after scandal until we are no longer welcome in polite society. Indeed, the more I think of it, the more I believe I *want* to create those scandals. Why should I be above reproach for the sake of people who would disdain me if not for fear of your reprisals? Why should I care what they think? Why not just live my life as I want to live it, and with the man I want to live it with?"

Her father's eyes glittered a little too brightly, and he held out his arms to her. Vivien went into them, hugging him. "So like your mother," he whispered. "Mr Lane-Fox is the luckiest man alive, beside myself, of course."

Vivien snorted. "I'm not sure he sees it that way, Papa. He wishes he'd never met me."

Papa chuckled and kissed the top of her head. "He told me he thinks you should marry Blackstone, or Ashburton, as he has already suggested. I said I would give you that advice by the by. If you actually considered such a thing, he'd be beside himself, naturally. I think the poor fellow just needs a little time to realise what's good for him. He's got spirit, that boy, else he'd have not got into that scrape today dealing out retribution for you. He's just overwhelmed. I believe he was at his wits' end before he even met you, and with good reason, from what I hear of his female kin. And now you've turned his world upside down and inside out, and believe me, I know the feeling. He'll come about, love. You wait and see."

"I hope so," Viv said, despondently. "Or else I shall have to kidnap him, or do something desperate."

"Please do not say things like that in my hearing," her father said, glaring at her. "You're turning me grey with worry."

"Who is turning you grey?"

Papa turned, his expression softening as Mama came into the room.

"Both of you. How is a man to keep his wits when he is husband to one of the two most beautiful and daring women in the country, and father to the other? I ask you. It's a wonder I am not entirely white."

"You know as well as I that a little daring is to be admired, Silas, and you are getting vain in your old age," Mama teased, lifting on tiptoes to kiss his cheek and touch a finger to the fine sprinkling of grey at Papa's temple. "Either that, or you do not worry half as much as you pretend, for there is barely any grey visible at all."

"There was none yesterday," he grumbled, though he was clearly enjoying Mama's attention, preening a little as she stroked his nape.

"Did you release Mr Lane-Fox and his friend from incarceration?" she asked him, worry in her eyes.

Papa sighed. "Your daughter asked me to, therefore it is done."

"Excellent. Such a relief. I hated to think of them locked up, the poor dears. Vivien, darling, Evie and Aisling came around earlier. They have asked you to go to Aisling's room. I believe they were worried about the young men, too. Put their minds at rest. Ash will escort you through the hotel."

"Yes, Mama,"

Vivien hurried to the door and smiled as she closed it firmly, so no curious servants could gawk at the sight of the Viscount Cavendish hauling his wife into a passionate embrace.

"Thank goodness," Aisling said, her relief palpable. The three of them had clambered onto Aisling's bed. Evie flopped back across the foot of the mattress, her arms outstretched over her head, while Aisling arranged the pillows behind her until she was comfy. The bed was barely visible beneath the froth of skirts and petticoats of their voluminous gowns.

Vivien smiled at her. "I might have thought you'd be happy to have Mr Cootes locked up. He *is* the most vexing man in the world, after all."

Aisling's dark brows drew together. "Just because I dislike him, does not mean I wish him any harm Only to be as far away from me as possible."

"You still dislike him, Aisling?" Evie asked, swinging her legs back and forth off the end of the bed and making her petticoats rustle. "Even after he stood up for you so gallantly?"

"He… He behaved well, I admit, but—"

"But?" Evie asked, turning on her side and propping her head on her hand to gaze at Aisling.

"He bothers me," Aisling admitted crossly.

Vivien chuckled. "He was right then."

Aisling sighed. "Yes, though I do not understand why he was so pleased by the idea. I don't like him, he makes me furious and most of the time I want to hit him. I never want to hit anyone! I don't have a violent bone in my body, and I can't abide fights. I did not know what to do when that scene erupted today, but…."

Vivien and Evie both waited silently until Aisling sighed with frustration.

"I couldn't leave. I couldn't bear the thought that he might be hurt," she admitted, her expression disgruntled in the extreme.

"Aisling, love. You know, sometimes when men *bother* you, as you describe, it's because you have feelings for them," Viv said gently.

Aisling threw up her hands. "Of course I have feelings for him!" She counted on her fingers as she listed them one by one. "Antipathy, irritation, indignation…."

Evie and Vivien laughed, and Aisling glared at them.

"That is not what I meant," Viv protested. "I mean, you find him… *attractive.*"

Aisling blinked, looking as appalled as if Vivien had suggested she found the idea of standing in a cesspit attractive.

"I do not!"

Vivien sighed. "Have it your own way, but I think your Mr Cootes might be right. He does bother you, and not for reasons you want to consider."

Aisling flounced off the bed and flung open the wardrobe doors. "Never mind that wretched fellow. I'm sick of thinking about him. This is more important."

She strode back and deposited a large hatbox on the mattress. "It's your turn, Viv."

Viv lifted the lid off the box to see the battered hat full of dares. "But I already took one. I was one of the first, after Lottie and Eliza."

"And yours was illegible," Aisling said.

Vivien shrugged. "But that's the luck of the draw. We agreed, we don't get to pick and choose, one go each. Otherwise we'd keep taking dares until we found one we liked."

Aisling shook her head, her expression determined. "No. I have been considering this, Viv. There is an element of magic in this hat, I'm certain of it. Therefore, giving you a blank dare was the hat's way of telling you it wasn't your time. You weren't ready."

"I'm still not ready," Evie said, eyeing the hat with misgiving.

"That's all right, Evie," Aisling said, patting her hand. "There's plenty of time for you yet."

"Oh, I see. I must take one now because I'm four and twenty and still on the shelf!" Vivien said, laughing with outrage.

"Hardly on the shelf, love," Evie said, snorting. "No one has had more offers than you."

Vivien snorted, remembering some of the disgusting satyrs who'd thought to try their luck with an offer.

Aisling nodded. "Exactly, but you are on the brink of something. I feel it, Vivien. This is your time, and, if you want to make things come out right with Mr Lane-Fox, perhaps the hat has the answer."

Vivien frowned at the battered top hat, a peculiar sensation squirming in her belly. Aisling often had odd notions about magic and fate and otherworldly things, and Viv never dismissed such talk. She'd been around Nani Maa and her bosom bow, Pippin, long enough to know better.

"Well, I suppose it wouldn't hurt, but should we not ask the others—"

Aisling sighed and sat on the bed, taking Viv's hand. "I know it's scary. I was terrified, and my dare gives me sleepless nights just thinking about it. I dread summer, but it is a rite of passage, and your time has come."

Viv suppressed a smile, amused that Aisling should think her unduly afraid, when she was only concerned the other Daring Daughters should not think she had cheated.

"Very well then," she said gravely, sitting up and peering into the battered hat. The neatly folded slips of paper were of varying sizes, some yellow with age, others a pristine white.

"Close your eyes, Viv."

Viv obeyed Aisling's order, smiling as she dipped her hand into the hat. The dares rustled and sighed as she stirred them about and finally made her choice. She pulled the slip out, realising it was one of the original dares, the paper yellow and brittle. Viv unfolded it, peering at the faded writing.

"Well?" Evie demanded, sitting up on the bed.

140

"Dare to reach great heights," Viv read aloud.

"What on earth does that mean?" Evie asked.

Aisling pondered this. "Well, great heights could mean an achievement, like becoming famous, but that seems rather a lot to ask. I think it means to be taken more literally. To get up high. Like to climb a tree or to the top of a tall building."

"Lud!" Vivien exclaimed.

"What will you do?" Evie asked Vivien, who laughed and stared at the slip of paper in consternation.

"I don't have the faintest idea."

13th April 1841, The Duke of York Hotel, Brighton

The ballroom was full, with everyone decked out in their finery. They had opened the large glass doors upon the terraces to let the mild evening air stir the fug of perfume and overheated bodies. Everyone was chattering and in high spirits, and the whirling dancers spun to a stop as the music faded.

August wished he'd not come, wished Sylvester had not talked him into staying, but that he'd turned around and gone back to London, or even home. God help him. Though what home looked like now, full of artists and eccentric types, he dared not consider. Instead, he pasted a smile to his face and tried to give the lady upon his arm his full attention now their dance was over.

"Do you enjoy Brighton, Miss Thrussell?"

His companion looked up at him, smiling, staring at him as though he were the most fascinating man in the world. He wondered if she practised in a mirror or if she really found him of that much interest. He had the sinking feeling the answer would flatter neither of them.

"Oh, certainly. It is most diverting, and the weather is so kind to us at present."

"Indeed, like summer has come early," August replied, wracking his brain for something other than the weather. Conversation with Miss Thrussell did not come easily to him.

"Do you read much, Miss Thrussell? I have just finished *Nicholas Nickleby*."

Miss Thrussell shook her head. "My father does not approve of novels, or poetry. He says it is a bad influence on the female mind and leads to unrealistic fantasies about life."

August's eyebrows shot up. "And what do you think?"

Miss Thrussell's expression became one of mild panic. "M-Me?"

"Yes, you are female, after all. What is your opinion? Do you think reading a novel would make you believe in fairy tales? Would it lead you into wickedness?"

The young woman's hand went to her throat, and she paled a little. "I —I am sure I would not like to test the theory. My father has my best intentions at heart, and it is not for me to question him."

August blinked. "Don't you ever question him?"

Miss Thrussell shook her head. "Of course not. It is not my place to do so. My domain is the running of the household, keeping it orderly and comfortable for him now Mama has passed on, God bless her. In due course, I hope to do the same for a husband and… and for any children, should we be so blessed."

She whispered the last and blushed prettily.

August stared at her in consternation. Everyone spoke highly of Miss Thrussell, extolling virtues that made her the perfect young lady. Everyone vaunted her exquisite manners, told him her charming company was a boon to any gathering, not only that, but she was also lovely to look upon and though her dowry was modest, they expected her to be snapped up before the season was over. This was the wife who would give him a comfortable home, a life with no upsets or dramas. They would have children, which she would dote upon and keep from under his feet. His life would be peaceful, organised, comfortable… and yet— an unaccountable surge of panic rose inside him.

"I'll return you back to your party," August said, wondering why his chest was so tight, why it was so hard to breathe.

"August, old man. Good evening."

August stopped in his tracks at the familiar voice. "Blackstone. I didn't know you were here." His gaze fixed, however, not on his friend Jules Adolphus, Marquess of Blackstone, but upon the exquisite woman on his arm. "Miss Anson," he said, the words catching in his throat.

She was beyond stunning. Her gown was a deep blue green, bringing out the colour of her eyes and highlighting the generosity of her curves. Vivien's face was impassive, beautiful but somehow devoid of her usual sparkle, too contained, any feelings she might have had ruthlessly suppressed behind a mask of polite civility. A necklace of sapphire and diamonds glinted against her golden skin, the glittering jewels as cool as her expression, and August wanted to weep with longing, wanted to fall to his knees right there in the bedamned ballroom and beg her never to let him go, no matter if she ought to… no matter if he was the last thing she needed.

Vivien curtsied, her lovely indigo eyes travelling to the lady beside him. Her expression never faltered.

"I was only supposed to be down for a few days, but then I bumped into this gorgeous creature and could not resist the temptation of staying just a little longer." Jules gave Vivien a wink, raising her gloved hand to his lips, and she lowered her eyes, blushing a little.

August felt the panic that had assailed him earlier bloom into something else, something wild and unreasonable as jealousy churned in his guts. Christ. Jules never spoke to Viv like that. They always bickered, insulted each other, unless… unless she had taken

August's advice. The advice her father said he would second. And perhaps Blackstone had realised he had something precious within his grasp and he ought not to waste a moment.

"The dance is beginning, my lord," Vivien said softly, avoiding August's eye.

"Oh, so it is. Well, excuse us. Duty calls," Jules said, grinning and leading Vivien out onto the floor.

Chapter 14

Monsieur,

Excuse me if my handwriting is erratic. I cannot stop giggling at the idea of you being a lapdog. Too funny! What a ridiculous comparison. Now, if there were such a thing as a lap tiger, or panther, or even a lion, that I could see, though it would be an uncomfortable thing indeed, to have such a creature in one's lap, I'm sure.

However, I am pleased you came, though do not make out it was only for my sake, for I shall not believe you. The entire world is here, and no doubt your latest amour among the throng. I admit I could not discover who your latest flirt is. I can usually tell as the women preen so and look so pleased with themselves, but whoever this lady is, she is remarkably sanguine. Have you met your match, Monsieur? Is she not as impressed with you as she ought to be when in the presence of such a godlike figure?

I should love to see Provence one day. To walk in the lavender fields and to gaze upon a sea of impossible blue. Yet, I wonder if I ever shall.

You know I am a homebody and travelling seems such a lot of bother.

—Excerpt of a letter from Miss Evie Knight (daughter of Lady Helena and Mr Gabriel Knight) to Louis César de Montluc, Comte de Villen.

13th April 1841, The Duke of York Hotel, Brighton.

"I wish we had not listened to Nani Maa's advice. That was not well done of us, Jules," Vivien said, her insides tied in a knot.

She wanted to run away from the ballroom and all its so elegant guests, but she was dancing in the arms of a man who was not the one she wanted.

Jules spun her into another graceful turn, and it was a moment before he replied. "I don't know why you'd say so. It worked beautifully. I'm wasted as a marquess, you know. I could do great things on the stage. I'm certain the poor dolt believes I'm halfway in love with you already."

"Oh, don't," Vivien moaned, utterly wretched. "I ought never have let him think it."

"Why did you not open your mouth, then? Perhaps the presence of a certain Miss Thrussell kept you from giving the game away?" Jules suggested.

Vivien glowered at him and allowed him two more turns of the room before she replied. "She's what he wants, you know that. A well-behaved wife who will give him the quiet life he longs for."

"Humbug. He doesn't want that, never has. He's just tired of trying to keep his female relations in hand. The sooner he realises he can't and leaves them to their own devices, the better."

"He worries for them because he's a good man and believes it is his duty to protect them."

146

Jules's rather cynical expression softened, and he nodded. "I know that. And he ought to protect them, up to a point. But if there is one thing I have learned from my sisters, it is that they have minds of their own and are quite capable of using them. His sisters are not children but grown women. How they choose to live their lives is their decision. No matter how badly he wants to protect them, if they refuse to be protected, that is their choice. Short of locking them in their rooms and holding them prisoner, what exactly can he do?"

Vivien smiled despite herself as they executed another turn about the room. He was a marvellous dancer. Also, she liked Jules a great deal. He made out he was a spoiled, idle aristocrat, but there was far more to him than that. "I heard your mama's voice in that little speech, my lord."

Jules snorted. "I should think you did. Good God, I've been fed *A Vindication of The Rights of Woman* since I was a boy, alongside the dos and don'ts of inheriting a dukedom. Try to reconcile those two worlds if you can."

Vivien laughed. "You seem to manage very well, Jules. You'll make a fine husband when you finally grow up."

"Ouch!" Jules said, his expression one of rueful amusement. "There's a backhanded compliment."

"Well, I can't be too nice to you. It would go to your head, and you are quite smug enough already. Good heavens, how anybody could ever imagine the two of us married is beyond me. We'd murder each other before the week was out."

"Wouldn't take that long," Jules replied with a grin. "I adore you, my dear girl, but we are both far too sarcastic and cynical about the world. We both need someone with a lightness of heart to keep us from becoming jaded and bitter."

"I am not cynical," Vivien retorted. "So you may speak for yourself. I am a realist, however, and I do not approve of sticking one's head in the sand. And in my opinion, you had better find yourself that special someone quick smart before you are in reality what you only pretend to be."

"As ever, your company is as soothing as a trip to have one's teeth pulled," Jules replied as the dance ended and he offered her his arm.

"And yours like being at a picnic in the company of a wasp," she countered, smiling sweetly at him.

Jules burst out laughing and patted her hand. "Good luck with your quarry, my dear. The sooner that fellow gives you a reason to be sweet-natured, the better."

Before Viv could match him with another stinging retort, they were among their friends again.

"Evening, Villen and I recognise you, don't I?" Jules said thoughtfully, staring at the man beside Louis César. "No, don't tell me. Never forget a face. Geoffrey? Godfrey? No, Godwin, that's it. You're a pal of Mr Lane-Fox."

"Pal might be overstating things, rather, but you're spot on, by Jove," Godwin said, looking exceedingly pleased at being remembered by the Marquess of Blackstone.

Jules nodded. "Blackstone, pleased to make your acquaintance. Who else is here? I've not had time to look about yet. Miss Anson nabbed me for a dance the moment I arrived."

"I did no such thing, you beastly man," Vivien protested. "Nani Maa gave you your orders, so don't go blaming me for it."

"True," Jules conceded. "And that is an order I would not dare refuse."

"I believe Lady Aisling is here, as is Mr Sylvester Cootes, Mr Lane-Fox. I think I saw Ashburton somewhere, but he was being elusive as ever," Louis César replied, his eyes on the dance floor.

"Miss Knight is here, dancing with Lord Vane," Godwin said, gesturing to where the two were dancing an energetic polka. Viv turned to watch her friend and smiled. Evie's face was flushed, and she was laughing, making her quite the prettiest young lady on the dance floor compared to all the others who were far more sedate and seemed taking it rather too seriously.

"How lovely she looks," Vivien said. "She is so full of life."

"She ought to watch herself with Vane," Jules muttered, scowling.

"Miss Knight is no fool," Louis César said, his voice cool.

"No. True enough, and anyone with half a brain ought to know there would be hell to pay if anyone upset Evie," Jules replied with a small laugh. "Universally adored is not something you can say of many people, but I think perhaps she might manage it."

Godwin nodded. "I agree. Do you know, she spent a full hour listening to my Aunt Ada drone on at some *musicale* we both attended the other night? I mean, Ada's a sweet old lady, but even her family can't manage that long when she starts off on one of her rambling stories. But it made Ada's night and she gets little company. She even promised to call on her to take tea, and she will. Heart of gold."

"That sounds like Evie," Viv said with a smile.

Turning back to her friends, Vivien's smile froze on her face as she saw August join their group. Everyone greeted him warmly and Viv gave him a polite nod but did not know what to say, how to act with him. She knew seeing Blackstone flirting and intimating his interest in her had shocked him, perhaps hurt him, and she was mostly horribly guilty for causing him even a moment of unhappiness. But there was a small, uncharitable part of her that hoped he'd felt as utterly wretched as she had felt upon seeing Miss Thrussell gaze up at him with such obvious warmth. Papa had told her what he'd said the day he'd got him out of that gaol cell, and had given his opinion that he only needed a little time to realise what it was he must do. But what if he continued to believe she ought to marry Blackstone? Would he leave her to her fate because he thought it for the best?

"Miss Anson."

Vivien looked up, her heart thrashing about like a wild thing caught in a snare as she realised he was speaking to her.

"I don't suppose by some miracle you have a dance free for me?" he asked, his voice soft.

Viv stared down at the dance card in her hand, though she already knew it was full. She had not expected to see him here tonight. She had assumed he would have left by now, would have gone back to town, or perhaps home. The pretty card with the hotel's initials embossed in gold upon it seemed to blur, and Vivien blinked hard.

"I am sorry, Mr Lane-Fox. I do not," she managed, though it took considerable effort.

"Ah well. Idiotic of me to have thought it possible."

He went to turn away, but Vivien reached out, touching his sleeve. "If I'd known you'd be here—"

He smiled at that, and the sight made her stomach do an odd little somersault.

"That eases my disappointment. Thank you."

Vivien frowned, fiddling with the dance card and betraying her agitation too obviously. "I thought you would be gone by now. But I suppose Miss Thrussell is temptation enough to keep you in the vicinity. She's lovely, and everyone says how nice she is, what pretty manners."

"She is all of those things," August replied, the words like a shaft of ice, spearing her heart. "And yet I don't have the slightest desire to see her again. I thought she was what I wanted, or at least I wanted what she represented. I've been a fool, Viv."

He whispered this last, and Vivien looked up, staring at him, the ice melting abruptly, replaced by a surge of warmth and hope.

"Truly?"

August nodded, glancing about in frustration, as there was not the slightest chance of a private conversation. "Tomorrow? Ireland's Pleasure Gardens. Will you come?"

"When?" Vivien demanded.

"When can you get away?"

"I don't know, though I'm never allowed out alone," she replied with a regretful smile, suddenly frustrated by the idea of her brother or some other chaperone dogging her heels. She wanted to be private with August, to spend time with him without someone looking over her shoulder. "But Evie might help me. If we just happened to be there and—"

August grinned at her. "Can you get word to me of when you'll be there?"

Vivien laughed, breathless now. "Yes. Yes, I'll find a way."

"Until tomorrow then."

"Tomorrow," she murmured, hardly daring to breathe in case she awoke, and discovered it had all been no more than a lovely dream.

"What do you think? Will you come with me?" Vivien asked.

Evie, still flushed and breathless from her dance, only laughed and nodded. "Of course I shall help. What a daft question."

"Oh, thank you, Evie."

Evie only grinned at her. "We shall simply take ourselves off for a stroll. The best time would be in the morning, I suppose, whilst most people are still abed. Do you think you could get out then? My maid will accompany us for propriety. She's a sweet creature and would never tattle on me unless I did something truly dreadful."

"Well, if you come and call for me? I shall be up early, and hope Mama doesn't insist on a chaperone if you're with me. Ash is never up before eleven, even on a good day, certainly not after a ball. But if I can get away, how shall we get word to August, though, to let him know?"

"Oh, that's easy. Monsieur Le Comte will do that," Evie said blithely.

"Will I indeed?" Murmured a low voice.

Evie turned to discover Louis César behind her. He held out a glass of lemonade for her.

"I thought you might be thirsty after your exertions, Miss Knight. But, pray, what is it you wish of me? Should I slay a dragon? Complete *les travaux d'hercule?* You need but name it. I am your servant."

"Foolish man," she said, laughing and accepting the glass of lemonade. "The labours of Hercules will not be necessary. Only, I wish you to help us. Miss Anson wishes to walk in the park tomorrow with Mr Lane-Fox, but without her brother or a chaperone, so they can speak privately. We think she can get away in the morning but won't know for certain until then."

"You mean you wish me to awaken *early?"* Louis said, widening his eyes as if this was a far greater sacrifice than Hercules had endured.

Evie rolled her eyes at him. "I thought you were ready to slay dragons for me?"

He waved this away. "Ah, and so I did. *Mais alors*, if this is what you ask of me, I will, of course, assist in any way I can and forgo my beauty sleep." His blue eyes twinkled with amusement.

"I should think foregoing your beauty sleep would be a public service," Evie replied tartly. "If you get any handsomer, you'll cause a riot one of these days."

Louis pressed a hand to his heart. "Ah, and she notices me at last. I may swoon."

Evie tutted, shaking her head. "Well, don't swoon just yet. I'm still thirsty. Would you escort me to the refreshments room for another drink, please?"

Louis held out his arm to her. "With the greatest of pleasure. Until the morning, Miss Anson."

"I'll call just before ten, Viv. Don't keep me waiting," Evie said, winking at her before Louis César bore her away.

Chapter 15

My Lady,

I was never more surprised and delighted to receive a gift. And such a gift it was, too. A small pot of greasy ointment that smelled so appallingly bad, I almost retched. I assume this is a token of your regard, in which case I am not entirely sure how to take it. I believe I shall conclude that you were worried to death for my wellbeing, that you could not sleep for your anxiety that I might suffer the slightest discomfort, that you cried into your pillow when you remembered my heroic behaviour.

In which case, my lady, I am most appreciative of your delightful unguent.

Having applied it tenderly to my many bruises, I must report it to be most efficacious. Though it renders me confined to my room in case I am ejected from the hotel or come to the attention of the neighbourhood's hungry dogs. They could hardly miss me.

—Excerpt of a letter from The Hon'ble Mr Sylvester Cootes to Lady Aisling Baxter (Daughter of the Right Hon'ble Luke and

Kitty Baxter, the Earl and Countess of Trevick).

14th April 1841, The Old Ship Hotel, Brighton.

Vivien's maid looked at her rather suspiciously when she rose far earlier than expected but, other than that, it was easy enough to be ready to go walking when Evie called for her at the appointed hour. After reassuring her parents that Evie's maid was going too and they were only strolling in the Pleasure Gardens as the morning was so lovely, she was free.

"Do they not approve of Mr Lane-Fox?" Evie asked her as they walked back through the hotel.

"I think they approve," Vivien admitted. "But that doesn't mean they don't worry, and with everything so up in the air I want to wait until I'm certain he means to court me. If they knew, they would have made Ash come, or Mama would have come, and it would have been far too awkward. I just want him to myself for a bit before things become official."

"To make certain he won't cry off again?" Evie said, with rather too much blunt honesty, though Viv could hardly deny it.

"Yes, I suppose so. It would be completely mortifying, and I don't think my heart can stand another disappointment. I am a little afraid to get my hopes up in case he's changed his mind again. Seeing me with Blackstone obviously shook him, but…." Vivien shrugged. "Ah, well, we'll see."

Evie took her arm. "I like him. He seems a good man. I'm sure he would not encourage you to hope if he wasn't certain."

Vivien nodded. She believed that too, but still, her nerves were all a jangle.

"Oh, look, there's Louis," Evie said brightly, as an elegant figure appeared at the top of the stairs. "He's such a dear man to help us. He loathes getting up early, you know."

Vivien studied Evie, curious to understand what was between her and the comte. She knew Evie considered the man as much a friend as she did Vivien or Aisling, perhaps more so, and yet.... What did the comte feel about this? It was certainly an unusual situation, not to mention scandalous if anyone outside of her friends discovered it.

"Good morning, ladies. I take it all is well?" the comte said, smiling warmly at Evie, who agreed that it was. "I shall perform my duty as commanded, then. If you will excuse me, we shall meet you in the park in, say, twenty minutes?"

"Oh, are you coming too?" Evie asked, brightening.

The comte returned a narrow-eyed gaze. "You do not seriously mean to say you made me awaken at this unholy hour without thinking of offering me the salve of accompanying you on your walk?"

Evie laughed, shaking her head. "It never occurred to me you would wish to, but I shall be pleased for your company, as I always am."

"Hmmm," the comte replied darkly, and went away to retrieve August.

"I think you hurt his feelings," Vivien said, though Evie frowned at her words.

"Don't be silly. He was only teasing. It's just his way."

Vivien shrugged and let it go, but was not entirely convinced Evie had that right.

The morning was beautiful, warm and blessed with a vivid blue sky, and Mr Ireland's Pleasure Garden was splendid in all its spring glory. Spread over ten acres of land, the area comprised a spacious lawn for cricket, and dedicated spaces for other manly exercises, which were separated from the gardens.

The gardens themselves included shrubberies, meandering walks, a bowling green and promenades adorned with tea-boxes.

Opposite was a canal with a bridge, which led to a Gothic castle with a battery mounted with six cannons. Beyond this stood a maze.

By the time the two men had reached the park, Vivien was in a dither of anticipation. August's expression was enough to banish any lingering butterflies and chase away her doubts. He smiled at her, his eyes warm and full of certainty, and Vivien knew he would not change his mind again.

"Miss Anson," he said, sounding as though he felt a little breathless, too. He bowed politely to her. "How fortuitous to meet you on this glorious morning. The comte and I were just taking a little stroll to clear our heads after last night's entertainments."

"A coincidence indeed," Vivien agreed for the benefit of Evie's maid, who was lingering at a discreet distance but was still within earshot.

"Oh, Vivien, shall we try the maze?" Evie asked, gesturing towards the dark square of high hedges. "It's usually dreadfully busy, but there's no one about at this hour."

"Oh, but Miss Knight," Evie's maid protested. "It's not really proper, what with two fine gentlemen beside you and no chaperone."

"But we have a chaperone, for you'll be there too, Rachel," Evie replied calmly.

The woman took a breath and shook her head, her expression regretful but determined. "No. Sorry to be difficult, miss, but I'd rather not. I got lost in one of those dratted labyrinth things when I was a girl. In there for hours, I was. I won't do that again, if you please."

"Oh," Evie said, her face falling. "No, of course you must not if it makes you uncomfortable."

"There is no one about," the comte said, looking around them at the acres of deserted gardens. "I think perhaps it is not so dreadful a risk. If anyone comes, you may say you have only just exited, having become separated from the rest of the party," he suggested to the maid.

Evie beamed at the comte and turned to Vivien, who nodded her agreement at once.

"Rachel?" she said to the maid, giving the woman a beseeching smile.

Rachel huffed and folded her arms. "It's not proper, miss."

"Oh, but it's only Monsieur Le Comte, and you know he is trustworthy by now."

Vivien watched Louis to see how this had gone down, but the Frenchman's beautiful face was inscrutable. Rachel, too, looked towards Louis and did not appear as convinced as her mistress.

"You do as you think best, miss, but please don't get lost in there or I shall have the devil's own job explaining things, and so shall you."

"I promise we shan't be long," Evie said, giving the woman an affectionate kiss on the cheek and taking Louis's arm. "Well, come along then. Don't dither."

August chuckled as Evie disappeared into the maze with Louis and they followed behind, their pace leisurely.

"Good morning, Miss Anson," he said when finally the dark pathways of the maze swallowed them up and out of sight of prying eyes.

"Good morning, Mr Lane-Fox," Vivien replied, feeling unaccountably shy.

"I didn't sleep a wink last night. I've been counting the hours," he said, reaching for her hand.

Vivien looked down at where their fingers tangled together and let out a shaky sigh. "I was so afraid you wouldn't come. That you would change your mind."

August drew her to a halt and Vivien was barely aware of Evie's voice growing fainter as she and Louis moved farther into the labyrinth.

"I've been a bloody fool, Viv," August said, his voice harsh. "Bainbridge tried to tell me, told me over and over if I'm honest, but I—"

"It's all right," Viv said, pressing a finger to his lips. "I understand. You don't need to explain, or to apologise."

"I do," he said fiercely. "My God. When I saw you with Blackstone all I could think was, August you blasted idiot, if you've lost her it will be the biggest mistake of your life."

Vivien bit her lip as guilt sat uneasily in her stomach. "Actually, August, I —I think I ought to confess. Blackstone has no interest in me. He put that entire scene on to make you jealous. I'm so sorry. It was unkind to do such a thing and—"

August kissed her.

Viv's breath snagged in her throat. His lips were warm and soft, and her brain dissolved like sugar in hot tea.

"Oh," she said dazedly when he drew away again.

"I'm glad you did it," he said fiercely. "And I shall thank Blackstone, too. He made me see sense, and I've never been more grateful for anything in my life."

Vivien blinked, not feeling entirely steady. "But you want a quiet life, August. Peace and quiet and—"

He kissed her again, this time his hands moving to clasp her waist, which was just as well as she felt increasingly giddy.

"I want you," he whispered, his voice firm as he pulled back again. "I want you and everything that comes with you. If I must fight for you every day of my life, Viv, it will be worth it. If society doesn't like us, that's fine. We have our own society, friends and family, people who care for us, whose opinions we care about. Anyone else can take a running jump as far as I'm concerned."

"Yes," Vivien said, hearing the echo of the words she'd spoken to her father as her heart soared.

August gathered her closer, and Vivien's heart raced. This was what had been missing before. She had allowed a suitor or two a stolen kiss, more out of curiosity than a wish to do so, but it had only ever been a press of one mouth against another. This was entirely different. August's hold on her was firm but gentle, and her entire being seemed to vibrate with tension, with anticipation, until she felt she would go mad if he did not kiss her.

"Viv," he murmured, stroking her cheek, staring at her with such a look in his eyes that she wanted to laugh and cry at the same time, for she was so thoroughly overwhelmed. "May I kiss you again?"

A breathless laugh escaped her. "I think you had better," she managed.

He grinned, a remarkably boyish expression, but then his smile faded, and a different light lit his eyes as he tilted her chin up and brushed his lips over hers. Vivien shivered, and he must have felt her reaction, for she was aware of his lips curving against hers, smiling as he repeated the tender caress. Slowly he pressed his mouth to hers, again and again, a long series of tiny kisses that melded into one bone-melting embrace. His tongue traced her lower lip and Viv's heart kicked in her chest.

"Let me in," he said, a sweet command she was pleased to obey.

Slowly, his tongue sought hers and he laughed softly as she sought to copy his movements. "A quick study, Miss Anson," he teased her, pulling back to look down at her. Viv was somewhat relieved to discover his breathing was as erratic as her own and did her best to unclench her fists, which had unknowingly grasped his lapels and likely wrinkled them beyond saving.

"I'm glad you think so, but… I believe I need further instruction," she said, endeavouring to give him her haughtiest tone of voice.

"Do you now?" he said, a rough quality to his words that made excitement skitter down her spine. "Well, then I had best oblige, hadn't I?"

Vivien gasped as he kissed her again, aware this time of how much he had held back as she was pulled hard against him, and his mouth captured hers. Heat swept through her, and a maddening sort of ache began low in the pit of her stomach. Instinct drove her closer, pressing her body against his, for only he could give her the antidote to this sudden burn in her blood that threatened to drive her to insanity. Her breath caught as his arousal pressed against her, tangible evidence of his desire that only made her pulse accelerate to an even greater speed. Eagerly, she sought more contact, needing to be closer still. August groaned, his hand skimming up her side to her breast. Vivien arched towards his touch, needing more, gasping as he thumbed her nipple. Even through the layers of her clothing, his touch was electric, making her giddy with wanting. August broke the kiss, burying his face in her neck and kissing her throat.

"Viv, Christ, stop, love. I —I can't… Hell!"

He thrust her away from him, holding her at arm's length, and regarded her with wary amusement.

"You are dangerous," he said, sounding as if he'd been running for his life, though his crooked smile reassured her his words were playful.

"*Me?*" Vivien said, fighting for breath. "You speak for yourself. I… I can barely stand. My knees feel most peculiar."

"Come here," he said, pulling her back into his arms and settling her head against his shoulder. He held her gently, his chin resting gently atop her head, one hand stroking her back as Vivien leaned into him. Oh, this was heavenly. She laid her hand upon his chest, feeling the steady thud of his heart beneath her palm. Closing her eyes, she savoured the moment, the closeness that felt so perfectly wonderful, even though the desire for more still simmered in her blood. She nuzzled against his coat, enjoying the masculine scent of clean linen and shaving soap, and something pleasantly spicey she could not quite name but hoped would become familiar and dear to her.

"I'll speak to your father when we get back to the hotel," he murmured against her hair.

Viv dared a glance up at him, wanting to read his expression, to be certain this was what he really wanted, that desire alone was not what motivated him. She had received too many offers of that nature, men who would marry her because they wanted her in their beds, and were prepared to overlook what they saw as her faults to indulge that desire. Rejecting their offers had not been difficult. She would never marry a man who viewed her in such a way. August stared down at her.

"I think you were made for me, Vivien Anson. I was a damned fool not to realise that sooner. It terrifies me now, to think I might have run away from you, when only you could make me this ridiculously happy. I was seeking something I didn't even want, for reasons that elude me now. Can you forgive me for being such a dolt?"

Vivien smiled, hearing nothing but sincerity in his words. This man would always stand beside her, and do it with love and pride, and no regrets.

"There's nothing to forgive. Will you kiss me again?"

He chuckled and pressed his mouth swiftly to hers, lingering for a moment before he pulled away with a sigh of regret. "Don't temp me any further, love, or we'll get ourselves in an awful pickle. The fine weather will tempt people to the gardens soon and I've no desire to explain myself to your father if we get caught in a compromising situation."

"It's early yet," Viv grumbled.

"Yes, and your father's an intimidating devil. Let me at least assure him of my honourable intentions before we get ourselves into mischief."

The regret in his eyes was reassuring, so Viv gave a heavy sigh but took his proffered arm. "He knows you're honourable, else he would never have bailed you out. He doesn't care about reputations and scandals in the same way other people do. Papa is not like most peers because he doesn't give a fig for what polite society thinks, and they know it."

August nodded, looking thoughtful. "I know that, and I have always admired him for going his own way. I've heard the stories, of course, about his past, about how he ran away from home as a boy and lived on the streets and still made a success of himself."

Vivien studied him, realising that August had lost his father far too young, had become the head of a household of unruly women at an age when he ought to have had no more worries than being told off for getting into another scrape at school. He had carried a significant burden and now, in marrying her, he might feel he was adding to it, but she would disabuse him of that notion as soon as she could. Marrying her would only mean they could share any burdens between them.

"I believe he admires you too, August."

"What on earth for?" he demanded, looking genuinely bewildered.

"Oh, August," she said, laughing ruefully and shaking her head. "I think I shall let Papa explain that to you."

Louis smiled as Evie let out a huff of frustration.

"Oh, drat it. Another dead end. I felt certain this was the right way. We shall be here all day at this rate." She glared at the thick green hedge in consternation and turned back to him with a swish of skirts and petticoats.

"Tant pis," Louis murmured, not minding the idea in the least.

"You're not helping much," she said, giving him a sideways glance.

Louis shrugged. "But you are doing admirably, *ma petite."*

"No, I'm not," she laughed. "We're horribly lost."

"Alas, such a dreadful fate to be lost in a labyrinth with me."

Evie's expression was one of amusement now as she took his proffered arm. "You're fishing for compliments," she observed.

"You know me too well," he replied with a mournful sigh. "But if I do not fish, they never surface of their own accord."

She made a muffled sound of outrage that made him smile. "Silly creature. You've leagues of women ready to pour the butter boat over your head. You know full well the reason you like my company is that I don't treat you like some earthbound deity."

"This is true, but a fellow becomes accustomed to such meaningless flattery, and so when it is entirely absent, one becomes... anxious. I am a restless fellow, truly. If I do not have constant reassurance, I fret, fearing my worth and my company do not bring you pleasure."

She darted him a curious glance, for despite his teasing manner there had been too much truth in those words, and she'd heard it.

"I believe you are still fishing, but I shall reassure you all the same, for you are my favourite person in the world outside of my family, Louis. Surely you know that much?"

He smiled at her, wondering why such a heartfelt compliment only made his chest tight.

"As you are mine."

They walked on in silence, the labyrinth leading them in ever decreasing circles. Evie was quiet and Louis watched her, aware something troubled her.

"Are you going to tell me what is worrying you, love?"

Her brow furrowed a little, and she pursed her lips. Louis tried not to stare, but she had a delectable mouth, a perfect cupid's bow and a full lower lip, soft and kissable, and he was going out of his bloody mind. Here they were, alone, in a romantic setting, and he was too terrified of scaring her off and ruining everything to make a move. *Putain.*

They reached another dead end, and instead of turning, Louis stopped. He reached out and gently lifted her chin, forcing her to look at him.

"Evie," he said softly. "Unburden yourself."

She licked her lips as she considered, and desire shafted through Louis, the need to take her in his arms so fierce it made his skin ache.

"It's silly," she said, looking adorably flustered. "You'll laugh."

Louis frowned. "I certainly will not. I would never laugh at anything that causes you a moment's disquiet."

Evie let go of his arm and tangled her fingers together nervously. "Well," she said. "Last night at the ball...."

Some instinct told Louis he would not want to laugh at what came next. He might want to do murder, or to destroy something, or more likely someone, but he would not laugh.

"I went for a walk about the hotel with Mr Cooper—it was all quite proper as lots of other people were doing likewise," she hurried on, probably sensing the change in his manner, for it was all he could do to keep his expression impassive.

Mr Cooper. Louis brought to mind the image of one of Evie's many suitors. A pleasant enough young man, a year or two her senior. Then he imagined the pleasant fellow's imminent demise.

"Am I to take it Mr Cooper took liberties?" Louis asked, his voice a growl, though how he'd got the words out at all he wasn't certain.

"Oh, no. Not really," Evie said, blithely unaware of the havoc she was wreaking with her words. "Only, we turned a corner and for a moment no one was about and so… and so he… kissed me."

So, this was what hell felt like, Louis thought wildly. Not only had it not been him kissing Evie, now he was reduced to the position of her confidant, forced to listen to a description of the advances of some panting boy. *Dieu ait pitié.* Had he really been so wicked in the past that he must now be punished so severely?

"If he did not take liberties, why are you so troubled?"

Louis prayed she wanted him to murder the blackguard, for he'd take the greatest pleasure in doing so.

Evie blushed, and the picture before him was one of such sweetness, such innocence, that he knew damned well why he was being punished. He could never be worthy of her, was not a fit husband for her, but he would have her all the same. *She would be his*, he swore. Not through force, not with bullying or underhand tactics. He would be patient. He would wait as long as she needed him to wait. But no one and nothing on earth would stop him. No matter how long it took for her to see him, no matter what he needed to do, she would be his wife, for he needed her as no one else did. He needed her generosity, her kindness, her endless patience, her love, for he hungered for that as much as he did her voluptuous curves. He had spent too much time of late imagining losing himself in her softness, exploring her splendidly lush body and resting his head upon her magnificent breasts. He wanted her to be his with a single-minded determination he'd felt for nothing before in his life. So he would not mess this up.

"I'm not troubled, exactly," she explained, though she sounded mortified. "Only it was so… disappointing."

Louis let out a breath. *Merci. Merci. Grâce à Dieu.* Gathering his wits, Louis forced himself to speak.

"In what way was it disappointing?"

Evie frowned, staring at the ground. "Well, everyone makes such a fuss, don't they, about kissing, I mean? Many of my friends have told me about the first time they kissed their husbands and—" She gave a despondent sigh. "Your first kiss is supposed to be memorable but… but it was just rather wet and sloppy and… and I didn't much care for it."

Louis' heart ached, and he consigned the bumbling young man to the devil. He'd known he would not be her first kiss, known he must let her have her freedom, though the thought had plagued him to death, but that some thoughtless prick had just snatched it from her with no regard, no realisation of the preciousness of what he stole made him wild with fury. His fists clenched.

"Je vais tuer le fou!"

"There's no need to kill him," she said, smiling at him and laying a reassuring hand on his arm. "Though I appreciate the sentiment. He was quite sweet, only…. Oh, I don't know, Louis. I just felt nothing at all. Was it me? Did I do something wrong?"

"Non!" he retorted, struggling to regain his composure before he did or said something he ought not. "No, you did nothing wrong. You felt nothing because this man means nothing to you. He is just a thoughtless boy who does not know how to go about such things. This is the trouble with very young men. They know nothing but act like they know everything and—"

"Louis," Evie said, interrupting him, her voice gentle. "It's all right. I'm not upset, I was just rather underwhelmed, that's all. Was your first kiss like that too, then? Or was it special?"

She could have said nothing better calculated to cut through his mounting fury and unbalance him. The memory swept over him like a toxic cloud, revulsion swirling in his gut like acid.

"Louis?" she said again, concern in her voice now.

Louis shook his head. "First kisses are seldom what one would hope for," he said, pushing the past back into the locked box where he kept it. He had long since learned to compartmentalise things he did not wish to think of, and he had buried deep those days of wretchedness, banishing them to a place so dark they need trouble him no more. He let out a breath and drank in the sight of the woman in front of him, letting her nearness calm him. His Evie. The pain of the past eased away, replaced with a longing to claim the peace she brought him for always.

"What is it, Louis?" she asked, reaching out and taking his hand. The worry in her expression made his throat tight. "You're awfully pale. What did I say? Do you want to tell me?"

Louis shook his head and managed something that resembled a self-deprecating laugh. *Merde,* he would never want to burden her with his past. She was too tender-hearted, and the knowledge could only distress her. *"Non.* It is only the strain of being up at such a lamentable hour of the morning."

Evie smiled at him but did not look entirely reassured, and Louis cursed himself. He stared down at their linked fingers and returned to the topic they should discuss, easing her concern over that ridiculous kiss.

"This business of first kisses is nothing to fret over," he said, reaching out and allowing himself the delicious torment of touching the back of his hand to her cheek. Her skin was like warm silk, and he savoured the knowledge, imprinting the moment upon his mind to be remembered over and over again when he was alone. "He was just a foolish boy, snatching an opportunity. Your reaction was inevitable. If you were kissed properly, you would not dislike it, I promise."

"If you say so," she said with a sigh.

"Shall I prove it to you?"

Louis knew he ought not to have said it, but he was damned if he'd take the words back. He was putting temptation in his way and threatening everything, but... but how could he not? She was so close. Her scent had invaded his mind and made him reckless. Sweet chamomile. Was that the soap she used? It was delicate and unpretentious, unlike the sophisticated perfumes he had become so heartily sick of.

"Prove it to me?" she repeated, frowning. "How?"

"I could kiss you," he said, fighting to keep his voice nonchalant. "Just to show you the difference between an ignorant boy and a man who knows what he's doing."

Her eyes widened.

Louis thought perhaps his heart stopped beating. He certainly held his breath. If she rejected him out of turn, or found the idea repulsive, he would die of misery.

"All right, then."

Marie, mère de Dieu. Merci. Mille mercis.

His heart leapt, and he stared at her for a long moment, hardly daring to believe he'd heard her correctly. Her cheeks were pink, but she stared at him unblinking, unafraid, trusting him.

Behave. Behave. Behave.

He repeated the words like a mantra, threatening himself with dire consequences if he took the slightest liberty. The moment hung suspended, as if they had stepped out of time into some other place. Louis caressed her cheek with fingers that were not entirely steady and then tilted her head up. Evie closed her eyes and Louis thought his heart might break the moment was so impossibly sweet. He was undeserving of her trust, surely, but he did not care. He would have this.

Slowly, he leaned down and pressed his mouth to hers, gently, kissing first that full bottom lip, and then that perfect cupid's bow, and then settling his lips a little firmer upon hers as emotion and desire swept through him, stealing his breath. *Mon Dieu.* Longing was a searing pain in his chest, the need to share his life, his body, the darkest corners of his soul with this woman, something he could neither explain nor fight. How long must he wait for this to be his alone? He gathered her a little closer, finding no resistance, and had to battle fiercely against the overwhelming desire to pull her against his body and kiss her properly, deeply, with all of his heart and soul, the way he wanted to.

Louis forced himself to draw back. Not stealing another kiss, and then another, and then all her kisses, was undoubtedly the hardest thing he had ever done in his life before, but he was laying the foundations of a future, building a deeper, binding trust between them, which he prayed she would return to when the time was right.

Her eyes fluttered open, and she stared at him, unblinking, lifting her fingers to touch her lips.

"Oh," she whispered.

"Better?" he asked, wishing he didn't feel like the rest of his life hung in the balance.

She nodded, the motion a little jerky. "M-Much better."

Louis let out a breath.

Needing the distraction, Louis tucked her arm in his and they carried on into the maze. They walked in silence for a while until he felt her gaze upon him.

"I suppose you've kissed a great many women," she said. "So you have had a vast amount of practise."

In that moment, Louis wished that were not true, but she already knew it was, and he was not about to tell her lies. More lies. For he was keeping the secrets of his heart from her, was he not? "I suppose so," he said, feeling every bit the wicked satyr leading an innocent nymph astray.

"Well, it was certainly very different from Mr Cooper, much… nicer."

"Nicer?" Louis quirked an indignant eyebrow at her.

"You're fishing again," she observed, with perfect accuracy.

Louis laughed. "I can hide nothing from you, my sweet girl."

"Well, it was nice. Very nice. Thank you."

"Nice," Louis repeated in disgust, shaking his head. "I wish to banish this word from the English language."

Evie giggled. "Oh, very well. It was lovely, truly lovely, thank you. You are very kind to be so patient with me when I know you must think me gauche and silly. I am so pleased you are my friend, Louis."

Louis sighed, knowing it was likely the best he could hope for in the circumstances. "You are neither gauche nor silly, and I am glad to be your friend too, Evie."

For now.

Chapter 16

Mr Cootes,

I must insist that you do not write to me again. It is most inappropriate.

I can assure you my sleep was entirely undisturbed, and I shed no tears on your behalf — not a single one — so you may rest easy on that point. To conclude, I have romantic aspirations towards you upon the receipt of that healing unguent can only be evidence of a weak intellect or a wilful disregard for the truth.

I have some skill as a healer and as the fight was in an honourable cause, I felt it my duty to offer you such aid as I could. I am pleased if it eased your discomfort. The smell is unfortunate, I agree, but suits you admirably.

I hope that this concludes our dealings with one another.

—Excerpt of a letter from Lady Aisling Baxter (Daughter of the Right Hon'ble Luke and Kitty Baxter, the Earl and Countess of Trevick) to The Hon'ble Mr Sylvester Cootes.

15th April 1841, The London to Brighton Road.

"*The smell is unfortunate, but suits you admirably*. Ha! She is in love with me," Sylvester pronounced, stretching out his long legs and propping his boots on the seat opposite as the carriage bounced over a rut.

"Where exactly does it say that?" August asked in amusement, regarding the sharply worded missive from Lady Aisling.

"Oh, it's not obvious. A lady is never obvious," Sy said with a grin, snatching the letter back and tucking it in his breast pocket. "But it's there. You notice, for such a shy little creature, she never hesitates to give me a splendid set down."

"I had noticed," August admitted, for it was true. Aisling tended to seek the background, to linger with the wallflowers and watch proceedings from afar. She rarely spoke in company with people she did not know, and even among friends could sometimes be reticent, but Sylvester seemed to provoke her so much she was positively outspoken.

"And what of your intentions towards her?" August demanded. For Aisling was Vivien's friend, and whilst Sy was an excellent fellow who would not cause a lady hurt on purpose, he had a reputation that suggested women fell for his charms all too often.

Sy shrugged, which did nothing to reassure him. "I don't know. Nothing untoward. Perhaps only to prove to the lady that she does not fool me. She shows the world this timid creature who doesn't dare open her mouth and who blushes at the drop of a hat, but I know better."

"How do you know better?" August asked, frowning now. "What do you mean?"

Sylvester shook his head. "I will not tell you that, but I'll make her give me the truth. You see if I don't."

"Sy, if you upset her, or cause her a moment's distress—"

"Steady on, old man," Sy said, regarding August with mild alarm. "I said I mean her no harm. No one will know but me and I'll take it to the grave, but I want to know why she pretends to be one thing when she is quite another. It makes no sense to me."

"*You* make no sense," August said crossly, still anxious and determined to keep an eye on Sylvester and Aisling.

"That's the way I like it," Sy retorted, folding his arms. "But what about you? How did your little tête-à-tête with the viscount go? I take it he looks favourably upon you courting his beautiful daughter?"

August nodded, still a little bewildered by that fact. Vivien was an heiress, and a beauty unparalleled among the *ton*, no matter some people's idiocy over her heritage. Everyone knew she'd had dozens of offers from men far wealthier than he and with impressive titles to boot. She had turned down a marquess if the rumours were to be believed. Not that August was about to ask her for that smacked of desperation.

"He did. He even seemed pleased."

Almost... fatherly, actually, and hadn't that been a surprise? August had been unprepared to be welcomed with such warmth, especially bearing in mind the muck he'd made of it and the weeks of misery his foolishness had caused Vivien, not to mention himself.

Silas, as he was to call his prospective father-in-law, had waved this away, however, and said all young men made cakes of themselves when they were in love, and it was only to be expected. He also gave some very sound advice about making his proposal a memorable one, the kind of thing his wife would enjoy telling their children in years to come.

His wife.

Mrs Vivien Lane-Fox.

August grinned.

"Oh, stop it," Sylvester grumbled. "You're making me queasy. Bad enough I'm being dragged back to town before everyone else without having to endure your incandescent joy all the way there."

August snorted, not giving a damn if Sylvester cast up his accounts. He was too happy to care if he looked like a lovesick sap skull. If the cap fits and all that.

"Silas needed to return to town and that meant Lady Cavendish leaving and Miss Anson with her. I wasn't about to kick my heels in Brighton when she was in London, was I? Apparently Gabriel Knight has some battle royale underway over the route of his new line and he needed the viscount to throw his weight about. Besides, if Miss Knight and her family are returning to town, that means Lady Aisling is going with her."

Sylvester waved this away, but August did not believe his interest in Lady Aisling was either as shallow or as calculating as he made out. The only trouble was, he didn't think Sylvester realised it himself, which might be a cause for concern.

22nd April 1841, The Strand, London.

August gave himself a mental shake and tried to remember to breathe. It wasn't easy, truly. Not when the woman sitting at his side was so unspeakably lovely. She wore a deep purple carriage dress this morning with a matching bonnet, resplendent with matching feathers that fluttered in the breeze as they trotted at a good clip. August could not help but keep casting glances at her, unable to believe his good fortune.

They were just returning after a pleasant ride about Hyde Park. August had borrowed Bainbridge's new Brougham and had decided he must invest in one. It was a far smoother ride and more stable than anything he'd driven before, and Viv would need something elegant. He could not have her feel she had come down in the world by marrying him. The carriage he'd left at home for his mother and sister's use was certainly becoming bit outdated and as he rode everywhere, he'd not felt the need for such an investment.

A stab of unease assailed him as he considered the motley lot currently installed at his home. What was he to do about that? The house was his and ought to be Viv's home, but it was his mother and sister's home too. Of course, with the hefty dowry Viv brought to their marriage, they could well afford to buy another property, but the solution depressed him, rather. He'd always imagined bringing his family up there. It was a fine house, and he'd hoped to banish the memories of the past by turning it into a home, filled with children and love and happiness, and perhaps, just a *little* less drama than it had become used to in the past few decades.

"What's wrong?"

August glanced at her as he turned into The Strand, but dared not take his eyes from the road for long. The Strand was a major thoroughfare in the city centre, and he needed his wits about him.

"Nothing," he called back cheerfully, setting the matter aside for the moment. He needed to discuss this with Vivien, but not now. For one thing, he'd not yet proposed. He'd thought perhaps to take the opportunity this morning in Hyde Park, but as lovely as the setting was, it didn't feel right. Certainly not memorable, as his soon to be father-in-law had counselled it ought to be.

As they drew up before Cavendish House, August frowned as he recognised a footman from Rother House. What the devil was he doing here in town? His heart plummeted as he realised there could only be one explanation.

"What's she done now?" he demanded of the footman, leaping down and handing over the reins to one of the viscount's men.

The footman thrust a sealed note towards him, shaking his head. "Mrs Lane-Fox told me to get this to you as soon as you could, but I've had the devil of a journey, sir. I ought to have been here yesterday only with one thing and t'other...."

August let the man's words wash over him as he broke the seal and scanned the words with a sensation like ice water washing down his back.

"Hell and the devil!" he exclaimed, crumpling the paper up and stuffing it in his pocket. "I'll wring her blasted neck for this."

"Whatever is wrong?" Viv asked, leaning over the side of the carriage. August cursed himself for not having had the good manners to see her safely down first.

"I'm so sorry, love. I've got to dash. I'd best help you down. My sister is about to do something dreadful. Not for the first time, and almost certainly not the last."

"How exciting," Viv exclaimed, looking vastly entertained by this information.

August held out his hand to her, but Vivien shook her head. "You can't think I'm going to miss out on the fun, August? Do be reasonable."

August frowned. "Viv, love, I don't think *fun* is the word you're looking for. Anna is dead set upon causing a scandal, and the last thing I need is for you to get caught up in it."

Vivien raised one imperious eyebrow at him. "Mr Lane-Fox, might I remind you of certain promises you gave me? You said we would have our own society with people whose opinion mattered to us, and anyone else could take a running jump. Did you not mean that?"

She studied him, the intensity in her indigo eyes suggesting his answer had better be the right one.

"Yes, love," he said with a sigh. "I meant it but, knowing Anna, things might get out of hand," he warned, hoping that she might err on the side of caution for once and stay home.

"Excellent," she said, settling herself back on the seat.

And... he was an idiot.

August climbed back into the carriage.

"Where are we off to, then?" Viv demanded once they were underway.

"Vauxhall Gardens. There's a charity gala with a fete and a balloon ascension and a grand luncheon for seventy members to celebrate their first year of the Royal Asylum for Destitute Females."

"And so?"

"And so Anna has a bee in her bonnet about such associations, and especially about the men who run them. For every one of those seventy members is male."

"Well, that is ridiculous, when it is a charity for women, I agree, but surely the charity itself is an admirable thing?" Vivien said.

August sighed. He had thought the same thing until he had sat through far too many lectures on the subject from his female relations. "It is, on the face of it, but Anna believes most of these women could be saved from becoming destitute or in trouble with the law in the first place with access to a proper education. Getting them out of such trouble should also be remedied the same way. The school purports to do this, but actually only teaches—"

"Needlework, cooking, cleaning, et cetera," Vivien guessed.

"Yes. Exactly. Anna says if any of these fine men were reduced to having nothing more to accomplish in life than a neat row of stitches, they'd likely drink gin and get into trouble with the law, too. She believes if they taught the women to read and write, perhaps even some basic mathematics, that they would become useful members of society, who would in turn teach their own children."

"I like your sister already." Vivien grinned at him, and August let out a huff of laughter.

"Yes, I rather thought you might. The trouble is, Anna would rather do something—anything—rather than simply write letters or talk about it. She says there is no point talking when men don't listen."

"You can't expect me to argue that point," Vivien replied.

August frowned until he felt her hand settle upon his knee. "Not all men," she amended with a smile.

"Thank you for that," he said, leaning over to kiss her cheek.

"So what is it your sister is up to, precisely?"

"*Precisely,* I don't know. But it must be exceptionally bad for Mama to be worried, for she is usually all in favour of Anna's dreadful behaviour. I suspect she has come up with something really dangerous this time."

"Then we had best make haste," Vivien said, holding onto the seat as August nodded and the horse picked up its pace.

22nd April 1841, The Royal Gardens, Vauxhall, London.

The fete was a large one, with perhaps a hundred market stalls and entertainers. To the right of the fete, a huge red and white striped silk balloon rose eighty feet above the crowd who watched from a large, two-tiered wooden stand.

"Heavens," Vivien said, staring at it in wonder.

"Have you never seen one before?"

Vivien shook her head. "It's rather beautiful."

"It is, but there's no time to admire it, I'm afraid. We must find Anna."

Vivien nodded, and they paid their entrance fee, hurrying through the crowd.

"What does she look like?" Viv asked breathlessly, almost running to keep up with him.

August paused, still scanning the crowds as he spoke. "She's a pretty blonde, rather petite with blue eyes, though she is fond of disguises, so she could appear to be anything from a flower seller to a dandy."

"A dandy?" Vivien repeated, wide-eyed and finding herself increasingly in awe of his sister.

"On one memorably terrifying occasion, yes," August said, his expression grim. "Where the devil would the wretched girl go?"

"Everyone is watching the balloon," Viv offered.

August nodded and took her hand before pausing. "Hell, you ought not be here alone with me. I didn't stop to think. A ride in Hyde Park is one thing, but—"

Vivien smiled and pressed a finger to his lips. "Do stop fretting," she chided him gently. "Let us find your diabolical sister."

He let out a breath and nodded. "Yes. All right, then."

Little by little, August elbowed his way through the crowd to the front, Vivien following close behind him. By the time they emerged, she was quite breathless. The sturdy rail kept the crowd away from the balloon itself and Viv leaned upon it with relief. It was an impressive scene, the vast balloon only a part of the spectacle, for behind it on enormous rollers turned a huge motorised panoramic backdrop of the balloon's most famous and record-breaking flight. The scene painted on a moving canvas roll depicted the voyage from Vauxhall, over the Channel, across France and Germany, with the descent near Weilburg. Viv stared at it in wonder, unable to comprehend the desire to undertake such a journey, let alone how they had contrived to achieve it.

"Viv?"

She turned in surprise to see Evie by her side.

"Evie! What a surprise."

"Papa loves balloons, or any new form of fast travel," Evie explained, as her father gave Viv a polite bow. Lady Helena held his arm, looking as exquisitely elegant as always.

"Good afternoon, Mr Knight, Lady Helena." Vivien bowed and introduced August to them, who said everything that was proper but was clearly a little distracted.

"We're looking for Mr Lane-Fox's sister," Vivien said, explaining his disquiet. "We appear to have misplaced her."

Mr Knight's expression became grave. "You may safely leave Miss Anson with us, Mr Lane-Fox, if you would like to carry on your search in the, er... other areas of the fete? If your sister has wandered off, she might have inadvertently stumbled upon the less salubrious side of such an event. I am at your disposal, should you wish for help."

"You are most kind," August said sincerely. "And I shall accept your offer of chaperonage for Miss Anson while I continue my search. My sister is not a child, and in all honesty, I fear for anyone thinking to take advantage of her, for she is a formidable young woman. However, I am concerned and... if you'll excuse me. Miss Anson, if you could keep an eye out here, I should be grateful."

"Of course," Viv replied, too aware of the worry in his eyes to complain about being abandoned. Evie took her arm as she watched him hurry away.

"Papa knows the fellow doing the balloon ascension, and he has offered us a closer look," Evie said, grinning at her. "We can even get in the gondola. That's what the bit they stand in is called, apparently."

Vivien turned back to frown at the gondola. The idea of going miles up into the sky in a construction like that with nothing but an enormous balloon to hold one up... her stomach turned a somersault.

"How nice," she said faintly.

"Well, he takes passengers, you know," Evie said, winking at her. "And what was it your dare said?"

"Lud!" Vivien exclaimed in horror. "You think… in *that*?"

Evie laughed, shrugging. "*Dare to reach great heights.* You'll not get much higher than in a balloon, but no, of course not if it frightens you. I thought it would me too, honestly, and it does, but… but I'm intrigued. Imagine being up that high, seeing what only the birds see. How magical that must be."

"Ah, indeed, it is magical. Like seeing through the eyes of God," said a jovial voice behind them. "Mr Charles Green, balloonist, at your service."

Chapter 17

Nic,

I have had the strangest sensation of late. I cannot put my finger on it, but I sense I am being watched, perhaps followed.

Tell me I am being paranoid.

—Excerpt of a letter from Louis César de Montluc, Comte de Villen to his brother, Monsieur Nicolas Alexandre Demarteau.. Translated from French.

22nd April 1841, The Royal Gardens, Vauxhall, London.

August pushed his way through the crowd, increasingly anxious. He would bloody murder Anna when he got his hands on her. He hurried on, and in his haste and concern, ploughed into something solid.

"*Merde!*"

"Steady on!"

August righted himself and prepared to make an apology when he recognised the three men.

"*Monsieur,* forgive me," he said, hoping the comte and his brother would not take offence. Jules, the Marquess of Blackstone, who appeared to be accompanying them, looked on with undisguised amusement.

"No harm done," replied the comte. "But you appear to be somewhat out of sorts. Is there a problem?"

"My dratted sister is the problem," August admitted. "I must find her."

"Is she in trouble?" the comte's brother, Mr Demarteau, asked in concern.

"Not yet, but at any moment, yes, I believe so."

The comte frowned, lowering his voice. "Then I must insist you allow us to offer you our assistance. What can we do? You can rely on our discretion. I give you my word of honour."

Both men turned to stare at Jules, whose eyebrows shot up. "Well, I'm no sneaksby," he retorted, looking affronted. "I'll hold my tongue."

August sighed, the offer relieving him more than he wished to admit. He took off his hat and slapped it irritably against his thigh. "I don't know. That's the devil of it. My sister is a passionate advocate for the rights of women. I know she plans for something to happen today, something to bring attention to her cause, but I do not know what."

"If she's looking for a spectacle, I'd suggest the balloon," Jules said, gesturing to the extraordinary thing.

August nodded. A nagging sensation in his guts had been telling him the same thing. "I've already been there and found no sign of her, but you're right. Though she could be anywhere in this blessed crowd."

"Well, shall we, then?" Mr Demarteau asked.

The men nodded, but Louis César hesitated, turning to look behind him. He rubbed the back of his neck, scanning the crowd.

"Again, Louis?" his brother asked, his expression one of concern.

"What is it?" August asked, wondering what he was searching for.

The comte shook his head. "Probably just my imagination," he muttered irritably. "Come along, we had better help find the young lady."

Jules strode beside August as they made their way back to the balloon.

"No hard feelings?" he said, watching August with interest.

August snorted and shook his head. "None. I owe you a debt, truth be told. Seeing her with you was the wake-up call I needed."

"Pleasure to be of service, and please don't trouble yourself with thoughts of jealousy. Vivien is a wonderful girl and I'm pleased as punch for you both, but I wouldn't marry her if you paid me. No offence to the lady. She'd say the same. We'd murder each other."

August grinned, remembering that Viv had said much the same thing.

"All's well that ends well. That is assuming my outrageous sister doesn't put the entire family beyond the pale with whatever it is she has planned."

"Lively girl, is she?" Jules said with interest.

"You could say that," August grumbled, pushing his way back through the crowds to where he'd last seen Viv with the Knights and fretting himself to death when he discovered Vivien was not where he had left her.

"*Sainte Mère de Dieu,*" the comte exclaimed, clutching at his brother's arm.

August followed his horrified gaze to the basket of the balloon. It was an extraordinarily shaped contraption, rather like a deep gondola, with large golden eagle's heads staring out from both sides. Attached to the balloon with white and crimson gores and draped in swathes of purple velvet, it was quite a sight. It was not, however, what held August's attention.

Both Vivien and Evie were standing in the gondola, staring up at the balloon, whilst Mr Knight was deep in conversation with the balloon's proprietor and captain, Mr Charles Green. Whilst all parties were so occupied, a lithe, blonde figure hurried up to the back of the balloon and climbed in, immediately disappearing as they ducked down and out of sight.

"Christ!"

August hurried up to the gate that separated the crowd from the gate to the private area immediately around the balloon where several burly guards kept the riffraff from causing mischief by interfering with the delicate contraption.

"I must get though," August said. "That's my fiancée," he added, which was jumping the gun rather, but he doubted Viv would mind in the circumstances.

"I don't care if that's your maiden aunt or the Queen of Sheba," the guard replied dryly. "Mr Green has all the guests with him. Ain't no one else gettin' in."

"Hell! But you don't understand," August said, and then snapped his mouth shut before he could explain. He could hardly give Anna away and cause a great scene. What the devil was he to do?

Murmurs among the crowd gradually turned to screams as the balloon swayed gently and began to rise.

"*Merde!*" Louis said, leaning over the fence. "There's no one with them."

August turned back to see Mr Green running for the balloon with Mr Knight beside him. Without another word, Louis had vaulted the fence, his brother following close behind. August did likewise, though perhaps less gracefully, dodging the guards who lunged after him.

"Viv!" he shouted. "Anna!"

Viv and Evie were clutching the sides of the basket, their eyes wide with horror as Mr Green tugged ineffectually at one of the dangling ropes, yelling for help as Mr Knight struggled, tugging on another. But the balloon was too heavy and too intent on its course.

"I must get up there!" Green shouted, clearly panic struck.

"Nic!" Louis shouted, leaping to catch hold of one of the dangling ropes. His brother did likewise. They were soon off the ground as the balloon continued to ascend, and the two men shouted for Mr Green, who caught their meaning and jumped. The brothers grabbed a hand each and heaved the man up until he could catch hold of the basket and clamber in.

"Wait for me!" August shouted, running full pelt. He jumped, relieved when the brothers caught him by the hands. A little less so when he looked down and saw the ground disappearing at an alarming rate.

"Don't look down," the brothers yelled in unison.

For a moment, August hung suspended, entirely reliant on the strength of the two men not to drop him. From this height, he'd likely break a bone or two at the very least.

"On three," Louis shouted at Nic before looking at August. "Ready?"

August nodded.

"Un, deux, trois!"

The two men hoisted him higher, and August let go of Nic's hand for long enough to grab Mr Green's, who was hanging over the side of the gondola. August grasped it with relief and climbed, helped over the side by Anna and Vivien.

"August, oh, August!" Vivien cried, clinging to him. She was trembling hard, and August clutched her to him, feeling entirely too shaky for comfort himself.

"It's all right, love. It's all right."

"Louis!" Evie shrieked in distress.

He turned then, remembering the comte and his brother were still on the wrong side of the damned basket. Mr Demarteau's dark head appeared, and he helped the man in. August's stomach lurched as he saw how high they were now.

"Monsieur!" he called down.

Louis looked up, not moving until he saw his brother safely in the gondola. He climbed then, with the same ease he had seen the man exhibit at the Fancy Fair.

"Oh, Louis! I was so frightened."

Evie flung herself at him and held on tight, which was a little shocking but hardly surprising in the circumstances. August was only amazed the lot of them weren't hysterical. He felt a little hysterical himself as he turned on his sister, who had emerged from beneath the sacking she'd hidden under.

"You little wretch! Was this your doing?" he demanded furiously.

"No!" Anna retorted, indignant at the accusation. "I was only a stowaway. I'm not fool enough to think I can navigate the dratted thing by myself, am I, you great lummox?"

August subsided, too exhausted by the excitement and anxiety of the past hour to protest further.

With a sniff of irritation, Anna flounced away—though not very far in the confines of the gondola—and picked up a small sack. Sending August a wicked grin, she tipped the contents over the side.

Pink bits of paper fluttered in the breeze, hundreds of leaflets rushing about them and then fluttering down, to fall upon the expanse of Vauxhall Gardens like rose-coloured snow.

August snatched one as it sailed past and let out a bark of laughter.

"What is it?" Vivien asked, taking it from his hand. She stared at it, smiling and reading aloud. *"'Virtue can only flourish among equals. Educate our girls and free them from poverty and vice.'* Well said." She grinned at Anna and held out her hand.

"We meet again," Anna said, clasping it warmly. "I knew I liked you. Are you the reason August was so wretched the last time he was home?"

Vivien regarded him with interest.

"Yes," he replied for her. "She is."

"Do you really like it?" Anna asked, gesturing to the leaflet in Viv's hand. "Of course, the first bit, *Virtue can only flourish among equals* isn't mine, it's—"

"Mary Wollstonecraft. I know." Viv grinned at her.

"Oh. I do like you. You ought to marry this one, August," Anna said loftily.

Before August could reply, the balloon gave a lurch as a current of wind caught at it and August held Viv closer to him. Anna clung to the side of the gondola, staring down at the tiny figures of the people below who were running about, catching her leaflets. She smiled happily.

"You've met before?" August asked her, deciding it was better to concentrate on conversation than the fact the ground was disappearing at an alarming rate.

"Yes. I... er.... Well, actually, I hid her from a policeman," Viv confessed apologetically.

August stared at her in consternation for a long, silent moment, and then he began to laugh. He laughed and laughed until tears streamed down his face and he was fighting for breath.

"Are you all right?" Vivien asked, an uncertain look on her face though her eyes glittered with amusement.

"I am," August agreed, gasping. "I am better than all right. I'm happy. And you… you are marvellous, magnificent, and…."

"And?" she prompted as he stared at her, realising that here, now, hundreds of feet in the air and flying like a bird, was the perfect moment. He took both her hands in his.

"And would you do me the very great honour of becoming my wife, Miss Anson?"

Viv gasped, a dozen different emotions crossing her face at once, all of them variations of joy. "Yes," she whispered, before adding rather louder. "Yes, yes, yes!"

She flung herself at him and kissed him, and August realised he really did know how it felt to fly.

22nd April 1841, High Above The Royal Gardens, Vauxhall, London.

"Dear me, I cannot understand how the balloon got free when it was so securely tethered. It's never happened before." Mr Green looked most indignant. "And no doubt there will be the devil to pay from my customers. It costs a pretty penny for a flight like this, you understand."

Evie wondered how much a pretty penny was, but did not like to ask. Anna Lane-Fox had no such scruples.

"How much?" she demanded with interest.

"Twenty-one pounds for men and ten pounds ten shillings for women," Mr Green replied.

Mr Demarteau whistled in appreciation of the small fortune. Louis glowered at Mr Green. "I will pay you double that, provided you get us down in one piece," he said darkly.

Mr Green's eyebrows went up. "Done," he said at once.

Evie laughed.

"I believe it might be worth even that price, for it is glorious," Mr Demarteau breathed in wonder as he gazed down at England spread beneath them like a beautiful patchwork in every shade of green known to man. "Look, Louis," he said, turning back to his brother.

Louis shook his head and didn't budge from the centre of the gondola. He looked rather green himself. Evie felt embarrassed and somewhat foolish now for the way she had mauled him, but honestly, she had been terrified. The shock of finding herself airborne had been bad enough, but watching Louis holding on to a rope over the side had been simply appalling. The relief of seeing him whole and beside her had been so overwhelming she'd quite forgotten herself. Now, though, the terror was fading somewhat, replaced by awe at the beauty surrounding them. It was, as Mr Demarteau had said, perfectly glorious. They floated in utter peace, as gently as the tiny wisps of cloud in an otherwise blue sky. If not for the fact it was exceedingly cold, it was wonderful.

"Stop dithering and come and see. It's astonishing," Louis' brother called, gesturing to them to move away from the centre of the gondola and look over the side.

Evie took a nervous step closer to the edge, but Louis shot out his hand and grasped her arm.

"Don't you dare," he said, tugging her closer.

"We're up here now," Evie replied gently, aware he was fretting. "We may as well enjoy it."

"Enjoy it?" Louis retorted, looking somewhat outraged.

Mr Demarteau turned to study his brother in consternation. *"Mon Dieu,* Louis. Surely… you cannot tell me you're *afraid of heights?"*

His brother found this utterly hysterical and went off into whoops.

Louis muttered something in French that sounded exceedingly rude and most uncomplimentary.

"Well, he has a point," Evie teased gently. "I mean, you climbed up to the rafters at the Fancy Fair without batting an eyelid, and you hung onto that rope over the side in mid-air too, and that didn't seem to bother you."

"Ce n'est pas pareil! That was within my control," Louis growled unhappily, his accent far more audible than usual. "If I fell, it was my own damn fault. This… this feels like being at the mercy of a gust of wind. I dislike being at anyone's mercy." He rubbed the back of his neck irritably and Evie regarded him with concern, realising he really was wretched. Though she knew she ought not, she took his hand, lacing their fingers together, and held on tight. He was her friend, after all, and in need of comforting.

"It's all right," she said softly. "Mr Green has done hundreds and hundreds of these flights. He even flew all the way to Germany. Can you imagine it? We will be fine, I promise."

Louis stared at her, his blue eyes electric.

"You're not afraid," he observed with a little huff of laughter. "My, *Little Miss Stay at Home* is enjoying herself."

Evie's lips quirked. "Well, I would not have chosen to come up, certainly not in these circumstances, but now we're here." She turned and gazed out around them. "Yes! Yes, I am enjoying myself. Though I wish it were not so dreadfully c-cold."

She shivered, and Louis frowned. "Come here."

He pulled her against him, her back to his chest, and wrapped his arms about her waist, resting his head atop hers. It was dreadfully scandalous and quite inappropriate, but August and Vivien only had eyes for each other, Anna was obviously a scandal all by herself, and his brother would be unlikely to say anything. Only Mr Green might tattle, and she suspected customers willing to pay double for a safe landing could be assured of discretion. Besides which, the heat of Louis' body radiated from him, warming her, and she relaxed into his embrace. Louis sighed, some of the tension leaving him as he held her. It felt good to be enveloped so securely in his arms. Evie stared about them. The beauty of England was simply breath-taking, with its dark forests nestled snug upon velvet pastures and twisting silver blue skeins of rivers unravelled around them, glittering in the sun.

"I shall never forget this," she whispered, leaning her head upon Louis' shoulder, filled with a sense of wonder and wellbeing of the like she had never known. "Not so long as I live."

Louis' arms tightened about her. *"Moi non plus, ma petite. Jamais."*

Evie smiled, pleased he felt the same now, despite his concern. She tilted her head to look at him, finding his blue gaze warm, if not entirely relaxed.

"Assuming we live long enough to remember it always," he added with a wry smile.

"Such a pessimist," she chided him.

"Ah well, if I must die, I should like it to be with a beautiful woman held in my arms," he murmured, his voice low and wicked.

"Louis!" she exclaimed, surprised, and a bit scandalised, even though she knew he was only teasing her, the wretch. "Hush. If Mr Green hears, he will get entirely the wrong impression."

"Will he?" he asked with a sigh. "Forgive me. It must be these dizzying heights making me misbehave."

Mr Demarteau turned and regarded them. Something in the way he looked at her, held in his brother's arms, made her blush and realise the dreadful impropriety of the situation. Louis was her friend, though, and she was no fool. She knew the embrace meant nothing to him. It was not as if he would ever glance twice at her in that light when he had women who truly *were* beautiful throwing themselves at him from all sides, but others would not understand their friendship. Surely he had explained it to his brother, though, so why did he look at her in that odd way? Suddenly embarrassed, Evie straightened and went to move away, despite the cold, but Louis held tight, refusing to relinquish his hold on her.

"Non, stay. Nic won't tattle, and you're cold. I'll be good, I promise."

She heard the sincerity in his voice and subsided. He was deliciously warm, after all, and it was freezing.

They floated in silence for some time, and little by little Evie found herself once more relaxed in his arms, and far more at home there than she ought to be. She knew she must not get used to such things.

"I don't want to return to earth."

Evie bit her lip, wondering where that observation had come from, but her worries about the future seemed far away up here, the decisions she must make of less moment, when set against the surrounding vastness.

"I can understand the impulse. Here we hang suspended between heaven and hell and reality is far away. Is the future so daunting, love?"

Louis' voice was full of understanding, and Evie nodded, grateful that he knew her so well, that she need not explain.

"Yes," she said simply. "It is."

Chapter 18

My Lady,

Me thinks thou dost protest too much. Why fight it? You know you adore me, really.

Rest assured, your secret – <u>your secrets</u> – are safe with me.

—Excerpt of a letter from The Hon'ble Mr Sylvester Cootes to Lady Aisling Baxter (Daughter of the Right Hon'ble Luke and Kitty Baxter, the Earl and Countess of Trevick).

22nd April 1841, Peregrine House, Grosvenor Square, London.

"My word, what a day!" Evie flopped back against the pillows of her bed as Vivien settled beside her. "I thought Mama would never stop crying and hugging me. The poor dear was frightened witless."

Viv nodded. "Not only your mama," she observed, for Mr Knight had obviously been beside himself, no matter how manfully he'd tried to moderate his display of relief so as not to overset Evie entirely.

"Still, they were endlessly grateful to Monsieur le Comte and Mr Demarteau for their bravery and quick thinking, which is wonderful."

"You mean so your father doesn't fret so much about your friendship with the handsome comte?" Vivien said.

"Yes," Evie replied with a shrug. "It's pointless him worrying when there's nothing to worry about. Perhaps now, after our adventures and Louis bringing me home safely, he'll realise that."

Viv decided she was too tired to argue the point. Clearly Evie did not believe there was anything to worry about, but she was an intelligent girl. She'd figure out eventually why her father fretted so. Viv had sent word to her parents that she was well and in the Knights' care after a slight mishap, and not to worry. They would not yet know about her adventures ballooning, but they would have been worried when the hour had grown late, and August had not returned her. There would be time enough to recount her astonishing day tomorrow, but now she was weary to her bones.

It was very late, for it had taken far longer to return home in a carriage than the distance they had travelled in the balloon. Thankfully, their landing had been smooth, but it had taken time also to arrange transport.

"Well, you certainly completed your dare in style," Evie observed.

Vivien snorted. "Unintentionally. Though I'll fight anyone who says it doesn't count, for I'm not going through that ordeal again." She stretched and smothered a yawn, making herself more comfortable.

"It *was* exciting, though," Evie said. "Strange, really. I truly don't like the idea of adventures and that kind of excitement one little bit. It always frightens me so. Yet I shouldn't have missed today for the world."

"You are a conundrum, Evie Knight."

Evie nodded, her expression thoughtful. "I know," she admitted.

Vivien closed her eyes with a sigh. "I feel like I've been dreaming, but I don't want to wake up."

"Yes. That's how I felt when we were up there. Like it wasn't at all real, just a fanciful dream."

Evie's voice was pensive. Vivien smiled.

"A dream, but not a dream," she said. "Instead, my happily ever after."

"Yes! Oh, Viv, I do like Mr Lane-Fox," Evie said, taking Viv's hand. "And he looks utterly besotted, the poor devil. I think you shall be very happy."

Viv nodded, quite unable to keep the foolish grin from her face. "I think I shall too."

Evie turned on her stomach, resting her head in her hands and looking pensive. "You knew he was the one, didn't you? Almost at once, I mean."

"Yes, I suppose I did."

Evie frowned. "I don't have the faintest idea," she admitted. "I just cannot imagine myself married to any of the young men who have deigned to show an interest in me."

"What about the devastatingly beautiful comte?" Vivien asked, curious now.

"Don't be silly," Evie said at once. "He's my friend."

"He'd be a difficult husband, I suppose," Vivien mused, observing Evie's reaction to the words. "Always being chased by beautiful women, and he's got a wicked reputation, too. The things they whisper about him are scandalous. They say he's astonishing in bed."

"*Viv!*" Evie blushed scarlet. "Don't speak of him so! And who are *they?* Where did you hear such a thing, anyway?"

Viv shrugged. "In the retiring rooms. Women gossip. Lots of women, considering he's had a string of lovers that he discards like his waistcoats."

Evie's expression had closed up, giving nothing away, but her voice was curt. "Louis does not treat women so shabbily. He is faithful whilst they are together. They just do not hold his attention long. He is easily bored, but he makes no promises and is careful not to cause hurt. That is why he never lingers long with a mistress, so they cannot grow too fond of him."

Vivien's eyebrows went up, astonished that Evie knew something so intimate about him. "You really do know him well."

Evie nodded. "I do."

Vivien hesitated, wondering whether she ought to push a little further, to make her friend consider another point of view. "He's been your faithful friend this age, Evie, but he's very attentive. Does that not seem odd to you?"

Evie sat up, annoyance flashing in her eyes. "No. Why should it? He does not trust people, or make friends easily, but he knows I do not flatter or tell him lies because I do not lust after him like the other women do. He knows he can trust me, and we *like* each other. Why is that so hard to understand?"

Vivien considered this and realised she could see the truth of it. She knew that when most men looked at her, they only saw something they desired, not a complete person. She had seen the women determined to be the Comtesse de Villen—or his next mistress—that hunted Louis at every *ton* event, hanging on his every word, batting their eyelashes, wanting him for his beauty and his wealth and his title, not for who he was. How precious would someone like Evie become in a world where he trusted no one to give him anything but meaningless flattery?

"Forgive me," Vivien said, meaning it. "I did not understand. But is there no one you fancy? Not even Mr Hadley-Smythe?" she teased, knowing he was among Evie's favourites, and her most faithful suitor.

"That's all right. I know our friendship is unusual. And yes, I do like Mr Hadley-Smythe," Evie admitted. "He's agreeable company and a gentle fellow. Of all of them, he is the only one I believe I could consider. I think he would be a kind husband."

Vivien pulled a face at her words.

"What?" Evie protested.

Vivien laughed, shaking her head. "Well, that's a start, I suppose, but… but don't you feel anything more than that? Don't you feel an odd fluttering in your belly when he's close? Don't you long to be near to him, to be in his arms? To be alone with him and for the rest of the world to be far away?"

Evie fell quiet, a puzzled frown drawing her brows together as a troubled expression settled over her. She shook her head suddenly, as if shaking away a bothersome wasp. "Well, Papa says I have ages yet, so I don't need to worry about it for the moment, do I? I probably just need to spend more time with him to get to know him better. We only ever talk at parties and share a dance or two. It's not much to go on."

"Of course, silly goose. You've plenty of time, for you're only eighteen, whereas I am almost an ape leader at the grand old age of four and twenty."

Evie snorted, amused. "Methuselah, that's you. So, when shall you be married?"

"As soon as may be," Vivien replied at once, grinning at her. "Because I *do* long to be alone with August, and for the rest of the world to be far away."

26th April 1841, Rother House, Burwash, Etchingham, East Sussex.

"Stop looking so anxious. Papa said this was a good idea, and I agree. It's not like you haven't told them all what to expect," Vivien said, taking August's arm.

August swallowed down the knot lodged in his throat with difficulty and could not bring himself to answer. Their families were meeting today for the first time, ahead of their impending nuptials next week. He felt sick. Viscount Cavendish and his lady were here, along with Viv's twin, Ash, and their grandmother. Though August had been forthright in explaining his family's rather unconventional situation, he could not help but wonder if he ought to have been plainer still. Perhaps he simply should have told them his kin were barking mad and they may as well consider their daughter to be marrying into a family of bedlamites, but he hadn't wanted to frighten them off. Now, as he stared up at his ancestral home, he regretted not having prepared them more thoroughly. There was a naked man at one of the upper windows, in what had once been August's bedroom, and he appeared to be conducting an orchestra. August tore his eyes away, cleared his throat, and prayed no one else had noticed.

"That fellow is naked!" Nani Maa exclaimed, staring up at the window with obvious interest. "Where are my spectacles? Mary, get them for me."

So much for no one noticing. August sighed.

"Dreadful creature," Ash muttered affectionately. "You're supposed to be past the age of wanting to look at naked men," he informed his grandmother under his breath.

The old woman looked back at him, obviously offended. "Don't be ludicrous," she retorted, snatching her spectacles from her maid and putting them on.

"Shall we go in?" August said, trying to ignore the sensation of impending doom pressing down on him.

"August, darling!"

Out hurried his mother to greet her guests, with his sisters close behind. Mama was resplendent in purple silk and beaming a welcome. He had to admit she looked well, and happy too. The reason for that happiness leaned nonchalantly against the front door jamb, grinning.

"How do, August, old man. Well met."

"Afternoon, Charlie," he said, holding out his hand to the woman as she pushed off the door frame and strode towards him. Charlie—Charlotte—Brooks, looked dapper and elegant in a casual country outfit of men's riding attire. She had cut her hair short in a masculine style, and her gaze was confident and self-assured as she shook his hand. No matter what the world thought of Charlie, she knew exactly who and what she was and didn't give a tinker's cuss for anyone else's opinion. August admired her.

"Congratulations," she said, her expression genuinely pleased. "She's a beauty and I'm so pleased you're happy. Your mama worries for you, you know. It will be a weight off her mind to see you settled."

"I know," August replied, suddenly relieved that Mama had someone to look after her and to feel concern about her worries, too.

He turned to see his mother hugging Vivien fiercely and felt a sudden swell of emotion.

"And you must be Charlie Brooks. I am pleased to make your acquaintance." Silas held his hand out to Charlie, who gave it a firm shake.

"My Lord Cavendish, I'm honoured."

"Silas will do," his lordship said blithely. "As it appears, we are to be family now."

And with that, Lord Cavendish accepted Charlie's place in his mother's household and made everything right. Mama stared at his lordship, her eyes glittering, and it occurred to August that she must have been dreadfully worried about today.

"Shall we go in and have some tea?" she said brightly, her voice a little unsteady.

"A capital idea, Mama," he said, offering her his arm and escorting her back into the house.

26th April 1841, Rother House, Burwash, Etchingham, East Sussex.

Vivien was in love with Rother House. The ancient manor cried out for someone to take it in hand, but its beauty and quiet dignity were undeniable. Not that it was in a terrible state of repair. The building had been well maintained, which she did not doubt was August's doing, but the ladies of the house had far more important things on their minds than properly supervising the staff. On her way to the parlour, Vivien observed that there were cobwebs lurking in dark corners. The portraits needed to be taken down and given a thorough dusting, and no one had blacked the andirons for some time. Upon the arrival of the tea tray, she could not help but notice the silver needed a good polish, too. When the maid and a footman carried the tea things through, Viv also observed a dingy apron and the air of staff who had given up looking for either proper orders or appreciation. She longed to put things to rights, but she had agreed with August that they could not turn his mother and sisters out of their home, and she quite understood that living under the same roof with them was a recipe for disaster. The sisters she could have managed, but two mistresses of a household were a terrible idea, even if one of them did not care for domestic details.

So, they would look for another property in which to begin their married life, though she understood now why August was so regretful that they would not be living in his family home.

Nani Maa gave a great cackle of delight and Vivien looked up to see both her and her father snorting with laughter at something Charlie had said.

"Wicked creature!" her grandmother said, chortling. "Tell us another."

"But I must introduce you to Lady Elizabeth Demarteau," Mama said to Anna. "For you know, she runs a school for girls, doing just as you wish for those poor young women in the asylum. They are indeed taught practical skills like sewing and cooking, but they are also taught maths and how to read and write, and even the practicalities of running a business—"

Anna's gaze was rapt as she listened to Mama explain about Eliza's charitable school and Vivien's attention drifted to her brother, who was standing by the fireplace whilst Gwen studied him with a frown of concentration.

"Move your hand, no, make a fist and put it on your hip. Yes… that's it. Oh, that's very good. You are dreadfully handsome, aren't you? Will you pose for me?"

"For a painting?" Ash said, his eyes lighting with interest.

"No, so I can hang my scarf up—of course for a painting!" Gwen said impatiently.

Ash's eyebrows flew up at being spoken to in such a blunt way, but he didn't protest. After all, he was used to his twin speaking to him so.

"I don't know what you were worrying about," Vivien said to her beloved, suppressing a smug grin.

August laughed and shook his head as he regarded the two families getting to know one another. "They like each other."

The astonishment in his voice was audible, and Viv set her teacup down and leaned into him.

"They do, and I like you, very much."

His gaze darkened, falling to her mouth.

"Aren't you going to take me for a tour?" she asked, suddenly breathless as the desire to be alone with him became quite unbearable.

August nodded and stood up, taking her hand and leading her to the door. "I'm er… just going to show—" His voice trailed away as he realised no one was paying him the least bit of attention. "Well, carry on then," he said, shaking his head, and closing the door behind them.

They turned to the entrance hall, stopping in their tracks at the sight before them.

An extremely tall, statuesque woman wearing a severe black gown and with a pearl choker at her throat, came down the stairs, reading aloud from a book of poetry, her voice deep and majestic as she spoke in tragic tones, her free hand making extravagant gestures to underscore the words.

"*A timid grace sits trembling in her eye, as loath to meet the rudeness of men's sight. Yet shedding a delicious lunar light, that steeps in kind oblivious ecstasy the care-crazed mind, like some still melody. Speaking most plain the thoughts which do possess her gentle sprite: peace, and meek quietness, and innocent loves, and maiden purity...* Oh, good afternoon."

"Good afternoon," August and Vivien said in unison.

The lady smiled serenely, scratched at her unshaven chin, and carried on out to the gardens, declaiming as she went. *"A look whereof might heal the cruel smart of changed friends, or fortune's wrongs unkind—"*

The voice faded and Vivien turned to gaze up at August. "Was that—"

"Lord Crenshaw reciting Charles Lamb, yes, it was. Come along," August said briskly, towing her up the stairs.

"I thought you were going to give me a tour of the house," she said, hurrying to keep up.

"Certainly I am. I intend to begin with the quietest and most private corner of the house, or at least it had better be," he added darkly.

Vivien grinned, quite happy with this plan.

"That used to be my bedroom," August sighed, gesturing to a door on their right at the same moment said door swung open.

To Vivien's—and likely August's—profound relief, the occupant had finished conducting his orchestra and was now fully attired, and carrying a small suitcase. *"Guten Tag, danke, dass Sie mich haben."*

"Er, you're welcome," August offered hesitantly.

The fellow beamed at them, executed a smart bow, and marched away.

"What did he say?" Vivien asked.

August laughed. "Well, dredging up my long-forgotten schoolboy German, I believe he wished us a good day and thanked us for having him."

"Oh, that's… opportune," she said, glancing up at him from under her lashes.

"Isn't it, though?" August replied with a grin. "Yet one hesitates to consider what a naked conductor might have left behind."

He pushed open the door and stuck his head in.

Vivien craned her neck, trying to see past him. "Is it as it ought to be?"

"Oh! Yes, it is. Good heavens, I think it's actually tidier. Do you know, I believe he cleaned it. Come in."

Vivien did not need asking twice and hurried inside, closing the door behind her. She looked around with interest at shelves stacked with many books and odds and ends. A row of small animal skulls, a stone shaped like a frog, and several tarnished silver cups for sporting events. "So, this is where young August Lane-Fox grew up."

August shrugged. "Not really. I was rarely here. Mama sent me to school early to get me away from my father who… was not a kind man. I rarely returned, not even during the holidays if I could help it. I'd stay with my friends whenever I could and be wherever they happened to be."

"I'm so sorry, August," Viv said, holding her hands out to him.

August shook his head, taking her hands and tugging her close, enclosing her in his arms. "I'm not, at least, not any longer. If not, I'd never have met Bainbridge and Dare and Raphe de Ligne, and I'd not have missed my adventures with them for the world. They're the brothers I never had."

"I'm glad you had them, that you weren't lonely."

"So am I. I'm even gladder that I have you, though," he said, tilting her chin up towards him. "I think I ought to warn you, I'm feeling reckless and wicked and, if you stay here, I'm likely to take liberties with your person."

His eyes glittered and Vivien's heart gave a little leap in her chest.

"Well, it's about time," she said, and tugged his head down for a kiss.

Chapter 19

Mr Cootes,

You poor, poor man. It troubles me to discover an otherwise healthy person afflicted with such severe mental disorders. I beseech you to find help for your malady with as much urgency as possible. You are clearly deluded and living in a world of make-believe.

I hate to be the bearer of bad news, but those friendly little imps that chatter in your ear are not real and only a figment of your imagination, which is running amok. Please do not let this news upset you unduly. I understand modern medicine can offer you several cures for what ails you.

Indeed, I understand ice baths to be of benefit and will gladly give you a dunking in the nearest body of water if you insist on continuing with this nonsensical correspondence. You are living in a wibbly wobbly world of your own, sir. I have no tender feelings regarding you. I have no feelings for you at all other than those of intense irritation. I hope I have made myself plain? So, you may keep writing to me until you are blue in the face, for you shall receive nothing but insults in return.

—Excerpt of a letter from Lady Aisling Baxter (Daughter of the Right Hon'ble Luke and Kitty Baxter, the Earl and Countess of Trevick) to The Hon'ble Mr Sylvester Cootes.

26th April 1841, Rother House, Burwash, Etchingham, East Sussex.

August knew he was a rotter. Knew it, and didn't give a damn. Vivien's entire family was downstairs. *His* entire family was downstairs, and here he was, intent on debauching his innocent fiancée in his bedroom well ahead of their vows.

Well, it was about time people realised he was as thoroughly wicked as Bainbridge, Dare and even Raphe. A point he wanted to make most especially to the woman in his arms. She seemed happy enough with the plan so far. She had certainly mastered kissing, and the art of getting him hot and bothered in a matter of seconds.

Kissing Vivien was something he did not believe he would ever get used to. She matched him for passion, yet there was tenderness and adoration and so much love behind every touch of their lips it went far beyond mere lust, though that was certainly a force rising through him with increasing impatience.

"Viv," he murmured, breaking the kiss to press his mouth to her throat. "Viv, I'm losing my mind. I cannot wait until next week to marry you. I'll run mad."

Viv giggled, and August lifted his head to stare at her. "You're not supposed to laugh. This is my sanity at risk. I can't sleep for thinking of you. If I do sleep, I dream of you and such wicked dreams they are, love. I'm wretched without you. I need you with me always, in my bed most especially for I'm going all to pieces."

"The date is set now. We can't change it. And what happens in these wicked dreams of yours that distresses you so?" she asked innocently, looking up at him from under thick, black lashes.

"I couldn't tell you that," he whispered in her ear. "You'd be so scandalised you'd run away and refuse to marry me."

"Heavens. I think you ought to tell me in that case. If my husband is so dreadfully depraved, I think I have the right to know."

August nipped at her earlobe, pleased when she shivered in response. "I shan't sully your ears with the wicked details, but I need to put my hands on you. I want to touch you, to kiss you everywhere, from your lips to your lovely breasts to your most secret places."

Vivien turned around. "Undo my gown!" she said desperately, glaring at him over her shoulder when he chuckled. "Hurry!"

"I can't undress you entirely, love, much as it pains me to say it. We can't disappear for too long or someone will come searching."

Nonetheless his fingers made quick work of the fastenings, enough that he could tug the gown and bodice lower. He pulled her back against him and reached around to cup her exposed breasts, letting out a shuddering sigh as she arched into his touch. Her lovely behind pressed against him and he urged his hips closer, his lust-filled brain clouding with pleasure as his cock nestled snugly against her. Vivien's head fell back against his shoulder as he teased her nipples, gently rolling and pinching. He ducked his head to kiss her elegant neck, aware her breathing had grown erratic. There was no maidenly shyness, however, no shock or bewilderment at his touch. She trusted him, and that made his heart so full of joy he was suddenly filled to the brim with emotion. What they had together was special, too special to throw away their first time in a hasty coupling, afraid they'd be interrupted at any moment. Yet he needed a taste of her, needed something to carry him through the days until she was entirely his.

"Sit on the bed," he told her, the words harsher than he'd meant them to his, his voice having taken on a rough, raspy quality.

Vivien only glanced at him though, the hint of a smile at her lips as she did as he asked.

August's breathing was laboured as he took in the sight of her, perched on the edge of his bed. He had mussed her sleek black hair, which was falling from its pins, framing her beautiful face. Her lips were plush and rosy from his kisses, and her breasts, the delicate little peaks of her nipples…. His mouth watered and he swallowed hard and moved quickly, kneeling before her. He caressed her breasts, nuzzling the valley between the splendidly soft mounds and trailing his lips across the delicious curves. His mouth covered a taut bud, suckling gently as Vivien gasped, her fingers tangling in his hair.

"Oh, that's… that's lovely."

August lifted his head, but she made an incoherent sound of complaint and guided his mouth back again. He laughed softly against her skin, content to indulge them both a little longer. When he finally looked up, her eyes were dark and hazy with desire. Oh, Lord. His cock throbbed, his entire body aching with a need which he could not indulge as he so desperately wanted to, but his beloved need not suffer such torments and he could not wait any longer to put his mouth on her.

"Lay back, love. Don't be startled, but I… I need to… I want…."

Vivien ignored him for a moment, reaching out to stroke his hair.

"I know," she whispered, looking somewhat smug even though she was blushing furiously. "Nani Maa showed me a dreadfully wicked book. She said she'd give me a copy as a wedding gift. It is a sort of instruction book, and it has… pictures."

August stared at her, eyes wide with shock. "An… instruction book?"

Vivien nodded, biting her lip. "Yes, for many things about married life, but also all the possible… positions."

"Positions," August repeated, his mind boggling at the fact her grandmother had given her such a thing.

"Nani Maa says women ought to know what they're in for, and to know how to find their own pleasure. She says knowledge is power, and men are easier to manage when you know how to… er… handle them."

August swallowed, somewhat stunned. "Well," he said unsteadily. "She's not wrong."

Vivien giggled and tugged at her skirts, pulling them higher with maddening slowness. August watched, holding his breath as she revealed her dainty ankles, slender silk clad calves, pink garters tied in a bow, and then—praise be—the smooth golden skin of her thighs.

"I want to touch you," he managed, though his ability to speak full sentences seemed to diminish in proportion to the amount of skin she exposed.

"Yes, yes," she replied breathlessly, reassuring him she was similarly afflicted. He reached for her, his touch reverent. August sighed as he discovered her skin, impossibly silky, warm and, as he leaned closer, she enveloped him in her scent, a faint trace of orange blossom and the heady perfume of a woman who desired him. He pushed her skirts higher, tantalised by the first glimpse of silky dark curls.

"Lay back."

She obeyed him this time and August pressed his mouth to her inner thigh, kissing a path until he could nuzzle the tender skin on either side of her sex. Her breathing hitched.

"You're so lovely, Vivien. So perfect. I am the luckiest man alive."

She gave a nervous laugh, and he decided not to tease her, for she was anxious despite her bold words before, and he only wanted to bring her pleasure. Carefully, he searched the springy thatch of curls with a finger, his own breathing increasingly ragged as he parted the delicate folds. August leaned in, continuing his exploration with his tongue until he found the tender peak of her sex.

Vivien gasped, her hips bucking as his touch made her body leap beneath his mouth.

August smiled. "Be still, love."

The command was gentle but firm and Vivien stilled, so he settled to his work, caressing and circling and occasionally sucking gently on the small bud until her hips rose again but this time in search of more, undulating, seeking and demanding he pleasure her. He smiled, pleased, and encouraged her.

"Tell me if I please you, love. Tell me the things you like."

"C-Can't speak," she stammered. "Don't stop!"

He huffed out a laugh, his warm breath sending goosebumps skittering over her. She was so perfectly delicious, and he wanted to spend the rest of the day exploring her, showing her the pleasure he could bring her, but he did not dare. The idea of her father or brother coming to find her was not a happy one, and Viv would be mortified. August suspected Ash would be more likely to murder him than Silas would, and so this perfect interlude must come to an end.

August found the opening to her body, slick with desire now as he gently slid one finger inside her and applied his mouth again, licking slowly but with increasing pressure. He caressed her intimately, his touch languid as Vivien moaned, quivering beneath him and clutching at the bedcovers. A second finger joined the first, working in measured thrusts as he suckled the taut little pearl beneath his tongue and she reacted at once, her inner muscles clenching around him as she cried out. It was all he could do not to spend himself, the sounds she made, and the taste of her pleasure were so erotic. Slowly he eased her through the climax, careful to ensure he wrung every last shudder of release from her body until she was panting and boneless, sprawled on his bed in a pose of utter abandon.

"Are you well, love?" he asked her, wondering what she'd made of it.

"Well?" she replied faintly. "*Well?* No. You've killed me. I... I'm... I hardly know what."

August chuckled, pressing tender kisses to her thigh before he straightened her skirts and began putting her back to rights. He sat on the bed beside her, staring down at her flushed countenance with such a sense of rightness he could not stop smiling.

"The French call it the little death for a reason," he said, feeling rather pleased with himself.

"*Le petite mort,*" she murmured dazedly. "Yes, I understand why."

August helped her to sit up and began doing up everything he'd undone as Viv seemed incapable of lifting a finger, much to his amusement. Once she was back to rights, he lent down and kissed her neck and she leaned into him.

"That was splendid," she said with a sigh. "Is that what making love with you will be like?"

"Consider that an *amuse-bouche*. A little taste of what is to come, before the main course," he murmured.

Vivien snorted, giving him a wry look over her shoulder. "You've been spending too much time with the Comte de Villen," she teased him.

August grinned and hoped his still obviously unfulfilled lust would subside if they continued their tour of the house, for he could not return her to her family like this.

Vivien's gaze snagged on his falls, and she bit her lip, which didn't much help. "Poor August," she said with sympathy. "Can I help?"

August groaned. "No!" he muttered, and grasped her hand, towing her from the bedroom and any further temptation.

26ᵗʰ April 1841, Rother House, Burwash, Etchingham, East Sussex.

By the time August was in a fit state to return to the parlour, the two families were obviously getting on like a house on fire as the conversation was loud, full of laughter, and unrestrained. Either their absence had been unremarked, or everyone had ignored them slipping away to allow them a little privacy. Vivien heaved a sigh of relief, for though she did not believe her parents would have been angry with August, it would have been embarrassing all the same.

She sat down again, glancing at her brother, who was beside her. Of everyone, he was uncharacteristically quiet.

"Ash? What's wrong?"

Her twin flashed her a bright smile and shook his head. "Nothing. Just a little in awe of this gathering. They're barking, the lot of them."

Vivien laughed as he'd wanted her to, but she knew her twin too well to be fobbed off. They needed to talk. She was about to suggest they go for a walk when August's mother chinked a teaspoon on the side of a china cup to gain everyone's attention.

She laughed at the look on her son's face. "Don't look so horrified, August, darling. I shan't give a speech, I swear. However, I do have news that I wish to share with you."

"Oh?" August said, and though his expression was calm enough, Viv suspected he was bracing himself.

"Charlie and I are moving out."

August blinked. "What? Oh, but mother, there's no need—"

Charlie cleared her throat, shaking her head. "Hold your tongue, dear boy. Your mother is speaking."

August subsided with a frown.

"A house cannot have two mistresses," Mrs Lane-Fox said with a smile. "And as much as we have enjoyed our little experiment with running a retreat, it's dashed hard work."

"We're packing it in and going travelling for the next year," Charlie cut in. "Through France and Italy."

Mrs Lane-Fox nodded, her eyes sparkling with excitement. "Not until after the wedding, naturally, but when we return, we thought we'd prefer something smaller and cosier, just for us. Like... Like the little farmhouse down by the brook on the far southern side of the estate, *if* you wouldn't mind having us so close?" she added anxiously.

August glanced at Viv, who nodded, smiling, so he got up and crossed the room, crouching down before his mother and taking her hands. "Of course we don't mind, but are you sure? This is your home. Viv and I were going to build something new and—"

His mother pressed her finger to his lips and shook her head. "You are so dear to me, August. You were always such a good little boy, but far too serious. You cannot know how glad I was when you fell in with those other dreadful boys and began causing mayhem. It was so wonderful to see you happy, though you never quite shook the habit of worrying about us. I have appreciated the way you have looked after us all, even if we do not always appear as grateful as we ought to. This is your home, as it has never quite been mine, and you love this place as I never have. You ought to have it to yourself with your new bride. I am so proud of you, proud of the man you have become. If all men were like you, the world would be a far, far better place."

"Mama," August protested, his voice choked as his mother embraced him and kissed his cheek.

"Don't look too pleased, though, because I am afraid I'm still leaving you with your sisters," she added wryly.

August snorted.

"Oh, don't worry," Anna said, grinning at him. "We're going to stay with friends of Mama's for a couple of months to give you some peace. But then we will be back to make your life far more exciting than it would otherwise be."

"Heaven help me," August murmured, but he was smiling.

Everyone laughed and champagne was called for so that they could toast the engaged couple. It was a merry gathering, with lots of loud chatter and unrestrained happiness, but Ash—who was usually the centre of attention at any gathering—was still quiet.

"Come for a walk with me," Vivien said, offering him her hand. "The gardens are ever so pretty, and I want to explore."

Ash frowned and shook his head. "No, your fiancé will want the pleasure of showing your around."

"Come along, lazybones. August won't mind," she insisted, getting up and giving him a look that suggested he do as she asked or else.

"You are such a bully," he grumbled. With a long-suffering sigh, Ash got up and followed her out. Viv smiled at August as they left and he just nodded, his expression warm. The twins walked the gardens arm in arm for a while, the sunshine warm upon their backs as they admired the bursts of spring colour from an exuberant display of bulbs and flowering shrubs. Much like the house, the garden had been allowed to run wild, but here it worked, giving the once formal borders a romantic, haphazard appearance that seemed to cocoon the building so that it embraced the surrounding landscape rather than dominating it.

"I am happy for you," Ash said, at length, but Vivien heard the part he did not say.

"It will be so strange to be apart from you, Ash. I can't quite imagine it. I'll miss you so very much, which is why August suggested you might like to stay with us this summer. Say you will, at least outside of the season. I know you could not bear to miss all the excitement in town."

Ash leaned over and kissed her cheek. "You are a sweetheart, but I don't want to intrude on your happiness. The last thing you and your new husband will want is your brother under your feet."

"Don't tell me what I want," Viv retorted, earning herself an eye roll. "You're not just my brother, you're my twin. I'm uncertain how I will feel about not seeing you all the time, but it's a little daunting."

"I feel like I'm being cut adrift," Ash admitted sheepishly, glancing at her. "I know I'm a grown man and that it's utterly stupid—"

"It isn't stupid at all. I feel the same. I love August with all my heart, and I want to be his wife and live with him, but…."

Her voice hitched, and she turned and hugged her brother fiercely.

"Oh, drat you, Viv. Don't… you'll start me off. There you see, now you've done it," he complained bitterly.

Viv laughed, fishing out a handkerchief and handing it to him.

"Such a watering pot," she teased as he wiped his eyes. "I never knew a fellow for blubbing like you do."

"I have a sensitive soul," Ash retorted.

"And yet you wear that waistcoat," Vivien observed, eyeing it with resignation. It was gold today and embroidered with a swirling black pattern that would likely induce a megrim if you stared at it for too long.

"There's nothing wrong with my waistcoat. It is elegant and sophisticated, which you would know if you weren't so lamentably gauche."

Viv laughed, relieved he'd recovered his spirits sufficiently to bicker with her. "Oh, I shall miss you. Say you'll come and stay in the summer, at least."

"Of course I'll come. Wild horses wouldn't keep me away, though you'll need to get me a chaperone or do something about Gwen. She's trying to get me out of my clothes already."

"What?" Vivien stared at him in alarm until she realised. "Oh, for her painting. They're rather scandalous, apparently, though I've not seen any yet."

"I should say so, if she wants me to stand before her in my skin. Asked without so much as a blush, too. Well, on her part, I can't speak for myself."

Vivien giggled. "Are you going to do it?"

"Certainly not!" He sounded aggrieved. "A man needs a little mystery, not his wares displayed for all and sundry. Besides, it would cause a riot. I'd have women beating down my door, begging me to make love to them."

"Ridiculous creature," Viv said with a sigh.

Ash shrugged, ignoring that. "Well, anyway. She's bound to fall in love with me, so I'm only suggesting you prepare for the inevitable," he said gravely.

Vivien pressed her quivering lips together and nodded, patting his arm. "Yes, dear. We'll do that."

Chapter 20

August,

Glad to hear you've come to your senses. Don't like to say I told you so, but… well, I told you so. Should always listen to my advice. Becoming sensible in my old age.* Married life and all that. Makes a fellow grow up. My marchioness is reading over my shoulder and insists I have a mental age of around nine years. Shan't argue. Life is far more pleasant if you just agree. *See sensible comment above.

Honoured to stand up with you. Pleased as punch you should ask.

Hope you like the wedding gift. You admired the new Brougham, so I've had it sent around. Your lady will need something dashing for jaunting about town. You too, come to that. Don't complain about expense or I'll be forced to pummel you. Please remember, I'm disgustingly wealthy.

—Excerpt of a letter from The Most Hon'ble Lawrence Grenville, Marquess of Bainbridge, to Mr August Lane-Fox.

27th April 1841, Cavendish House, The Strand, London.

They held the wedding at Cavendish House, a private affair followed by a lavish breakfast for friends and family that was expected to go on all day.

"Here." Bainbridge handed August a silver hipflask, which August took with gratitude.

Several large swallows produced a pleasant glow in his belly, but did little to diminish the jittery sensation that was making him pace up and down whilst he awaited his bride. He was about to try another large swallow when Bainbridge snatched his flask back.

"That's enough."

"Tell my guts that," August grumbled.

"There, there. All be over soon. You won't feel a thing," Bainbridge soothed him, resting a comforting hand on his shoulder.

August snorted, but felt oddly reassured by Bainbridge's certainty. A peculiar thing that the big, brash fellow's presence could be soothing, but somehow it was. Perhaps he really was behaving like a grown up at last.

"Last man standing," Raphe said, coming up to shake August's hand, with Dare beside him. "You didn't hold out long."

August shrugged. "Well, longer than you did, at least. I tried to fight it, but there was no use. She decided she must have me and there was no gainsaying her."

"Well, just think of it. The four of us, married and respectable," Dare said, grinning broadly.

"Well, married, anyway," Raphe added with a smirk.

"Speak for yourself. I'm respectable," Bainbridge retorted, folding his arms and looking indignant. Frowning across the expanse of chairs to where people were taking their places, he made the entire room jump by bellowing at his father. "Pa! *Pa!*

Your grace! Down here, you daft beggar. *Bella!* Bella, sort him out, love."

Bella sent her husband a look of fond exasperation and guided the Duke of Axton to his place where a footstool had been put out to accommodate his gouty foot.

August, Dare and Raphe exchanged glances of delighted amusement but held their tongues.

"August."

August turned to see Viv's twin regarding him. He was ridiculously handsome, all deep golden skin and black hair gleaming like a crow's wing, and for once his waistcoat was the height of elegance but otherwise quite unremarkable. Today it was white, with subtle gold embroidery, for August knew he would do nothing to upstage his sister on her special day.

"Ashton," August said, reaching out to shake the man's hand.

"I'm not losing a sister, but gaining a brother. That's what Viv tells me," Ash said, smiling warmly at him. "I hope you feel you are gaining a brother, too. We don't know each other well, but you seem a decent fellow. Don't prove me wrong on that, will you? I would hate to have to kill you."

"I'll take good care of her. I swear it," August said, recognising the anxiety behind the man's words. "If I do anything less than make her exceedingly happy, you have my permission to plant me a facer."

"Oh, I shall," he replied with the utmost seriousness. Then his mouth quirked in a wry smile. "She's head over ears for you, and Viv's no fool. I know you'll be happy."

"I love her," August said simply. "And the invitation to come and stay for the summer was a genuine one. It's a big enough house for everyone to have their space, and I'll do my best to keep Gwen from importuning you."

Ash laughed. "Thank you. I appreciate that, and I shall be glad to come for a visit. He went to turn away, but August put a hand on his arm.

"Wait. Viv asked me to give you this." August reached into his pocket and withdrew a neatly folded white handkerchief. "She seemed to think you'd need it."

Ash flushed as the other fellows chuckled and gave a huff of indignation. "Well, she's not wrong," he grumbled, and snatched the handkerchief before stalking off.

Suddenly, a hush fell over the room, and everyone settled down.

"Here we go," Bainbridge said, ushering August into place and then taking a moment to look him over, adjust his cravat and smooth his lapels. Nodding, apparently satisfied that August passed muster, he patted his own pocket. "Damn, the ring. Hell. *Bella!* The ring. In your reticule, love. The *ring!*"

There was a moment of frantic rustling as Bella fished for the small box, withdrew the ring, and handed it to Bainbridge.

"I told you to take it earlier," she protested under her breath, blushing as everyone watched the exchange.

"Didn't want to lose it," Bainbridge groused, hurrying back to stand beside August and ignoring a glare of outrage from the minister. "Right ho. *Ready now,*" he yelled down the aisle as the congregation snorted and giggled with amusement and Dare and Raphe laughed themselves sick.

August laughed too, discovering he was delighted to see the smiling faces of the people he cared about. His dreadful family, his ridiculous friends, and... his beautiful bride.

Vivien appeared and stole his breath, his wits, and every last piece of his heart.

Her gown was red, though so heavily embroidered the red was barely visible. This gown had been a gift from her mother, a part of her trousseau, and was quite literally worth its weight in gold embroidery. Viv had told him the traditional Indian embroidery, or zardozi, was made with thread wrapped in gold and then twisted into tiny spirals and tacked into place. The spring sunshine flooded in through the windows and Vivien sparkled like the jewel she was. The light caught the fine precious metal and the stunning traditional jewellery that her mother had given her to begin her married life, and glittered and twinkled as she moved. Vivien said her grandmother had guarded the jewellery with her life when she had fled India, and had refused to sell a single piece of it, even when times were hard. Instead, she had worked her fingers to the bone to provide for Aashini, until Silas Cavendish had come along and helped her take her rightful place in the world. The pride of that history, pride of her heritage and in the women whose blood ran in her veins, shone from Vivien with such joy that August's throat felt tight. She was stunning.

At last she stood beside him, and the minister began the service, though August barely took in the words, too dazed by the glorious creature beside him. When finally it was time to speak their vows, it took a sharp elbow from Bainbridge before he snapped out of his reverie.

"Wake up, dolt. This is the important bit," Bainbridge hissed, in an undertone that could be heard all around the room going on the subsequent snickering.

Finally it was done, and August leaned in to kiss his bride. It was a chaste kiss, barely more than a touch of lips, but filled with all the promises they had just spoken to each other.

All at once everyone was on their feet and crowding about, congratulating the happy couple. August turned to see Bainbridge surreptitiously wiping his eyes on his sleeve, only to have Ash thrust a handkerchief under his nose. "Lucky for you, I brought a spare," he said, smirking, though his eyes were glinting just as brightly.

Vivien laughed and embraced her brother tightly. "I'm so happy!" she squealed, making everyone laugh, and August's heart felt as if it could soar like a hot-air balloon.

Sylvester regarded Lady Aisling as everyone began taking their places for the wedding breakfast. She had lingered in a corner, waiting until last as usual, and he barely resisted the urge to reach up and touch her perfectly arranged hair. It was dramatically dark, almost black, and he suspected if let free it would curl dramatically about her delicate face. Lord, but he wanted to see that. There was something in him that longed to put her all in disorder, to needle her until that meek little façade fell away and the real Aisling showed her true colours. She did not look at him but must have noticed him watching, for her sweet rose petal mouth tightened, settling into something mutinous.

"No."

"You don't know what I was going to say yet," he observed mildly, irritated that she'd not even deigned to turn her head.

"It doesn't matter," she said, her cheeks flushing the most becoming shade of pink. "Please, leave me be."

Her chest was rising and falling far too quickly, and for a moment Sylvester toyed with the idea she was afraid of him. "Lady Aisling, I love nothing more than to tease you, and hearing you scold me is the highlight of my day, but... I would never hurt you. You do realise that?"

She looked at him then, a direct look that made him feel *seen*, in a way no one else ever really saw him. Which was ridiculous, and exceedingly disconcerting.

"Why must you persist?" she demanded, bewildered rather than angry, her voice little more than a whisper.

"Faint heart," he said, giving her his most winning crooked smile.

She tsked and shook her head. "Really," she said, clearly unconvinced, her voice flat. "Why?" she demanded again. He stared at her, his heart thudding far harder than the situation warranted.

"I don't know," he admitted. "Except that you're not what you purport to be, my lady. I know it, and you know it, but I want you to admit it to me. I want to know the real Lady Aisling. The one who isn't the least bit shy, the one who has dangerous secrets. I want all of your secrets. I would keep them safe for you."

Her eyes widened at that, her colour heightening to dramatic effect.

"You're deluded," she said, but he heard the tremor in her voice, the breathless quality of someone who fears they have been found out. He held her gaze, aware he was standing a little too close for propriety, and vibratingly aware that she had not given ground, and stepped back.

"It's you that's deluded if you think I'm going to give up. Besides which, you don't want me to."

"What?" She stared at him in outrage.

Sylvester bent until his lips grazed her ear. "Tell me to leave you alone," he whispered, aware of the way his breath had goosebumps shivering over her skin. "Tell me to go away and leave you be now, and I'll do it."

Her breath hitched, and she closed her eyes. "*D'anam don diabhal!*" she whispered, the words furious if incomprehensible. With an angry swish of her skirts, she swept away to take her place at the table and Sylvester watched her go. For a moment he was too stunned to think, but then a slow, wicked smile curved over his lips.

She had likely wished him to the devil in some foreign tongue, but she had *not* told him to leave her alone.

Louis regarded the happy couple, something horribly like envy settling with an unwelcome weight in his chest. He frowned down into his wineglass, twisting the stem back and forth between his fingers. The desire to fill his glass again was overwhelming, but he could not get drunk at such an affair, and he was liable to become maudlin if he did not do a proper job of it. His gaze settled on his brother and his wife, leaning into each other, speaking softly, their hands touching. Loneliness yawned like a great wasteland inside him, promising him endless days of emptiness if he could not make Evie love him. His attention drifted back to the happy couple and the longing for the happiness they shared, the security of knowing *someone* cared for him, ate at his heart.

"Wonder what it would feel like, to be that happy and that much in love?"

Louis turned to see Barnaby Godwin was considering the bridal couple, much as he had done. Louis had been sitting between Lady Aisling and Mrs Bonnie Cadogan, but Lady Aisling had excused herself, complaining of a headache. Barnaby, who'd been sitting on her right, appropriated the lady's seat and leaned in, his voiced dropping to a confidential tone.

"Makes you feel a bit… bereft, don't it?" he said wistfully, and Louis heartily wished him to the other side of the room.

Yes, damn him to hell, it did, but he didn't need someone to underline the point for him.

"You wish to marry, Barnaby?"

"Oh, yes," Barnaby said, his face lighting up. "Like the idea of a little wife to toddle home to. Someone what's pleased to see me… well, assuming I choose right, and she *is* pleased to see me. Though at the rate I'm going, it ain't going to happen. I just don't have a knack with the ladies. Not like you, though I suppose with a physiognomy like yours, you don't even need a knack. They throw themselves in your path."

Louis laughed bitterly and shook his head. *"Non, ce n'est pas vrai. Women* might be easy. The right woman is not easy at all," he muttered, folding his arms and trying to keep his gaze from the far end of the table where Evie sat.

"Well," Barnaby said, impressed by this observation. "If you can't manage it, what hope is there for the rest of us poor blighters?"

Louis sighed and regarded the man, who was clearly disinclined to leave him in peace. "Who is the young lady you desire?"

Barnaby shrugged. "Don't have a particular lady in mind," he admitted.

Louis refrained from rolling his eyes heavenwards with difficulty. "Well, who do you fancy?"

Barnaby pondered this. "Miss Ackerson is a pretty sort."

"Non." Louis shook his head at once. Miss Ackerson was no better than she should be and had once groped Louis at a formal dinner when he'd been sat next to her. The wretched creature had been remarkably persistent and difficult to dislodge. She also had a sharp tongue and a nasty habit of spreading malicious gossip. Yes, Miss Ackerson seemed an unlikely choice to be the sweet-natured, loyal wife Barnaby fondly imagined.

"Oh? No good?" Barnaby's face fell.

"Not no good," Louis said carefully, unwilling to slander the girl despite his animosity. "Just not for you, I think. Who else?"

"Miss Pilchester?"

Louis frowned, recalling an enthusiastic horsewoman and an energetic, forceful lady with extremely firm opinions. He suspected Barnaby might get trampled underfoot.

"Next?"

Barnaby sighed, and then a soft look came into his eyes. "Lady Millicent Fortescue."

Oh, now this one had possibilities. "A shy young lady. Plays piano very well, a sweet smile and pretty eyes."

"That's her!" Barnaby said. "By Jove, you know everybody."

"Not quite," Louis replied, dryly. "But she would suit you very well, I think. Why did you leave her until last?"

"She's an heiress," Barnaby said gloomily. "Her papa adores her, and he has his sights set on a bigger prize than I. I'm a younger son. No title. No blunt, neither. Not that I've pockets to let. I can afford a nice little home and a wife, but I've not enough for a prize like that."

"Then you must charm her, make her see the man you are. Make her want you, above the titles and the wealth and all the rest of it."

Barnaby looked dubious, which was fair enough. It was a tall order.

"Don't reckon I could do that," he intoned, shaking his head.

Louis stared at him. Barnaby was a good man, a decent, kind man who would make a loving and loyal husband. Why shouldn't he get the woman he wanted? Suddenly, it seemed that Barnaby ought to have his chance, because if he succeeded, maybe Louis could too. Why the two things were suddenly linked in his mind, he could not fathom. It wasn't as if he and Barnaby had the least thing in common except... except they both wanted a woman who appeared to be out of their reach. For now, at least.

"You can do it," Louis said, his voice firm. "I shall help you do it."

Barnaby blinked, looking a little as though he'd been staring at the sun too long.

"You?" he said, such incredulity infused in that one word, Louis had to smile. "You'll help me woo Lady Millicent."

"Oui," Louis nodded and held out his hand. "A deal."

Barnaby stared at his outstretched hand, back at Louis, and then at his hand again, as if uncertain what the catch was. Finally, he reached out and shook Louis' hand so firmly his enthusiasm nearly sent their wineglasses flying.

"Well," he said, shaking his head in wonder. "Well. Fancy that."

Vivien shrieked with laughter as they ran for the carriage whilst their friends pelted them with rice and shouted good wishes, amongst some ribald advice for August from his friends.

They were journeying back to Rother House, which was blessedly empty of artistic types or the females of August's family. It would be just the two of them for the next couple of months. They would take a trip to Paris later in the year but, for now, Vivien was more than content to get to know both her new husband and her new home, with no interruptions.

The carriage swayed as it set off, amid cheers and waving handkerchiefs, and Viv waved back, blowing kisses to her parents and Ash. She blinked back tears, remembering how mama had wept and laughed when she'd seen her walking down the aisle.

"Your father looked like he wanted to take you back," August observed, pulling Vivien against his side.

She sighed and rested her head on his shoulder. "I know. The poor darling. I had to scold him quite soundly before he gave me away. He got all sentimental and teary, saying how like Mama I looked on their wedding day. Honestly, I was on the verge of sobbing my heart out. A fine sight I should have looked, walking down the aisle to my husband in floods of tears."

August chuckled. "Poor devil. Though Ash will struggle the most, I think. He's going to miss you."

"Oh, don't you start," Vivien said with a huff. She gave August a playful smack, and he chuckled, holding her tighter.

"No regrets?"

Viv shook her head but looked up at him, studying him carefully. "Not on my part, but what about you? You'll have your mama and Charlie on your doorstep, and me and your dreadful sisters in one house. Shall we drive you to distraction?"

August laughed. "Yes. I'll be stark staring mad before the year is out and my hair will turn grey overnight. I can't wait."

Vivien leaned in and kissed his cheek. "I shan't let that happen, you know. I shall take your sisters in hand. I approve of their ambitions, and of their commitment, but I believe they might find less scandalous ways of achieving their ends if they think more carefully. As Mama is fond of saying, a little daring is an admirable thing, but there are limits. After all, they won't be taken so seriously if they make themselves into pariahs."

"I've been trying to tell them that for years, but do they listen?"

"You're a man, my love. You simply cannot understand the frustration and fury a lively and intelligent woman like your Anna must keep hidden simply to get through a day acting as a well-behaved young lady ought. But don't you worry. We shall think of a way to channel her energies more productively. She's very excited about Eliza's school, for a start."

August stared down at her, a smile at his lips that Vivien could only describe as besotted. Which was handy, really, as she was thoroughly besotted herself.

"We don't have to worry about them for at least two months," August said softly, tugging at the ribbons of her bonnet.

"No. We don't," Vivien replied, allowing her new husband to toss her frightfully expensive new hat aside without a murmur of protest. "Mr Lane-Fox, are you planning to disarrange my coiffure?"

"At the very least," he said gravely.

"Well, it's about time," Vivien replied with a sigh, and allowed him to get on with it.

Chapter 21

Monsieur,

I was sorry not to get the chance to speak with you at the Lane-Fox wedding. Papa was breathing down my neck, though, so I thought I had best be a little circumspect. I had hoped your heroics might change his mind about you, but I have just endured a lecture about wicked men and their wiles, which I believe was supposed to put me on my guard in your company. Can you believe it? The trouble is, Papa was a wicked man before he married and knows how enticing they can be. The poor dear is terrified I will get myself in a fix. I have tried to reassure him, but he does not trust you or your motives and will not be reassured. Mama is more reasonable, at least, though even she warns me to have a care for my reputation.

It is becoming increasingly difficult to get letters to you, but I have enlisted one of the footmen. He has been with us since he was a boy and I trust him to retrieve your letters and to send mine. He is well compensated for the risk he takes, naturally, but I wish I did not have to rely on such underhand measures.

Oh, you'll never guess. I had my first proposal of marriage yesterday! Mr Cooper, of whom I spoke to you, asked to speak to Papa. It surprised me that Papa agreed to it, except I believe he knew I would turn the fellow down and thought I ought to speak to him myself. Honestly, it was mortifying. The poor man blushed and stammered so. I don't know which of us was the most embarrassed. I almost accepted him just to make it stop.

I think I let him down gently. I hope he doesn't hate me now, but I only told him the truth, though I fear that I might have left him room to hope, which may not have been a kindness. I am far from ready to think of marrying anyone, though. I want to have some fun before I tie myself to a husband and a household. Goodness, how flighty I sound, but you know that is not what I mean. I just don't want things to change. Not yet.

—Excerpt of a letter from Miss Evie Knight (daughter of Lady Helena and Mr Gabriel Knight) to Louis César de Montluc, Comte de Villen.

27ᵗʰ April 1841, Rother House, Burwash, Etchingham, East Sussex.

It was early evening by the time they reached Rother House, and the last vibrant streaks of a lavish sunset fading from the sky as the carriage rolled up the drive. The mullioned windows reflected the fiery colour, making the house appear all ablaze.

August helped Viv step down, and she sighed with relief, stretching her spine after too long in the confines of the carriage. Her hair was in disarray, as August had promised, and she had been thoroughly kissed. Her new husband had refused anything more than this on the grounds he was going to enjoy his nuptials in a proper bed and not in a jolting carriage. Vivien had been as much frustrated as relieved by this, but wished she did not feel so worn out after their long day.

August slipped an arm about her waist as she stared up at Rother House.

"Happy, love?"

"Mmmm," she said with a sigh, leaning into him.

He chuckled and kissed her cheek. "Poor thing. You're worn to a thread. I don't suppose you slept a wink last night."

Viv shook her head. "I was far too excited to sleep, and then I was up early as there was so much to do to get ready."

August guided her into the house, where their new housekeeper hurried to greet them. Mrs Meacham looked pleased as punch to see them arrive. She was a spare, short woman who vibrated nervous energy and Viv had hired her on the spot when she had interviewed for the position. The rest of the staff would stay on for now, and could show their worth before Vivien made any further decisions, but it had pleased the old housekeeper to retire rather than get used to a determined new mistress who would undoubtedly set the place on its ears.

"Good evening Mr and Mrs Lane-Fox," Mrs Meacham said, dipping a curtsey. "Your baths are ready as you requested, and the staff will bring a light supper up the moment you ring for it. Don't hesitate to let me know if there's anything else you require."

"That sounds perfect, Mrs Meacham, thank you," Vivien said, noticing dusted portraits and a sparkling entrance hall. "And I see you have taken the place in hand."

"We've made a start," the woman said, her expression suggesting she had only fired her opening shot and a battle royale was yet to begin.

"Excellent. If you'll excuse us, my wife is weary after our long day," August said, putting an end to any further domestic discussions and towing Vivien up the stairs.

"Oh, of course, sir," Mrs Meacham replied with a knowing smile that made Vivien blush and hurry to keep up with her husband.

The master bedroom was a splendid, well-proportioned room. In daylight, it looked out upon the lovely gardens and the gently rolling hills of the Sussex Weald though it was cosy now with the heavy curtains closed and the lamps lit. The bed was a hefty looking four poster of an age with the building, but the hangings and bedcovers were quite new and a lovely shade of forest green with a pattern in gold thread. They had clearly been chosen by August's mama.

August kissed Vivien tenderly but swiftly released her. "I'll see you after your bath," he said with a gentle smile.

Viv let him go a little reluctantly, though she was also relieved. A bath sounded heavenly, and so did a moment to prepare herself for her wedding night. Not that she was nervous, only full of anticipation. Between Mama and Nani Maa's forthright advice—and that rather wicked book! — she felt she had been well prepared. Besides, she trusted August, and knew he would be a considerate lover, as he was considerate in all things.

Once she'd enjoyed a wonderful soak in sweet-scented hot water and brushed out and secured her long hair in a loose coiffure, Viv went to the bed. With nervous fingers, she picked up the wicked creation of silk and lace that had been a private wedding gift from Eliza. Unsurprisingly, it was French. She smiled, remembering how reserved and well-behaved Eliza had been before she had married so scandalously to Mr Demarteau, the

Comte de Villen's illegitimate half-brother. Eliza had proven that a little daring went a long way in her determination to wed the man she desired, and so Vivien took a deep breath and shimmied into the black silk nightgown. There was a far more demure white creation amongst her trousseau which was perhaps more in keeping for a virginal bride, but August knew she was not always the well-behaved young woman she ought to be, and he loved her anyway. Vivien bit her lip, skimming her hands over the sleek material that clung to her breasts and hips, and reached for the matching robe, leaving the sash undone. The silk was cool against her skin as she walked to the door that August had showed led to the adjoining parlour. He was waiting for her, standing by the fireplace, its glow casting him into bronze and copper and gold as he contemplated the flames.

"I hope you're not having second thoughts," Vivien said as she closed the door behind her.

"Of course not, I—" August's words came to an abrupt halt as he looked up and saw her. His mouth fell open as he took in the confection of black silk and lace, and Viv felt a moment's anxiety at the shock in his eyes.

Perhaps the white would have been the better choice after all?

"Vivien," he said, her name a breathless sound above the crackle of the fire.

"Don't you like it?" she asked, hesitant now.

"Like it?" he repeated, blinking at her in bewilderment. "I may fall to my knees and thank my maker for his bountiful gifts, but *like it* does not express my sentiments."

Oh. He did like it. Vivien grinned. "I was worried for a moment there. I thought perhaps I had shocked you."

"You have shocked me," he murmured, moving closer. "But I realise a fellow needs shocking now and then. Keeps him on his toes, makes him remember he's alive."

237

He stopped in front of her, one hand sliding over the silk at the curve of her waist, down to her hips.

Viv smiled. He wore only a loose shirt and trousers, his feet bare, and his hair still damp from his bath. She placed her hand on his chest, discovering his heart pounding fiercely beneath her palm. "You are certainly alive."

"You're not wrong," he murmured, leaning in to nip her ear. "That's not the only evidence, either."

Viv bit her lip, her attention riveted by the part of him he alluded to, pressing urgently against the fall of his trousers.

"I have been out of my mind with wanting you, but we had best eat first, love," he said ruefully. "Before you discover you are the main course."

Vivien did not mind the sound of that, but she was hungry and too afraid that her stomach would grumble and mortify her at an inopportune moment if she did not attend to it.

They sat down to a splendid supper of salmon en croute and buttered haricots verts with a deliciously tart lemon sorbet to finish. August kept her wine glass topped up and Vivien did not remonstrate, for the wine was excellent and soothing to any last-minute nerves.

All the same, her stomach did an odd little flip when August rose and walked around the table, offering her his hand.

"Time for bed, lady wife," he said, his voice gentle as he smiled down at her.

Vivien took his hand, feeling his warm fingers curve reassuringly around her own as he guided her back to their bedroom. Her bath and all the evidence of her preparations had been removed, and the covers turned down, though the room was still scented with the perfume of her bath oils.

"Orange blossom," August said, breathing it in appreciatively as he closed the bedroom door.

"It's my favourite," she said, moving to the bed and leaning back against one of the heavy posts.

"Mine too, now," August replied, following her.

He reached up and pushed the dressing gown from her shoulders. Viv shivered as she let it slither to the floor. His gaze skimmed down over the black silk of the indecent nightgown, lingering on the lacy edge that barely covered her nipples.

"Nervous?" he asked, stroking the upper curve of her bare breast with the back of his finger.

"A little perhaps," she admitted. "But I trust you."

"Perhaps I ought to confess that I am more than a little nervous," August admitted with a wry smile, though it was hard to concentrate on his words as his finger moved lower, gently caressing a nipple that grew hard beneath the black lace. His touch provoked the most deliciously distracting sensations in places besides where he caressed her.

"You... You... are nervous?" she managed, struggling to keep her mind on the conversation.

"I want it to be good for you, perfect, but sometimes, the first time—"

"I know," she said impatiently, and pressed her mouth to his, kissing him passionately.

August gave a brief huff of laughter against her lips before gathering her against him and giving her the kiss she wanted. He kissed her until she was giddy, plundering her mouth as his hands roamed over her, the silk whispering in their wake. He drew back to regard the damage he'd wrought.

"Less talking, more action. I have my instructions, then," he said, his eyes glinting mischievously as he tugged his shirt over his head.

"Yes," Vivien squeaked, scurrying onto the bed and kneeling down in the middle to watch the marvellous spectacle of her husband disrobing. Her heart thudded as she took in a splendidly broad chest with a scattering of gold hair that trailed down, arrowing beneath the line of his trousers. He dispensed with these efficiently too, pushing trousers and small clothes down past strong thighs and kicking his discarded clothing aside. August stood still for her, letting her peruse her bridegroom at her leisure.

"Do I meet with your approval?"

He arched one eyebrow, the rat, for he must know that he was gorgeous, all long limbs and sleek muscle, his belly taut and well defined. Her gaze fell inevitably to that most masculine part of him and everything feminine within her quivered in anticipation.

"I am on my knees and thanking my maker for his bountiful gifts," Vivien said, fighting a smile.

August laughed, pleased with the comment. "As you should be, for if you do not admire me now in all my magnificence, I shall be in a sorry taking ten years hence."

"You'll still be magnificent when you are an old, old man, and I shall still adore you," Vivien said, her heart kicking with excited anticipation as he climbed onto the bed.

"Do you adore me, love?" he asked, moving until they sat opposite each other, knees touching.

"Yes," she said simply.

"What a lucky devil I am," he murmured with a sigh, whilst he pushed one delicate strap from her shoulder. The night gown slipped lower, the lace catching on the taut nub of her nipple so that it didn't fall.

August's lips quirked, and he pushed the other strap down too. Once again, the lace only fell part way. He huffed out a laugh. "Devilish thing means to torment me. Take it off at once."

It was a command, but his eyes were warm and teasing, and so Vivien obeyed him, wriggling the nightgown up over her hips and then tugging it over her head. She cast it aside, feeling a blush warm her cheeks as she turned back to her husband.

He was gazing at her with such reverence her nerves subsided.

"Mercy," he whispered. "I may not survive the night. What is the price for making love with a goddess? Surely some angry god will come and smite me for my temerity."

"Such nonsense," Vivien tsked, rolling her eyes.

"Take down your hair for me." It was less of a command this time, more of a plea, and his breath caught as Viv raised her arms to remove the simple clasp that she'd secured her hair with. It fell, cascading over her shoulders and breasts to her waist.

August reached to touch it. "More black silk," he murmured. "Such wickedness."

Gently he eased her backwards onto the mattress, his gaze hungry with wanting her as his hands explored, caressing, stroking, until Vivien wanted to stretch and purr like a cat in the sun. August lay beside her, leaning down to kiss her as his hands continued a languid exploration of her body, his long fingers dipping occasionally between her thighs to wreak havoc upon her self-control. Viv's reaction to this sensuous assault was not the least bit languorous as his lazy attentions stoked her from a pleasantly simmering warmth until her body felt all ablaze.

"August," she panted, needing him now, understanding what the hollow ache inside her was clamouring for.

"Not yet," he said, kissing a path down her neck to her breasts as his fingers returned to the sensitive place between her thighs to provoke more of that deliciously maddening sensation until she felt she would scream. Quite beyond shame or maidenly reserve, she spread her legs, begging him for more or she would lose her mind.

"So beautiful."

His words were full of adoration and Viv sighed as he bent his head, stroking his hair. He covered her nipple with his mouth, suckling hard, and slid his fingers inside her.

It was perhaps not quite a scream, but her reaction was fierce and her cry loud enough to shock herself as the pleasure took her over, rolling through her with such force that by the time she could remember her own name she was utterly boneless.

"Heavens," she panted, staring up at her husband, whose blue eyes were dark and heavy lidded. "And we haven't, you haven't even…."

She couldn't quite remember where she'd been going with that observation, though August seemed to understand.

"No, though I intend to rectify the oversight now," he said, moving between her legs.

"Now?" Vivien replied, still dazed and floating in a pleasant fog that might easily have had her drifting to sleep. "I'm not sure I have the… *Oh!"*

Vivien's breath caught as August's arousal slid over her slick flesh and desire burst to life all over again. He chuckled, the bad man, and Vivien slid her arms about his neck.

"Still sleepy?" he asked, all innocence.

"Certainly not."

He grinned, and Vivien held her breath as he nudged the blunt head of his arousal inside her. She closed her eyes for a moment as he pushed and retreated, gaining a little more ground with each forward motion.

"Viv?" She heard the question behind her name, the concern, so she opened her eyes and smiled at him. He let out a shuddering breath and sank home, stealing her breath as the strange fullness of his invasion became absolute.

Viv waited a moment and let out a shaky exhalation, taking stock of the situation and finding there was no pain, just a slightly peculiar sensation that was not quite comfortable. August kept still, resting his forehead against hers and breathing with quiet deliberation. She suspected he was counting.

"I'm all right," she whispered.

His eyes cracked open, and he stared down at her. "Thank God," he muttered and withdrew, pushing back inside her with a sinuous motion that made the not quite comfortable sensation dissolve into something entirely different.

"Oh," she gasped, clutching at his shoulders. "Oh, that's...."

"That's?" he asked, a rather smug look in his eyes.

Vivien bit her lip, for the urge to laugh was undeniable, and she was uncertain he'd appreciate it.

"Are you laughing at me, wife?" he demanded, nipping at her ear.

"N-No," she managed, fighting to keep her composure. "Only you l-looked so very pleased with yourself."

August snorted. "Good God, pleased with myself? I am the smuggest man in the entire world. Now be quiet. I'm trying to make love to my new wife."

Vivien dissolved, and August made a choked sound. "Oh, Lord, stop, *stop* jiggling about. You're killing me!"

Apparently deciding enough was enough, August took a firm hold of her hips, tilting her just so, and thrust forward. The laughter abruptly ceased as Vivien experienced a jolt of pleasure that made her catch her breath.

Her husband made a pleased, masculine sound and repeated the action, again and again until Vivien was mindless, head thrown back and incapable of ceasing the soft, incoherent murmurs he tore from her. Her hands glided over his lean flanks, stroked the damp, satiny skin of his back and grasped at his muscular shoulders.

"More?" he asked, his voice husky.

"Yes, yes," was the most she could manage in reply, but it was enough.

He loved her tenderly, thoroughly, and with increasing vigour, his movements becoming urgent and less coordinated. Vivien held her breath, chasing the bright, gathering sensation that was building inside her until it exploded in a rapturous burst of white light. August made a harsh sound, his hold on her tightening, his powerful body surrendering as pleasure overtook him and he shuddered, spending inside her with a rush of heat. His breathing was ragged as he laid his head on the pillow beside hers, his eyes hazy as he looked at her.

"I was right," he murmured, his voice unsteady. "I won't survive the night."

Vivien laughed, and he grinned at her, looking inordinately pleased with himself.

"I love you," he said, reaching out to caress her cheek. "And I adore making love with you. It's my new favourite thing."

"I love you too," she said, still laughing, turning her head to kiss his palm. "And making love with you is my favourite thing, too. It's like flying, only without the cold and fear of plummeting to one's death."

"Better than a hot-air balloon?"

"Oh, certainly. That was my dare, you know, to reach great heights. I thought I'd achieved it accidentally, but now I think I flew far higher with you."

August looked impressed and pleased by this observation. "I did not realise you had accomplished a dare with me. Bainbridge and Raphe told me about the hat. What scandalous creatures you Daring Daughters are. Whatever am I in for?"

"A wonderful time," she said, her voice firm. "Life with you will be far more daring and exciting than that little jaunt in a hot-air balloon, I'm sure."

"It had better be," he murmured, rolling to the side of her and pulling her back into his arms. "I have prepared myself for nothing less than absolute mayhem."

"Excellent. Absolute mayhem it is," she said with a sigh.

He stroked her hair, a soothing touch that made her eyelids feel heavy. "Do you mind if we begin in the morning, though, love? It's been a long day."

Vivien snorted with amusement and cuddled against her new husband, who made a firm but delightful pillow. "All right, if you insist. But first thing, mind."

"First thing, I swear it, and all the days of the rest of our lives."

"Perhaps not every day," she said, smothering a yawn. "I'll give you time off. For bad behaviour."

"Well, that sounds perfect," August sighed, and found he meant every word.

Epilogue

Dear Sylvester,

I hope you are having a marvellous time in town. Well, not too marvellous, for I want to interrupt your cavorting and ask a very great favour of you, which Greer and Raphe said I might, as you are my brother now.

I have been invited to stay with Lady Cara Baxter at Trevick Castle. I have my governess and my maid to accompany me, but I have been staying with my aunt and uncle, Lord and Lady St Clair, whilst Mama and Papa are away, but they have commitments and so cannot escort me. Gee and your brother are too busy with the restoration works at Marcross. Raphe said that he would be happy to give you more time off if you would accompany me to Trevick for my stay and see me safely returned home. I am to be there for two weeks, perhaps three. I have checked with Lady Trevick, who has extended the welcome to include you.

Please say you will come. I haven't seen Cara in an age and Trevick is a marvellous place to visit.

—Excerpt of a letter from Miss Alana
Cadogan (youngest daughter of Mr and
Mrs Jerome and Bonnie Cadogan) to
The Hon'ble Mr Sylvester Cootes.

27th May 1841, Rother House, Burwash, Etchingham, East Sussex.

It had been a perfect day and, by some minor miracle, no one had misbehaved.

"What's wrong?" Vivien asked, reaching for August's hand.

He looked up and smiled at her, and then returned his gaze to their guests, shaking his head.

"My sisters are here, my mother and Charlie are here, your twin is here, Dare and Elspeth and their baby daughter are here, and worst of all, *Bainbridge* is here with Arabella, and nothing has erupted, shattered, or exploded in my face. It's making me nervous."

Vivien snorted with amusement. "We've had a lovely picnic. The sun is shining, and everyone is content. Why, even Araminta is cooing happily. Isn't she just darling?"

"She is, but I'm still feeling anxious," August said, though the baby *was* adorable, all blue eyes and blonde ringlets. He wondered what their children would look like and smiled as he considered little girls with jet black hair and indigo eyes. His attention was taken as Bainbridge got up and moved away from the group. His expression was sombre, the lines about his mouth tense, and that was so unusual for Bainbridge since he'd married that August got to his feet. He leant down and pressed a kiss to Vivien's mouth. "Back in a bit."

August followed Bainbridge, noticing his wife, Bella, fast asleep on one of the picnic blankets as he passed. The marquess walked through the orchard to where a small stream curled, burbling over rocks. He stopped then, staring down into the water, but August did not think he saw it.

"Laurie?"

Bainbridge looked up, but his expression was so bleak August did not bother beating around the bushes.

"What is it?" he demanded. "What's wrong?"

Bainbridge shook his head, his dark brows gathered. "I don't know. I think Bella is sick, or… or she's sick of me. I'm too afraid to ask her. I am a lot to deal with, August, you know that. Too much for any sane woman. I've been too difficult, too… dreadful. She's tired out and fed up, I just know it. I try to behave, I swear I do, but—"

August held up a hand, stemming the tide of self-recrimination, which looked as if it might go on for some time. "Of course you're too much. Everyone knows you're a big loud lummox, especially Arabella, but that's why she loves you. Why don't you tell me exactly what's happened? Has she said something?"

Bainbridge shook his head miserably as Dare sauntered up, glancing at Bainbridge and then at August. "What's amiss?"

"Bainbridge is afraid Bella's had enough of him," August said, certain enough that this was preposterous not to tread more cautiously. Besides, you couldn't be subtle around Bainbridge. He wouldn't understand it.

Dare snorted and slung an arm about his friend's shoulder. "Barking mad. What's brought this on?"

"Then she's sick, and that's worse," he said, folding his arms over his chest. "I'll die if anything happens to her. If she was only sick of me, I might win her back, but to lose her… I won't survive it—"

"Good God, Bainbridge!" August said, reaching out and grabbing his shoulders. He endeavoured to give the man a shake, which was akin to shaking Royle House and about as effective. "Explain."

Bainbridge glowered, but offered something resembling an explanation. "Well, we're… you know, at it like rabbits usually. But the past few weeks… She's not been in the mood. Said she was tired. Retired early three nights in a row and then fell asleep when I was talking to her the following afternoon. Then yesterday morning she seemed more cheerful, so I… well, we… and then she ran off into the bathroom. I think she was sick," he said morosely.

Dare exploded into laughter.

August, who felt for the poor blighter, tried manfully to keep his composure. "Laurie," he said, struggling to stop his voice from quavering. "Did no one ever have a little talk with you, about the birds and the bees—"

Bainbridge looked at him in disgust. "She can't be pregnant. Bella doesn't keep secrets from me, she would have told me."

"Would she?" August asked mildly. "Before she was certain? Knowing what a great overbearing, overprotective lout you are?"

"Perhaps she didn't like the idea of being confined to her room for the next nine months and wrapped in cotton wool?" Dare suggested helpfully.

The big man paled dramatically.

"Bella!" he said faintly and then set off at a run back to the picnic.

"Oh, that's torn it," August muttered, and hared off after him with Dare at his heels. "Not in front of everyone!" he yelled after Bainbridge, but did not expect to be heeded.

August stopped on the edge of the gathering, causing Dare to run into the back of him and nearly knock him to the ground. At the same moment, Bainbridge fell to his knees beside his sleeping wife.

Everyone's conversation stopped as they turned to look.

Bella stirred, blinking up at her husband. "What?" she said dazedly, sounding alarmed. "What's wrong? What's happened?"

"Bella?" Bainbridge said, sounding choked. "Bella?"

Bella stared at her stricken husband for a long moment and then sighed. "Oh, Laurie. Who told you?" She shot a glare at Elspeth, who shook her head.

"Not me, I swear. I never told Dare, either," Elspeth protested.

"We worked it out," Dare said smugly as August elbowed him.

"Shut up. I don't want the blame," he hissed.

Vivien smothered her mouth with her hand.

"I thought you were sick," Bainbridge said, sounding wretched. "I thought you'd had enough of me."

Bella's face fell. "Oh, Laurie," she said, her expression full of tenderness. Bella got to her knees to embrace her husband. "You foolish man. How could you think such a thing? I'm only going to have a baby."

"Only!" Bainbridge exclaimed, looking appalled. "*Only*?" He sounded a little hysterical.

"Oh, dear," she said with a sigh. "*This* is why I didn't tell you yet. It's only been a few weeks. Come along, my love. Come for a little walk with me."

Arabella got to her feet and took her husband's arm, towing him back to the house where she could soothe him in private.

"Poor devil," Dare said cheerfully. "He's no idea what he's got coming."

"What has he got coming?" August asked, a little nervous at the idea. He wanted a family of his own very much, but not just yet. He still had fond if forlorn hopes of getting his blasted sisters safely married off before he had to fret over babies.

Dare walked over to his wife and plucked their daughter from her arms. "Come along, Minty, my dearest darling."

"I thought *I* was your dearest darling," his wife complained, settling herself back against the pillows arranged for her and stroking the burgeoning swell of her stomach. A brother or sister for Minty would be along soon enough.

"Of course you are my dearest darling, too. My dearest darlings," he said tenderly and then blew a raspberry against his daughter's neck, which made her squeal with laughter. "This is what he has coming," Dare replied, answering August's question.

"Well, that doesn't look so bad," August replied.

"No, it's perfectly wonderful, but alongside the joy is the terror."

"Terror?" August replied uneasily.

"From the moment they're conceived," Dare replied, kissing his daughter's soft cheek. "Terror of losing them or their mama, of illness, of anything that might hurt them now or in the distant future. I fainted when Araminta was born," he admitted ruefully.

"You didn't?"

Dare nodded, looking sheepish. "I did, though I shall kill you if you breathe a word to another living soul, and you'd best not tell Laurie. He's shaken enough as it is, poor bastard."

"Word of honour," August muttered, frowning.

"It wasn't the blood or the screaming, if that's what you're thinking. Though it looked like a damned butcher's shop, and my ears were ringing for days."

August swallowed, wishing fervently he'd never begun this conversation. "Oh?"

Dare nodded, gazing down at his daughter with misty eyes. "She was just so beautiful, and Elspeth had to work so hard to bring her into the world and… and I was just overwhelmed." He looked up at August and grinned. "Also, I'd not eaten or slept for twenty-four hours, which likely didn't help."

August laughed, shaking his head, and left Dare to talk nonsense to his beautiful little girl. He made his way back to Vivien, who was smiling, her head together with Anna and Gwen as they plotted something dreadful, no doubt. Gwen gave a little shriek and fell back, laughing fit to burst her stays… assuming she was wearing them for once. Ash only just snatched an uneaten slice of cake out of the way before she planted her head in it. He caught August's eye and shook his head before accepting Charlie's timely invitation to play billiards. Timely, for Gwen was gazing up at Ash in a most uncivilised manner. August sighed and wondered what to do about her. Ash sauntered off with Charlie, though it was an invitation he might live to regret, for Charlie was a demon with a cue. August almost warned him not to play for money, but decided against it. Ash was a big boy and would figure it out.

He turned and stared back at Rother House, turning gold in the late afternoon sun. Vivien got to her feet and slid her arm through his.

"Do you think Arabella and Bainbridge are all right?" she asked.

"Weeping and hysterical, I expect," August said thoughtfully.

"Ah, well, Arabella will watch after him."

August snorted and pulled her into his arms. "I love you, Mrs Lane-Fox."

"I love you too, Mr Lane-Fox," she said, leaning into him.

"You never think you'd have been better off marrying a duke or a marquess?"

She gave him a look of disgust that made his heart lift.

"Not ever. Not even for a second. I love our life. Your dreadful sisters are wonderful, and your barmy friends are my friends, too. It's quite marvellously perfect."

"You're perfect," he murmured, leaning down for a kiss.

"No, I'm not," she whispered back. "Not even nearly, but I'm perfect for you."

And August knew she was perfectly correct.

Next in the Daring Daughters series…

Their mothers dared all for love.
Just imagine what their daughters will do…

An Enchanting Dare

Daring Daughters Book Ten

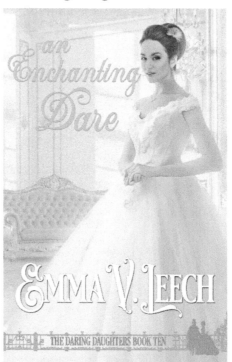

A Wary Young Woman…

Lady Aisling Baxter does not enjoy the company of the gossipy, judgemental *ton,* but she does need a husband. Another season has come and gone, and Aisling still hasn't found a suitable match, though that is perhaps unsurprising when she spends her time hiding behind potted plants. The only fellow who has shown the least interest in her is the most vexing man that ever lived, and

Aisling will be relieved to bury herself back in her beloved countryside and attempt to forget all about him.

An Irresistible Puzzle...

Mr Sylvester Cootes is a man with an obsession. It's been over six months since he first set eyes on Lady Aisling, and he cannot get the perplexing young woman off his mind. Whenever he sees her, he cannot help but force her to notice him by being as aggravating as he knows how. Shy Aisling is beautiful and mysterious and draws him to her for reasons he does not understand. But Sylvester is certain the lovely young woman is not all that she appears. The lady has secrets, and he means to discover them. Sadly, the lady also has a firm opinion about Mr Cootes.

She hates him.

A Twist of Fate...

No matter how much Aisling wishes to keep away from Sylvester Cootes, the fates keep pushing them together again. So perhaps it is time to trust in destiny, and a man she doesn't even like, because there's magic in the air, and even Aisling can't fight the enchanting spell Sylvester has cast over her.

Pre-order your copy here

An Enchanting Dare

The Peculiar Ladies who started it all…

Girls Who Dare – The exciting series from Emma V Leech, the multi-award-winning, Amazon Top 10 romance writer behind the Rogues & Gentlemen series.

Inside every wallflower is the beating heart of a lioness, a passionate individual willing to risk all for their dream, if only they can find the courage to begin. When these overlooked girls make a pact to change their lives, anything can happen.

Twelve girls – Twelve dares in a hat. Twelves stories of passion. Who will dare to risk it all?

To Dare a Duke

Girls Who Dare Book 1

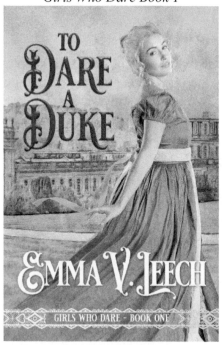

Dreams of true love and happy ever afters

Dreams of love are all well and good, but all Prunella Chuffington-Smythe wants is to publish her novel. Marriage at the price of her independence is something she will not consider. Having tasted success writing under a false name in The Lady's Weekly Review, her alter ego is attaining notoriety and fame and Prue rather likes it.

A Duty that must be endured

Robert Adolphus, The Duke of Bedwin, is in no hurry to marry, he's done it once and repeating that disaster is the last thing he desires. Yet, an heir is a necessary evil for a duke and one he cannot shirk. A dark reputation precedes him though, his first wife may have died young, but the scandals the beautiful, vivacious and spiteful creature supplied the ton have not. A wife must be found. A wife who is neither beautiful or vivacious but sweet and dull, and certain to stay out of trouble.

Dared to do something drastic

The sudden interest of a certain dastardly duke is as bewildering as it is unwelcome. She'll not throw her ambitions aside to marry a scoundrel just as her plans for self-sufficiency and freedom are coming to fruition. Surely showing the man she's not actually the meek little wallflower he is looking for should be enough to put paid to his intentions? When Prue is dared by her friends to do something drastic, it seems the perfect opportunity to kill two birds.

However, Prue cannot help being intrigued by the rogue who has inspired so many of her romances. Ordinarily, he plays the part of handsome rake, set on destroying her plucky heroine. But is he really the villain of the piece this time, or could he be the hero?

Finding out will be dangerous, but it just might inspire her greatest story yet.

To Dare a Duke

Also check out Emma's regency romance series, Rogues & Gentlemen. Available now!

The Rogue

Rogues & Gentlemen Book 1

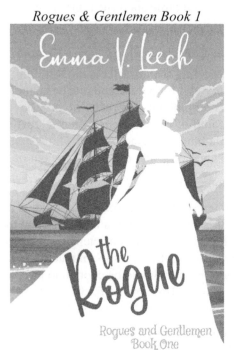

The notorious Rogue that began it all.

Set in Cornwall, 1815. Wild, untamed and isolated.

Lawlessness is the order of the day and smuggling is rife.

Henrietta always felt most at home in the wilds of the outdoors but even she had no idea how the mysterious and untamed would sweep her away in a moment.

Bewitched by his wicked blue eyes

Henrietta Morton knows to look the other way when the free trading 'gentlemen' are at work.
Yet when a notorious pirate bursts into her local village shop, she

can avert her eyes no more. Bewitched by his wicked blue eyes, a moment of insanity follows as Henrietta hides the handsome fugitive from the Militia.

Her reward is a kiss, lingering and unforgettable.

In his haste to flee, the handsome pirate drops a letter, a letter that lays bare a tale of betrayal. When Henrietta's father gives her hand in marriage to a wealthy and villainous nobleman in return for the payment of his debts, she becomes desperate.

Blackmailing a pirate may be her only hope for freedom.

**** **Warning**: This book contains the most notorious rogue of all of Cornwall and, on occasion, is highly likely to include some mild sweating or descriptive sex scenes. ****

Free to read on *Kindle Unlimited*: The Rogue

Interested in a Regency Romance with a twist?

A Dog in a Doublet

The Regency Romance Mysteries Book 2

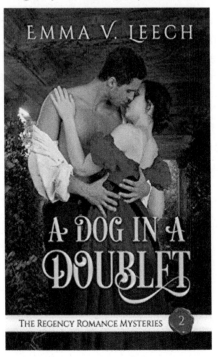

A man with a past

Harry Browning was a motherless guttersnipe, and the morning he came across the elderly Alexander Preston, The Viscount Stamford, clinging to a sheer rock face he didn't believe in fate. But the fates have plans for Harry whether he believes or not, and he's not entirely sure he likes them.

As a reward for his bravery, and in an unusual moment of charity, miserly Lord Stamford takes him on. He is taught to read, to manage the vast and crumbling estate, and to behave like a gentleman, but Harry knows that is something he will never truly be.

Already running from a dark past, his future is becoming increasingly complex as he finds himself caught in a tangled web of jealousy and revenge.

A feisty young maiden

Temptation, in the form of the lovely Lady Clarinda Bow, is a constant threat to his peace of mind, enticing him to be something he isn't. But when the old man dies his will makes a surprising demand, and the fates might just give Harry the chance to have everything he ever desired, including Clara, if only he dares.

And as those close to the Preston family begin to die, Harry may not have any choice.

A Dog in a Doublet

Lose yourself in Emma's paranormal world with The French Vampire Legend series.....

The Key to Erebus

The French Vampire Legend Book 1

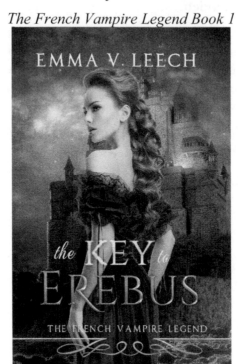

The truth can kill you.

Taken away as a small child, from a life where vampires, the Fae, and other mythical creatures are real and treacherous, the beautiful young witch, Jéhenne Corbeaux is totally unprepared when she returns to rural France to live with her eccentric Grandmother.

Thrown headlong into a world she knows nothing about she seeks to learn the truth about herself, uncovering secrets more shocking than anything she could ever have imagined and finding that she is by no means powerless to protect the ones she loves.

Despite her Gran's dire warnings, she is inexorably drawn to the dark and terrifying figure of Corvus, an ancient vampire and master of the vast Albinus family.

Jéhenne is about to find her answers and discover that, not only is Corvus far more dangerous than she could ever imagine, but that he holds much more than the key to her heart ...

Now available at your favourite retailer.

The Key to Erebus

Check out Emma's exciting fantasy series with hailed by Kirkus Reviews as "An enchanting fantasy with a likable heroine, romantic intrigue, and clever narrative flourishes."

The Dark Prince

The French Fae Legend Book 1

Two Fae Princes
One Human Woman
And a world ready to tear them all apart

Laen Braed is Prince of the Dark fae, with a temper and reputation to match his black eyes, and a heart that despises the human race. When he is sent back through the forbidden gates between realms to retrieve an ancient fae artifact, he returns home with far more than he bargained for.

Corin Albrecht, the most powerful Elven Prince ever born. His golden eyes are rumoured to be a gift from the gods, and destiny is calling him. With a love for the human world that runs deep, his friendship with Laen is being torn apart by his prejudices.

Océane DeBeauvoir is an artist and bookbinder who has always relied on her lively imagination to get her through an unhappy and uneventful life. A jewelled dagger put on display at a nearby museum hits the headlines with speculation of another race, the Fae. But the discovery also inspires Océane to create an extraordinary piece of art that cannot be confined to the pages of a book.

With two powerful men vying for her attention and their friendship stretched to the breaking point, the only question that remains…who is truly The Dark Prince.

The man of your dreams is coming…or is it your nightmares he visits? Find out in Book One of The French Fae Legend.

Available now to read at your favorite retailer

The Dark Prince

Want more Emma?

If you enjoyed this book, please support this indie author and take a moment to leave a few words in a review. *Thank you!*

To be kept informed of special offers and free deals (which I do regularly) follow me on *https://www.bookbub.com/authors/emma-v-leech*

To find out more and to get news and sneak peeks of the first chapter of upcoming works, go to my website and sign up for the newsletter.
http://www.emmavleech.com/

Come and join the fans in my Facebook group for news, info and exciting discussion…

Emma's Book Club

Or Follow me here…

http://viewauthor.at/EmmaVLeechAmazon
Facebook
Instagram
Emma's Twitter page
TikTok

Can't get your fill of Historical Romance? Do you crave stories with passion and red-hot chemistry?

If the answer is yes, have I got the group for you!

Come join myself and other awesome authors in our Facebook group

Historical Harlots

Be the first to know about exclusive giveaways, chat with amazing HistRom authors, lots of raunchy shenanigans and more!

Historical Harlots Facebook Group

Printed in Great Britain
by Amazon

20168839R00161